U

"Ever hear of the Filus murder case?" Meara asked. "It's maybe two or three years old by now. Never has been solved."

Dorsey turned in his chair to face Meara. "Maybe something in the paper. Or maybe I remember seeing something about it on the TV news. But that's about it. Should I know more?"

"Not really," Meara said, toying with the end of his tie. "Guy about our age, he steps off the bus on his way home from work, walks about two of the three blocks to his nice home in Point Breeze, and then takes two bullets to the head and goes to the sweet bye and bye. Never solved that one, never even came up with a suspect. The man left behind two sons and a widow."

Dorsey turned to Monsignor Gallard and then back to Meara. "And?" he asked. "You want me to do something about that? Is the bishop under suspicion? Has he been questioned under the hot lights yet?"

"No, no, not the bishop," Monsignor Gallard said, allowing a slight laugh to escape before continuing. "Just a priest."

STEEL CITY
CONFESSIONS

A MYSTERY

THOMAS LIPINSKI

AVON
TWILIGHT

AVON BOOKS, INC.
1350 Avenue of the Americas
New York, New York 10019

Copyright © 1999 by Thomas Lipinski
Inside cover author photo by Will Waldron
Published by arrangement with the author
Library of Congress Catalog Card Number: 98-93547
ISBN: 0-380-79431-4
www.avonbooks.com/twilight

First Avon Twilight Printing: March 1999

AVON TWILIGHT TRADEMARK REG. U.S. PAT. OFF. AND IN OTHER COUN-TRIES, MARCA REGISTRADA, HECHO EN U.S.A.

Printed in the U.S.A.

WCD   10   9   8   7   6   5   4   3   2   1

Written in memory of Bruce Miller,
the best writer I ever met

1

The retreat house and church at St. Paul's sit on the curve of Monastery Avenue that forms a rocky shelf in the cliffs above Pittsburgh's South Side. The architecture reflects the thinking and building materials of several ages: a chapel of dusty red brick with walls perhaps triple thick, and a courtyard, the final resting place for dozens of dead clerics, enclosed by several walls. The original sections of the retreat house are of the same construction but clash with more recent additions of glass and vinyl siding. The entire compound retains the image of an impregnable fortress, commanding the high ground against all would-be attackers.

As Dorsey pulled the Buick into the church lot, the engine coughed from the strain of climbing South 18th Street to Monastery in the mid-August heat. He maneuvered into a slot beside a steel mesh fence that stood as the last barrier to a cliff that gave way to steep, wooded hillsides and commanding views of both the city and the nearby Monongahela River Valley. Dorsey shut off the engine, reached into the backseat for his suit jacket, and climbed out from behind the steering wheel, stretching to his full height of six-four and tugging his shirt away from the sweat that had pooled at the small of his back.

Leaning into the fence, looking down at a cityscape partially obscured by gray summer haze, he again reviewed the phone call that had brought him to St. Paul's. The voice, which had the cracking tone of a teenager, was identified as

Father Ambrose's. No, he had said, he wasn't calling on his own behalf; he was calling at the behest of Monsignor Gallard. And, yes, it most certainly was business related. "Related to your specific business, as a matter of fact."

Gallard, Dorsey thought as his eyes turned from the city he loved to the river valley and the current of the Monongahela meandering through impoverished and bankrupt mill towns. Four years . . . nearly that since you last spoke to him, and it's been fourteen years before that when you last sat half asleep through his theology course at Duquesne. Monsignor Gallard . . . retired professor and close friend of dear old Dad.

Dorsey pushed off from the fence, starting for the monastery office as he slipped his arms into his jacket. The summer-weight suit was a well-cut shade of khaki, new, one sign of the upturn in Dorsey's fortunes. Work was coming in again these last fourteen months. Not an avalanche, but a steady stream of cases that kept the wolf from his door. He was popular again with attorneys and insurance companies, and all it had taken was one dead teenager and a policewoman's suicide. Ah, Dorsey thought, the price of success is low when paid by others.

Once inside the air-conditioned reception area, Dorsey identified himself to an elderly brother who led him down a short corridor of dark wooden walls adorned with crucifixes and icons. He was shown into what might have been either a conference or dining room. The first thing Dorsey noticed was the long table of matching dark wood that ran the length of the floor, surrounded by eight ladder-back chairs. There was a wall of three windows overlooking the city, and between each window hung a religious portrait. Beyond the head of the table was a second door.

"The others . . ." the brother said, "the others will be joining you in just a few moments. Take your time. Relax."

Dorsey moved to the windows, again checking the gray haze that hung above the downtown area like a cloud of auto exhaust, then took a chair on the far side of the table. He ran a finger across the table, admiring the wood shine from polishing he thought must occur daily. "The others," his guide had told him. Monsignor Gallard was in the singular. So there's to be a surprise guest, he thought. At least one. Which should come as no surprise to you.

The door behind the table's head slowly opened. Monsignor Gallard entered the room in a wheelchair guided by a very young and smooth-cheeked priest. Dorsey remembered the voice on the phone and figured him for Father Ambrose. He had heard of Monsignor Gallard's additional strokes, similar to his father's, but had not asked after him and certainly was unaware of his need for a wheelchair. The strokes and the four years since their last meeting had thinned the prelate's face and deepened the creases in his forehead and caused his jowls to droop. He smiled benevolently at Dorsey as the young priest slipped the chair into place at the head of the table before silently leaving the room. Dorsey returned the smile, remembering the case four years before in which the monsignor had assisted in leading him by the nose to a prearranged conclusion, and he wondered how deep his involvement had been then. Dorsey also had to wonder if that smile was all he had left, if speech was still within the man's abilities. He was immediately disabused of that notion.

"Thank you," Monsignor Gallard said, "for agreeing to see us so quickly. There's a good bit that has to be done, and from what I've been told it should be done quickly. Most quickly."

"Something special in mind?" Dorsey watched the monsignor's eyes drift toward the windows.

"You know I asked to be sent here"—Monsignor Gallard maintained his smile—"for purposes of retirement, once I learned that I wouldn't be allowed to reside in the Duquesne campus housing. So I asked to be sent here. Passionist Priests, that's the order that resides here. I'm not one of them, but I asked to come here as a reward for nearly sixty years of service. At least I can look down at the college grounds and guess at what's happening from day to day. Otherwise, for me anyway, the day holds some prayer time and relaxation when I'm not being bedeviled by that shrimpy Father Ambrose and his need to look after me.''

Dorsey leaned deeper into the chair and considered the performance. At first he thought that the monsignor was slipping with old age and infirmity, the first stages of his dotage, but he soon saw this as a chosen role: well-meaning *and* dissembling. Strategically timed nuggets of information would be dispensed as planned, for maximum effect. Dorsey saw he was marking time, filling space until everyone was assembled and accounted for.

''So who are we waiting on? How many?'' Dorsey asked. ''The brother who escorted me from the front door said I should wait for the others. You're an *other,* not 'others.' ''

Monsignor Gallard lost his smile for a moment. ''I wish I were sufficiently healthy to be in charge around here, not that they would ever allow such a thing. I think the good members of the order should learn to follow instructions and carefully weigh each of their words before speaking. But no matter, I suppose, it's no church secret. Another of your old acquaintances, a fellow colleague, should be arriving soon.''

Dorsey ran through a quick mental listing of names and found none to his liking. The days that Monsignor Gallard recalled were part of a false bonanza of employment followed by a hard fall into reality. And none of his then business colleagues remained family favorites. He was about to ask for a name when the brother on front-desk duty again opened the side door. He stepped aside to admit a square box of a man whose temples had grayed since Dorsey's last encounter with him in the county courthouse.

Former Assistant District Attorney William Meara had the look of an ex-prosecutor now doing well in private practice. The suit he wore was cut to fit and the shirt was of a quality that could withstand an August day in Pittsburgh. Dorsey knew he was gone from the courthouse because his boss had been defeated at the polls by Douglas Turner, a Republican. Suburban Protestant Republican. Dorsey had often wondered if that alone had brought on his father's second stroke.

"Goddamned, Meara"—Dorsey shook his head—"What a surprise. What a lousy, totally unexpected and totally unwanted surprise."

Meara took a seat opposite to Dorsey, unbuttoning his jacket and pulling at his trouser legs as he sat. "Have you gotten into any of it with him?" Meara addressed Monsignor Gallard. "Sorry to be running a little behind."

"Not a concern," the monsignor said. "We've just been saying hello."

"Is this it, then?" Dorsey asked. "Can we drop all this top-secret mystery crap and get started? I'd love to hear all about it. And then clear out and get back to my work."

Monsignor Gallard nodded to Meara who returned the gesture. "Ever hear of the Filus murder case?" Meara asked. "It's maybe two or three years old by now. Never has been solved."

Dorsey turned in his chair to face Meara. "Maybe something in the paper. Or maybe I remember seeing something about it on TV news. But that's about it. Should I know more?"

"Not really," Meara said, toying with the end of his tie. "Guy about our age, he steps off the bus on his way home from work, walks about two of the three blocks to his nice home in Point Breeze, and then takes two bullets to the head and goes to the sweet by-and-by. Never solved that one, never even came up with a suspect. The man left behind two sons and a widow."

Dorsey turned to Monsignor Gallard and then back to Meara. "And?" he asked. "You want me to do something about that? Something like solving the case, finding the murderer, personally strapping him in the chair and flicking the switch? That's somewhat beyond my level of expertise. Surprised, right? And why in the world are the two of you interested in this graybeard of a case?"

"Firstly," Meara said, "we agree. Solving this matter is far beyond the likes of you. And our interest has been generated by the interest, intense interest it seems, of others. I may no longer be involved in law enforcement, but I still own a telephone. Which people call me on. Old friends, new friends, buddies from my days in the DA's office. And one of these buddies has had a lot to say about the Filus case. He tells me that a new witness has surfaced and that our beloved District Attorney Turner is putting a lot of man-hours into the case. Seems he may have a suspect, and it also seems that he's on the verge of going after an indictment—''

"Perhaps," Monsignor Gallard said, interrupting, "perhaps I should mention that Bill is now with a law firm that represents the interests of the diocese."

Dorsey laughed. "Okay, what is it you're trying to tell me in this beat-around-the-bush conversation? Is the bishop under suspicion? Has he been questioned under the hot lights yet?"

"No, no, not the bishop," Monsignor Gallard said, allowing a slight laugh to escape before continuing. "Just a priest. Remember Tommy Crimmins, he played ball for St. Bonaventure University? He's a priest now. I'll bet you didn't know that."

"Holy shit," Dorsey said.

2

"**The DA**, he thinks he has a murder he can hang around Tommy Crimmins's neck? Well, hell. This is starting to get interesting." Dorsey slipped back against the rungs of his chair. He wasn't sure which was more surprising, Tommy Crimmins in the priesthood or Tommy Crimmins at the defendant's table. For three years, twice a basketball season, Dorsey had matched up against Crimmins, Duquesne against St. Bonaventure. Crimmins the work-boy forward, spending the last year of his college career throwing picks for a young Bob Lanier. Dorsey recalled him as thinner than himself but a few inches taller. And more than just a touch meaner. But, hell, not that much meaner, Dorsey thought. Not enough for this kind of thing.

"He's been pastor of St. Anne's for a little while now," Monsignor Gallard said. "That's where this poor Mr. Filus and his family attended Mass. The man, what was his first name again? . . ."

"David," Meara said, "David Filus. He was a CPA with some accounting firm in the Mellon Building. Made a pretty nice buck from what I understand."

"Let's get back to this murder business," Dorsey said. "How's about you telling me all about it so I can figure out what it is you have in mind for me?"

"Saving Father Crimmins, of course," Monsignor Gallard said. "And saving all of us, including Holy Mother Church, a lot of unnecessary bother so that we can go on

7

with our work, the work of saving souls. These religious pedophiles are one thing, but an allegation of murder is something else again. This business of being with young boys, well, that can be dismissed as a person's having cracked under the strains imposed by a celibate life. The pedophiles are just a small group of weaklings among us. But the church being seen as possibly harboring a killer would be ruinous. Murder, a calculated act. This one especially, ambushing a man on his way home. It requires plotting and observation before the act and covering one's tracks afterward. No, this can't be played off as an act of an unbalanced mind. This sort of thing could drastically change how the people of the diocese perceive the priesthood. Not good at all.''

"You said save Father Crimmins?" Dorsey asked. "Don't you mean clear him? Or does he need saving?"

Meara waved off the monsignor before he could respond, as if he were in court, urging his client to keep his silence. "Semantics," he said, "saved or cleared. Or both. I don't know what all the DA's got, but one thing he has for sure is the burden of proof. He has to at least convince a grand jury to indict, which can seem like a lot of bother if you know that you won't ever get a conviction because the defense has a potentially stronger case than your own."

"So," Dorsey said, "the job is to find something to derail the indictment process. To dissuade the DA's office from wanting to prosecute. I take it that as of now DA Turner has no problems with taking on the church because it wouldn't hurt his own political base. What with him being your new breed of non-Catholic politician?"

"That's how it sizes up," Meara said. "We need to kill this thing before it goes anywhere. And if we don't succeed, we need the basis for a plausible defense. Either way, you've got to get going on this right away. As far as we're concerned, you're on the clock right now."

Dorsey thought of the other work he had pending. Some of it could wait, some couldn't. "There's a little calendar shifting I'll have to do. You'll get first shot at my time, but there are some other irons in the fire.''

Meara produced a pen and notepad from the inside pocket of his suit jacket, then did some quick scribbling and passed the notepad to Dorsey. ''Guaranteed hourly rate is that number. Bonus if this goes away fast.''

Dorsey considered the number for only a second. ''I'm all yours.''

''Good.'' Meara rose from his seat. ''I'll fill you in on what we know on the walk to your car.''

Must be tons of information, Dorsey thought, it's such a hike to the parking lot. He rose and said good-bye to the monsignor.

''I hear you're giving some aid to Mrs. Leneski's case, the old woman in Lawrenceville,'' Monsignor Gallard said. ''That's good. If you need to spare a few moments for her, we'll understand.''

''Thanks loads,'' Dorsey said.

3

・・・・・・・・・・・

Both front windows of the row house were propped open by fans. Dorsey, sitting bare chested at his desk, used a variety of items as paperweights to keep his papers down. His wallet held down a week's worth of incoming correspondence and an empty coffee mug kept his invoices in place on the desk's far corner; a warm, unopened Rolling Rock anchored the notes he had just typed on the Filus matter. Behind him, wedged into the middle of a shelving unit stuffed with paperbacks and mementos of his basketball career, a tape player cruised through Ellington's "Caravan" and made way for "Perdido."

There was damned little that Meara could tell him and deciding where to begin remained an open question for Dorsey. Cloaking the Olivetti with its dustcover and then slipping the typed pages into a manila folder, he again replayed his stroll with Meara, who had begun his rundown by saying that he had only scant information and nothing on paper.

"It's like this,' Meara had said, wrenching loose his tie as they stepped out into the heat. "Looks like Crimmins may have had something going on with Louise Filus, the widow. And maybe this fling had been going on for some time, before and after the husband's death. Anyway, the DA's supposed to have a witness that's willing to say so. And this witness is supposed to be in a position to provide a motive for the killing. A money motive."

"Life insurance?" Dorsey had asked.

"Seems most likely. As I mentioned, Filus was well-off. And with his being a CPA, you'd figure him for having the estate-planning end of things pretty well covered. Anyway, the witness is this woman on the parish council who says she knows everything that went on between Crimmins and the Filus woman. This witness, she's an ex-nun of all things, which the woods are full of these days. How about that? Who in the hell knows where her heart really lies? Talk about possible axes to grind. That's something to explore. By the way, her name is Alice Sutton. Supposedly works as a substitute teacher in the city schools and at some food co-op during the summer."

Dorsey lifted the unopened beer and slipped the file beneath it. So, he thought as the fans' airstreams washed across him, it has to be a love triangle—if this Sutton woman has things straight. And that means she can't accuse Father Crimmins without implying that Louise Filus had a hand in her husband's death as well. Not if Sutton wants anyone to buy her story. Not if there's a money motive, like Sutton claims. So it's maybe a case of a man and a married woman wanting to be together and living on the old man's money. That made it a conspiracy with planning and intent and made for one nasty pot full of shit if it ever saw the light of day.

Dorsey left the swivel chair and went to the lone filing cabinet he kept in the converted living room-office. He extracted another file from the top drawer and took it to his desk, avoiding the midget refrigerator on the floor behind his chair. We'll understand, Monsignor Gallard had told him, if you have to put in some time helping Mrs. Leneski. Who gives a shit what you understand? Dorsey thought, opening the file. In two days he was to testify on Mrs. Leneski's behalf. And he still wasn't sure how best to go about it.

Mrs. Leneski, former client, grandmother of a lost teenaged girl that had needed finding, and current defendant before the Court of Common Pleas of Allegheny County. She thought a lot of you, Dorsey, he reminded himself. Hired you to find her granddaughter when you couldn't get hired to find a lost puppy. And you found the girl, all right. It was just that you found her four feet below ground and a few months dead. Dead before you ever heard her name. And then Grandma Leneski asked you the question that had your stomach flopping over. Asked you to kill the son-of-a-bitch doctor who wrote the illegal prescription for the drug that ripped open her granddaughter's heart, the drug that filled her chest with blood. At least you had the good sense to turn her down. A bright spot in your career.

The file held all the facts of the case. On a freezing cold afternoon that past January, Mrs. Leneski had entered the Butler Street office of Anton Novotny, M.D. A few of the neighborhood women were in the waiting room and several of them claimed to have voiced complaints when Mrs. Leneski bypassed the normal office procedure and marched herself into the doctor's examination room. That done, she withdrew from her oversized handbag a well-kept army-issue .45 from the Second World War, a relative's souvenir from the European campaign. Managing a two-hand grip, she got off one shot that put a hole the size of a grapefruit in Dr. Novotny's chest. There was only one shot, because the force of the gun's recoil had shattered the bones in her left wrist.

And there was a further complication to this matter. Dr. Novotny had not been alone. The records showed that Dr. Novotny had been in the process of conducting a rectal examination when the bullet struck. The patient, an elderly Medicare recipient like most of the doctor's clientele, had not only witnessed the act but now had a civil suit pending against Mrs. Leneski for mental and anal damages.

Dorsey was more worried about another facet of Mrs. Leneski's plight, the one that paralleled her case with Father Crimmins's situation. Again, this was no mad act of passion. Seven months earlier she had asked Dorsey if he would kill the doctor for her. For all Dorsey knew, there had been others who had refused over those seven months, and her doing it herself had been the last resort. On direct examination, Dorsey was sure that the attorney would avoid the subject. Cross-examination, under oath, was a different matter.

"So then I made a few calls," Dorsey told Al across the bar countertop, "to set up a few things for tomorrow. Take a look at some of the official and unofficial papers on this case."

Al slipped a fresh Rolling Rock in front of him and took a bill from Dorsey's stack on the bar. The barroom was air-conditioned and getting crowded, half filled with off-duty laborers and retirees from J&L Steel. Retirees, Dorsey thought, from a plant that has been torn down and hauled away. Retirees from a now empty plain running along the river. He looked at his green beer bottle and thought of the company's motto, "Same as it always was." Jesus, if only that were the case around here.

"Henry returned yet?" Dorsey asked, addressing Al by way of the backbar mirror, watching him as he worked the cash register.

"Not yet." Al moved his heavy frame halfway down the bar to wait on another customer as he spoke. "Still down in West Virginia as far as I know. That cabin he rented from Smitty is supposed to be pretty nice." He drew two beers from the tap then set them on the drain shelf, allowing the heads to settle. "He knows about Saturday, though. Told me when he left, said he'd be back to help you out on it. You reserve the truck yet?"

Dorsey took a pull on his beer. "All taken care of. It'll be waiting for us at the U-Haul center at Carson and twenty-ninth. Franklin's almost a two-hour drive, so the earlier the better." He took another drink of beer. "Henry better make it back here some time Friday night."

Al looked over the barroom crowd, wiped his hands on his white linen apron, and worked his way along the bar to Dorsey. He was a little heavier these days, Dorsey thought, an overall weight gain that had the buttons of his white shirt gaping at his chest. Otherwise, he remained unchanged, a big man lost somewhere in his sixties or seventies. And entirely in charge whenever he stepped behind that bar. Same as it always was.

"It'll be good," Al said, smiling. "Always liked Gretchen. And I think I like you better when she's around. Seriously, it's true. Sometimes you get that hangdog look like nothing's what it's supposed to be. You never had that when you two were an item." Al smiled again. "Yeah, yeah. You're gonna be easier to put up with when she gets back here."

"We'll see," Dorsey said, pulling himself from the bar stool and stretching out his legs. "We'll just have to see if my overall mood improves. But I certainly hope that it does. This being a burden on my friends has weighed heavily on my mind for a while."

"The cure will arrive on Saturday," Al said, heading for a customer at the far end of the bar, "with a truckload of furniture that has to be carried up to the second floor."

Dorsey settled back into his seat, watching himself in the mirror beyond the rows of liquor bottles that fanned out on either side of the cash register. His hairline reflected his forty-two years, both temples pulling backward but with a shock of curly hair hanging tough at the forehead. The shoulders were still broad and well-muscled, while the soft stomach was still somewhat under control and out of view beneath the bar. Presentable, Dorsey thought, still presentable. He sipped his beer and continued to stare into the looking glass.

He and Gretchen had remained in contact, even when she had been seeing another physician at Franklin Regional Hospital. Their continued contact had made little sense to Dorsey and for a while he had thought that this was the time to make a thoroughly clean break. But that hadn't been possible, and he had somehow exchanged his position of estranged lover for that of confidant and intimate friend. But now her fling with the young doc was over, Gretchen had assured him. And she was moving back to the city, to a new position at Mercy Hospital. And, Dorsey reminded himself in the mirror, it might not mean a damned thing. Remember your rule of thumb, he told the face reflecting back at him. Take what comes, romantically speaking, and settle for it.

"Al," he shouted down the bar. "You sure about Henry being back here in time?"

4

Looking down from a second-story window within Pitt's Hillman Library, a manila envelope held beneath his arm, Dorsey realized how much he hated the building. Not for what it was but for what it had replaced. Just outside and across a curving road that led into Scheneley Park was the last length of redbrick wall that had once enclosed the warning track at Forbes Field. In whitewash across a portion of the brick was the 457-foot demarcation. Another change, Dorsey thought, one that so many now lament.

Dorsey was no great fan of baseball, but he had been a fan of that old ballyard. The players who had passed through during the fifteen or so years he had sat in the left-field bleachers were of little consequence. Even Mazeroski and Clemente had been only temporary tenants as far as Dorsey was concerned. In his mind the place made the men and not the other way around. What was important were the cement bleachers, the rows of wooden drop-seat chairs that lined the grandstands, and the food booths doing business across the street from the ballpark. The players may have been the clergy, but they were nothing without a venerated worship site.

''The machine's all set for you, the fiche is in place.''

The voice pulled Dorsey back from his memories and futile wishes and he turned to face the assistant librarian. The man was in his late teens and ponytailed, his glasses

16

thick and finger-smudged. Dorsey thanked him and followed along to the workstation.

"Most people don't need this kind of help," the man said as Dorsey slipped into a chair facing the screen. "Really, it's a pretty simple machine. The fiche loads real easy, and then all you do is work this joystick to move things around." He took a firm grip on the directional knob and demonstrated. "See what I'm saying? You shouldn't be so put off by these machines."

Dorsey slowly placed the envelope on the workstation's countertop and produced a pen and small notebook from the hip pocket of his khaki slacks. "A guy your age," Dorsey said, turning to the man, "you or any of your friends, you ever see a guy working as an elevator operator? Maybe in a department store or an office building downtown? Never, I'll bet. And where oh where did they go? Whatever happened to that hard-working breed of men? Let me tell you. Everybody learned how to do their job for them. Especially after all the elevators were refitted with push buttons. So, now tell me, where do you see yourself in five years time?"

Abruptly left to himself, Dorsey concentrated on the screen, maneuvering the fiche of newspaper records for the *Post-Gazette*'s frontpage of November 7, three years earlier. Pen in hand, he began to scribble notes on the death of David Filus, forty-six years old on his most recent and final birthday. He had spent the last eleven years of his life as a CPA with the firm of Lambert and Associates, an independent accounting and investment firm located downtown in the Oliver Building, not the Mellon Building as Meara had suggested, Dorsey thought. Where they used to have elevator operators. Filus and family lived in the Point Breeze section of the city, and he had traveled daily to and from work by bus. The night before, November 6, he had stepped down off the bus and begun the three-block journey to his house.

He only lasted a block and a half of that journey. Someone, that mysterious unnamed someone, placed the business end of a .38 gun barrel to the back of his head and let a couple shots rip. No witnesses and only a few neighbors could remember a loud noise, and only then with the help of police-enhanced hindsight. The body had been discovered by a visiting nurse, running late that night, who had arrived to change the dressings on the leg of a diabetic patient on whose sidewalk the body was sprawled.

Dorsey pushed on through the next few weeks worth of murder coverage. A bullet casing was never found, so it looked like a revolver was used. The funeral was large but apparently dignified, and Father Thomas Crimmins had officiated. Left behind was his widow Louise and a set of twin sons who at the time were freshmen at a small college in the panhandle of West Virginia. From her photo, Louise was a looker, that early to mid-forties type that is regarded as handsome rather than beautiful. The boys, Greg and Mark, were short but broad and muscular in their dark mourning clothes, their hair full and neatly combed and parted. Dorsey figured them for bodybuilders, maybe small-time football players.

From the address, Dorsey estimated that the Filus home was at the far end of Point Breeze from his father's house. He pictured it sitting near the lower end of Frick Park, a forest donated to the city by the family of another dead steel baron—a forest into which any assailant could easily disappear, emerging without suspicion miles away. And there was another possibility based on geography, one that Dorsey saw as a ready-made defense theory.

Dorsey clicked off the microfiche light and settled back in the plastic scoop chair. Also not far from the Filus home, in the opposite direction from the park, was Thomas Boulevard. An attractive, landscaped thoroughfare lined with once elegant homes; it served as the stark frontier between affluent Point Breeze and a black and desperate Homewood. Just north of the boulevard, the slope of Westinghouse Park led toward Kelly Street and Frankstown Avenue, areas that were continuously mentioned on the local TV news in conjunction with sidewalk shootings and drug deals gone bad. So, Dorsey figured, the police theory was that one or two strung-out spades had crossed the boulevard and killed Filus for what he carried in his pockets—which, the newspaper reports mentioned, had been emptied. It was the obvious alternate theory in the murder and Dorsey knew that the new DA must have considered it. It was the strong and obvious choice. So the new DA must have convinced himself he's really on to something with this Crimmins thing.

Gathering up his belongings, Dorsey moved from the microfiche to a study table. He undid the clasp on the manila envelope and turned it open-side down, allowing two stapled reports to fall to the tabletop. Earlier that morning he had made two stops at the county courthouse and was now ready to consider the results.

The first document was the final disposition of the dead man's estate obtained at the County Registrar of Wills. Just as Meara had suggested about the dead CPA, the estate and will had been well-prepared long before death. Most everything passed on to Louise Filus. Two cars, the house that was then valued at a little under $100,000, and the proceeds of two life insurance policies amounting to $425,000. Mrs. Filus was also the custodian of two trust funds established for the twins. Each fund held $35,000 and control of the funds would not pass to the sons until their twenty-fifth birthday.

So, Dorsey thought, the woman had cash, heaps of it, and that by itself always raised eyebrows when dead bodies were found. And the police certainly knew about the insurance at the time of the initial investigation. But the newspaper records suggested an alibi. She had been attending a parish fundraiser that night. Dorsey wondered if Tommy Crimmins had been in the seat next to her. He could use a good alibi himself. Regardless, with an entire parish hall of corroborating witnesses, the police must have fallen back on their black-junkie theory. Especially with the boys away at school.

The document held no hope, Dorsey decided. Nothing unusual with the money being given over to the grieving widow. But he made a note to himself to ask her what she's been doing with it.

The second item was a copy of the coroner's postmortem report, which Dorsey had obtained for a two-dollar copy fee at the morgue. Most of it was standard, and boring: age, length of the corpse, and the metric weight of a variety of internal organs. In summation, David Filus was a healthy mid-forties, with the exception of having a good portion of the back of his head traumatically insulted by several bullets. One thing did catch Dorsey's notice, however. The report suggested that the shot had been point-blank and the strained musculature of the neck suggested that the victim's head was half turned to the left when the bullet struck home. Dorsey wondered if Filus was twisting about to get a look at his killer or just gazing off to his left, unaware that death was a breath away?

Dorsey stuffed the reports back into the envelope and checked his wristwatch, wishing he could avoid his next appointment. This wasn't of your making, he reminded himself. You've never shot a soul. Even when you were asked to.

The coffee was strong and bitter, and after more than a year of drinking it at least once a week, it still took Dorsey by surprise. He just lipped the rim of the cup and set it back in the saucer, watching Mrs. Leneski do the same across her kitchen table. "So what did they cover this morning?" Dorsey asked.

"More of the same. How I did it." Mrs. Leneski wore a high-necked black dress, the same one Dorsey had seen her in at her granddaughter's funeral and at each of her courtroom appearances. She looked no older for all that had happened, but then again, Dorsey thought, how could she? She had been a work-worn mid-eighties the day you met her and nothing had really changed. Not her looks, her attitude, or the white appliances and Formica-topped table that filled out the kitchen.

"They act like I lied and said I didn't shoot the son of a

bitch,'' she said, her voice filled with the distant echoes of
Eastern Europe. ''They make me sit there and listen to it all
and I wanna scream at the judge, 'Sure I did it, wouldn't
you?' But instead that goofy lawyer—he's a nice man, but
he's goofy—he takes my hand and holds it. Tells me to shut
my face and let him handle things. Then I tell him that I
already took care of things, that's why we're all here.''

''The state still has to make its case to the court,'' Dorsey
said. ''They have to show that an offense took place. They
have to establish the elements of a crime.''

''One year of law school and you know all that, huh?''
Mrs. Leneski lifted her cup and stared at him over the rim.
''Sometimes I wonder if my lawyer went as far as you did.
Maybe I should fire him and let you take over.''

''You could've done better than a lawyer who's spent
most of his career writing wills and handling juvenile probation hearings,'' Dorsey said, reminding her that his father,
Martin Dorsey, former county commissioner and grand old
man of Pittsburgh politics, had offered to cover her legal
expenses. An offer that Dorsey knew to be a thank-you for
tying off an old and annoying loose end for him. A loose
end by the name of Novotny.

''I pay,'' Mrs. Leneski said, leaving her seat and dumping
the remainder of her coffee in the sink. ''All them years on
the line at Kress Box; I got my money and don't use nobody
else's. I paid you, right? So I pay my lawyer. And I take
what I can afford.'' She rinsed out the cup and saucer and
put them in the drying rack. ''Ziggy will be here any minute
now to take me back. There's supposed to be some doctor
guy talking this afternoon. Tell how the bullet killed Novotny.''

''Pathologist,'' Dorsey said.

''What?''

''Pathologist,'' Dorsey repeated. ''This afternoon's doctor
guy?''

''Yeah, well, sure.'' Mrs. Leneski headed for the front
room and Dorsey followed. In the living room, she took a
chair by a window and watched for her ride. Dorsey sat on

the sofa, folding his legs to the right to avoid kicking the coffee table.

"Tried to get hold of your attorney yesterday," Dorsey said. "Left a message, two or three times, and never got a return call. You better let him know that we have to talk about my testimony. It's important. And it's supposed to take place tomorrow."

"So, tell them what you know." Mrs. Leneski turned from the window. "Tell them the truth, so what?"

"It's not that easy, not so simple." Dorsey leaned forward, resting his arms on his knees. "Long ago, at that very kitchen table, you offered me the job of killing Novotny. That was almost seven months or so before you got around to doing it on your own. And if I'm asked about it, I'll have to tell about it, which makes you, in the eyes of the law, a premeditating killer, not a sad, old grandma who was swept away by an irresistible impulse. And that makes the mercy of the court, even at your age, a lot harder to find."

"This supposed to mean something to me?" The old woman cut her eyes on Dorsey. "You were there; you went to my granddaughter's funeral. You know how old I am. You tell me what's left? You tell me that."

"How the hell do I know what's left?" Dorsey asked, pleading. "But I do know that it's senseless to suffer when you don't have to."

"You know suffering?" Mrs. Leneski said, turning back to the window. "You know shit."

5

At midafternoon, Dorsey swung by his Wharton Street row house to check on mail and phone messages. He dumped the letters on his desk and cracked open the office windows, putting the fans in place before dropping into his swivel chair. Reaching backward, he turned on the tape player, and with a strings backup, Charlie Parker put his own stamp on "Laura."

The mail was all for the good; mostly checks from insurance companies and law firms for services rendered. The message tape, Dorsey would soon realize, was another matter.

The first batch of calls had been from two adjusters at Blackwell Insurance, looking for reports on assignments that Dorsey had yet to complete. These things take time, Dorsey thought, taking solace in the hourly rate quoted by Meara and Monsignor Gallard. The next message was from Meara himself, wanting a status report and mentioning that a meeting between Dorsey and Father Crimmins had been arranged for that evening. Lastly, there was Irene Boyle, his father's long-time personal assistant.

Dorsey recalled his last encounter with her, just after his father's second stroke. It was in his father's room at the University Medical Center, just before what now appeared to be his permanent transfer to long-term nursing care. His father had been medicated into a sound sleep, and Dorsey and Mrs. Boyle had lingered near the door. "You have to

23

prepare for his death," she had told him. "You have to start thinking about it, we both do."

"Funeral arrangements?" Dorsey had asked.

"No, that's been planned out for years now. No, I meant that we have to start thinking about how we're going to get along without him. Once he's gone, you know."

Dorsey recalled her strange suggestion and how blandly she had made it. None of the hidden anger or disapproval that had colored most of their lifetime of conversations and none of the scattered confusion that had characterized her recent breakdown.

And now, with that same tranquillity, she had left a message asking that he call her with a time when he could meet with his father. It was important, but it was to be at his convenience. Oh, Dorsey thought, whatever happened to those command audiences of yesteryear?

He placed one quick call to Al, confirming that Henry had yet to return from vacation but was still expected for Saturday. Next he called Mrs. Boyle, but had to settle for her answering machine. His third call caught Bill Meara at his office.

"Around seven this evening," Meara said, "at the parish office. And let me tell you something, I'm not entirely sure Father Crimmins knows what this is all about. He may not be aware of all that's going on."

"The fuck are you talking about?" Dorsey asked. "You've kept him in the dark about this? The guy just might get his ass indicted on a killing and no one's mentioned it to him? Jesus, man, what the hell are you people doing?"

"Keep your goddamned shirt on already," Meara told him. "The diocese wanted to handle that part. Maybe they decided to handle it through you, what with you being an old buddy and all. Anyway you're getting paid, so you'll do it. Tell me what you've accomplished with your day so far. Then it can be my turn to be critical."

"Just getting my feet wet," Dorsey said and told him about his research. "When I talk to the Father tonight, I'll have him set up a time for me to see Louise Filus, which reminds me . . . I need something else from you guys. This Sutton woman, the former nun, I can find her easily enough on my own. But I'd like to know a little about her before I take her on. Why don't you see if you can find her old mother superior, or whatever, somebody I can talk to about her. The diocese must keep some kind of personnel file on these people. And while you're at it, see if you can conjure up any file they might have on Tommy Crimmins. I'd like to see what all he's been doing with himself these last twenty years."

"You won't have that by tonight," Meara said. "And I'm not so sure you'll need it, considering the assignment that's been laid out for you."

"You hired me for my expertise, remember?" Dorsey told him. "Just see about getting those files."

Dorsey parked the Buick at the corner of South Dallas Avenue, just up from St. Anne's parish compound, along the black wrought-iron fence that held back the grounds of a cemetery containing the remains of the city's founding families. It brought a quirky smile to Dorsey's face, thinking that so many of those rich WASP pioneers were forced to spend eternity so close to people they had spent a lifetime keeping at arm's length.

Once across the street, he walked past the engraved stone piece that proclaimed the parish title and along the low, well-tended hedges that surrounded the wide lawns. A thin walkway led to the parish residence, a large house of green brick crowned with several floors of whitewashed clapboard. Dorsey climbed onto the wraparound porch that housed two Adirondack easy chairs, and pressed the doorbell.

Dorsey waited a few minutes and was about to hit the chime again when a young man in his early twenties opened the door. His light brown hair was full and combed straight back, and he had the rounded wire-rimmed eyeglasses that mixed an intellectualism into his athletic appearance. Dressed in sweat shorts and an oversized T-shirt, his sneakers and legs smeared with dirt and loose grass, Dorsey wondered if he was meeting the parish groundskeeper.

"Help you?" the young man asked, filling the door frame.

"I'm here to see Father Crimmins," Dorsey told him. "We have an appointment. It was scheduled for right about now."

A light seemed to go on in the young man's eyes. "Oh, jeez, sorry," he said, stepping backward and to the side, inviting Dorsey to enter. "You're Mr. Dorsey, right? I'll get Father for you. We were just finishing up, anyway."

He left Dorsey in a parlor room that was furnished with several easy chairs and a small ebony-colored piano with matching bench. A hymnal rested on the music rack, and Dorsey wondered if Tommy Crimmins was the pianist. He ran through a few alternate approaches that he might try on the priest, ways to break the bad and frightening news, and found none to his liking. Just let the music flow, he told himself, the tune will call itself. The young man quickly returned with a much taller fellow who had changed little since Dorsey had last seen him some twenty years ago. He wore a short-sleeved clerical shirt with the Roman collar pulled free and the white tab shooting wildly off to the side. There were thin lines of gray in his thick, once jet-black hair, but the build was the same, thin and lightly muscled. He had Dorsey's shoulder width but not the bulk, and his waist showed no sign of expansion over the years. He smiled warmly at Dorsey, extending his hand.

"Carroll Dorsey," Father Crimmins said, taking Dorsey's hand. "Good to see you. My ribs still ache from your elbows. Guys on the team used to wonder if you put them through a pencil sharpener before each game."

"The way I remember it," Dorsey told him, "it was you that caused a lot of people to rethink this business about basketball being a noncontact sport."

Father Crimmins laughed and turned to the light-haired man at his side. "Carroll, let me introduce you to Bill Sargent. Bill helps out with the local kids' soccer team that the parish has a hand in. Soccer, it's all these kids talk about, like basketball when we were young. Imagine the two of us trying to stand upright and play a game with our feet at the same time.''

Dorsey shook Bill Sargent's hand and was told by Father Crimmins that Bill was only a temporary assistant coach and would be heading south in a week or so to begin his senior year at Tulane. "Not even Catholic," Father Crimmins said, "but he helps out with these kids, on parish grounds of all places. If this were thirty years ago, I'd have to assign an altar boy to follow him at all times, keeping notes."

Dorsey briefly smiled and nodded his agreement, hoping that the priest would pick up on some sense of urgency and send Bill packing for the evening. There was a silent moment among the three and then Father Crimmins worked his way through a graceful dismissal of the young man. Bill Sargent made a quick promise to be back for the next day's soccer practice and was soon out the door.

"The housekeeper went home early this evening," Father Crimmins said, leading the way from the parlor into a central corridor and then a private office. He offered a chair to Dorsey. Instead of installing himself behind the grand cherry-wood desk, Father Crimmins sat in a matching chair, turning it slightly to face his visitor. Dorsey figured it as an offshoot of some intimate counseling technique.

"I thought it would be best if she didn't know about your visit. The housekeeper, I mean," Father Crimmins continued. "Not that I'm in any way sure why you're here. But it seemed best to keep it discreet. Regardless, it's good to see you again."

Dorsey's eyes roamed the office and he concluded that it was done in a style best called clerical well-to-do. Beyond the desk was a matching wood credenza and the far wall had a sideboard and bar. Only one piece was out of place, an autographed photo of Bob Lanier in a Detroit Piston uniform, framed and standing by the liquor bottles.

"Dave Filus," Dorsey said. "David Filus to be formal. That's what brings me here."

Father Crimmins adjusted his weight on the chair. "I missed you, too. No time for catching up, right? If the mention of that name is supposed to shock me, it doesn't. It was a terrible thing that happened and the whole parish and I mourned him grievously. But I'll let you in on a little secret. Time passes and it heals things, and you don't feel so bad anymore. And it works for priests, too. I knew him and I liked him, but he's been gone a few years, and I've been busy. So I haven't given him much thought."

"How about the widow, Louise?" Dorsey asked. "She ever creep into your thoughts?"

"Okay," Father Crimmins said, again shifting in his chair. "Let's not fence around about this. What exactly brings you here this evening?"

"Alright," Dorsey said, "here we go." He laid it out for him, all that he knew and all the names he had. "This new DA," Dorsey said, "I figure he'll move slowly. But believe me, he'll move on you if he thinks he can. I'm here to come up with enough to convince him that it's not worth his while to raise a stink. So you and I have a lot to talk about."

"You're not interested in solving the crime?" Father Crimmins asked. His voice was weak and much of the color had left his face. He stripped off the white tab of his Roman collar and twisted it in his hands. From a hip pocket he produced a handkerchief and worked it along his brow and cheeks. "Christ, this is really something. But really, you're not going to solve this?"

"Me?" Dorsey said. "I wouldn't mind doing that, although I think that's one hellacious long shot, if you're a betting man. More importantly, your bosses who are now my bosses are not particularly concerned with it. They just want your problem to go away, and I think you'd do well to settle for that." Dorsey reached over and gave Father Crimmins a light slap at the knee. "Take a deep breath, buddy. Then we have to get started."

Father Crimmins shook his head, as if clearing his thoughts, and neatly refolded his handkerchief. "Ah, wow. You think that something is done with, completely behind you, and then, well, you get a night like this." He let a deep sigh deflate his chest. "What do you say we take a walk? I talk a lot better when I'm on my feet."

"Lead the way."

They headed along the cemetery borders in the direction of Frick Park and the museum that held that family's once private art collection. There were neighborhood kids playing on sidewalks and porches across the street. Each small group called out a hello to their pastor, and each effort was rewarded with a friendly wave. "Don't take this question the wrong way," Father Crimmins said, turning to Dorsey. "But have you ever been in a situation in which people, almost everyone, try to kiss your ass? I mean *really* kiss your ass?"

"Never," Dorsey said, laughing. "Not even once."

"Then how do I explain my life to you, how do I tell you what my version of religious life is like? Without that common experience?"

"Just keep going," Dorsey said, content to allow the priest to find his own way. There were questions to be asked and their time would come.

"I'm in a position where everybody wants to do everything for or with me. They want me to go out on their boat, they want to have me to the club for golf. I never have to eat at home; there's always an invitation. And have you ever seen a priest wait in line? For anything? At the movies or a restaurant? And never at church functions. I walk into a church-sponsored dinner, no matter how crowded the place might be, a horde of old women come out of the woodwork and fret over me. Here's a chair, they say. Or they make a mad dash into the kitchen and come running back to me with a double order of whatever's on the menu."

"Sounds like a sweet deal."

"For a while," Father Crimmins said. "Don't get me wrong, there are those who never get tired of it. The treatment is their due for hard work in Christ's name. Or so they say."

"You have some doubts about your fellow members of

the cloth?'' They had come to an intersection and Dorsey stopped to watch the light traffic before proceeding forward with the priest. ''Think they might be riding some kind of religious gravy train?''

''Always were a smart-ass,'' Father Crimmins said. ''That was the word on you, back in college. We used to wonder if we could get you out of a game on technical fouls by pissing you off, by getting you to complain and insult the referee.''

''I don't recall that ever working.''

''Given time, it would have,'' Father Crimmins said. ''But as I was saying, this being lavished over can be awfully smothering. And believe me, being taken care of can't replace being cared for. Or the sense, the security, that another person cares for you. Even with my faith, my religious sensibilities, and my desire to be a priest, that being cared-for stuff is pretty attractive.''

''And then there's that lack of intimacy.'' Dorsey shot a brief glance over his shoulder. ''There is that lack, isn't there?''

''Yes and no,'' Father Crimmins said, ''and not always in the way you couch that term. There is intimacy without sex and the lack of that can be just as devastating, if not more so. In this life, I have a whole parish with problems to listen to. That means I have to stretch myself pretty thin. So there's not much left for me. Or for me to share with someone I'd like to concentrate on.''

Dorsey found himself unable to find fault with the priest's position. Without Gretchen, even when other women had been available and attractive to him, there had been something missing. That sense of security, the feeling that at least one other person gave a damn was a rare and pricey item at times. He wondered if that feeling might accompany her physical return. He set that thought aside, returning to business.

''Time to end the philosophical discourse, Father. We can save the stream of free thought for later.'' Dorsey took the priest by the elbow and moved in close to him. ''Time is short. Just two fast questions. You have something going on with this Filus woman, right? And you can arrange for me to have a private and candid talk with her?''

"Aren't you forgetting to ask if I shot her husband?"

"Not really. It's not important just yet, and I may not want to know in the long run." Dorsey shot another quick glance over his shoulder. "I need you to answer my questions, right now so we can break this off. I wouldn't have expected you to have noticed, and to be honest I almost missed it myself, but we're being watched. When I pulled up to your place, there was this kind of dull-looking sedan, a Chevy, parked about half a block away with a bored-looking guy in the driver's seat. I should've pegged the guy right off as a cop or some DA's man. After all, I used to be one of those bored guys in a dull car. Anyways, the same guy has been trailing us. He's a little ways back there, on the far sidewalk.

"So, this is how it is. He was watching you and now he's watching me. And when he gets to the office in the morning, he'll check my license-plate number and the DA will wonder what's up. He'll maybe get nervous and try to move faster. So we have to move even faster than that.''

Father Crimmins squared up with Dorsey. "Well, as I'm being thought of as a murderer, I suppose I can confide in you about my personal life, which suddenly seems less important. Yes, Louise and I have a thing going. She and I are together. Someday, perhaps, I'll give you what you'll no doubt find to be the rather boring details. She'll talk to you."

"Okay," Dorsey said. "Arrange the meeting. Just me and her. And for our next talk, try to remember all you can about Alice Sutton. Then we can figure out why she hates you so much."

6

Dorsey sipped at the green beer bottle then set it to rest on the bar's countertop. "So, just like that, tomorrow's been canceled."

Al, hunched over as he filled the bar cooler with bottled beer, looked up at him in wonder. "They canceled Friday?" he asked. "Took it right off the calendar did they? Jesus, is this gonna hurt business."

"Don't take things so literately." Dorsey smiled. "We've discussed that problem of yours in the past. The Leneski trial, my testimony, it's off for tomorrow. Something about the judge having the flu. So it picks up again on Monday."

"Well," Al said, tossing an empty beer case across the floor, "that's gotta be good news. Gives you more time to figure out a way to help out the old woman."

Dorsey was the bar's lone customer at that late hour, and the quiet that wrapped about him made for a reflective mood. "We'll see. It's this lawyer that worries me. By the way, it was his secretary that called me about tomorrow, left a message on my answering machine. The guy's name is Artie Meeker. Ever tell you much about him?"

"The name doesn't ring any bells," Al said. He had finished with the cooler and moved on to dusting the liquor bottles on the backbar. "The guy been in business long?"

"Long enough, I suppose." Dorsey took another hit of his Rolling Rock. "But not as a criminal law specialist. Meeker's like a lot of guys I used to know. Worked as a claims adjuster while he plowed his way through night school at Duquesne. That's not an unusual thing, adjusters going on to law school. But most of the ones that do, they practice law for insurance companies. They defend companies against compensation claims or product liability cases, stuff like that. But this guy, Meeker, he didn't catch on anywhere. So he opens his own little firm, hangs up his shingle in Mrs. Leneski's neighborhood, and grabs any kind of case he can. Including Mrs. Leneski's case. Christ, I wish she had taken up my old man's offer. He would have gotten the best for her, and for free.''

''She's old and she's stubborn,'' Al said. ''And you never had a snowball's chance in hell of changing her.'' Al inspected the liquor bottles and stuffed the dust rag in the pocket of his linen apron. ''Tell ya' what, though. Must be nice being a judge. Calls in sick at least twelve hours ahead of time. Most people don't have that luxury. Most people have to wait to the next morning, you know, get up and see how you feel? Maybe you can drag yourself into work after all?''

''Maybe it's a matter of getting the proper treatment,'' Dorsey said, smiling. ''My doctor and your doctor would prescribe a week's trial of antibiotics. His doctor is probably more enlightened and suggested a three-day weekend at a cabin in the mountains. Next to a secret trout stream.''

Dorsey picked up on the tail early the next morning as he pushed along East Carson Street on his daily walk. Dressed in gym shorts and a dull gray T-shirt, five-pound weights strapped to his ankles, he chugged on toward the foot of the Smithfield Street Bridge. And for the entire round trip, a nondescript Chevy Corsica lagged a block behind. Dorsey hadn't expected to come under scrutiny until at least midday. Well, hell, he thought. The DA's office must really be burning the midnight oil. And they only do that when they have a real hard-on for a guy. Like Father Crimmins.

Back behind his desk, still dressed in his soaked workout clothes, Dorsey put in a call to Bill Meara. ''The guy's sitting across the street, in a car I think I used to use on the job.'' He used the front tail of his shirt to mop the perspiration from his face. ''Thought you'd want to know about this little development. And by the way, quarter after seven, and in the office already? That's good. Hope your bosses know what a great guy they have in you.''

''They know,'' Meara said, his voice sounding a little weary. ''That I make sure of, by staying a step or two ahead of the pack. And of you, too.''

''Tell me how.''

''Had a call late last night,'' Meara said. ''Remember what I said about keeping alive a friendship or two at the DA's office? Well, one of them gave me a buzz. Jesus, this Turner guy must really keep them late at the office. Seems they had a tail on Father Crimmins, which I assume you know already, and who comes acalling but Carroll Dorsey. The city's hottest young detective and the son of Douglas Turner's personal Antichrist. From what I'm told, Turner just about shit his pants. Started shouting orders to the staff about doing this and finding out about that and putting you under the microscope. The guy must be antsy as hell, trying to figure out what you're up to.''

''Doesn't sound so good,'' Dorsey said. ''If Turner's so worked up, he'll move faster. And maybe he'll be just a little meaner when he does move.''

''Depends on your outlook.'' Meara's voice was growing stronger, more reflective. ''Antsy can be good. For us, I mean. Didn't you ever screw up something, didn't you ever know anybody who screwed up something, because they were antsy? Just plain fucked up because they moved too fast. It could happen. Maybe it will. Something to hope for, dream about.''

''Well,'' Dorsey said, ''while you're at it, how about dreaming up those records I asked for on Crimmins and Sutton.''

''In the works,'' Meara replied. ''And if you can hold for a second, I have the phone number on that Mother Superior you asked about. She's free this morning for a talk. Just be sure to behave like a little gentleman and maybe she won't rap you across the knuckles with her ruler.''

Dorsey fished a pencil from the desk's center drawer and took down the number, scratching it into the desktop blotter. He told Meara that he'd call later if anything broke. ''And get those files.''

''Relax,'' Meara said just before hanging up. ''And don't forget who's working for whom.''

Through his shower and shave, Dorsey considered what he might do about the man following him. A few possibilities sounded like fun: high-speed getaway, going against traffic on a one-way street, switching cars with Al in the alley. But in the end he chose to do nothing. Because, he told himself, there is nothing you can do, nothing that would change matters. Turner knows you're involved and that's that. He's got a brain, at least half of one from the way some people talk, and he can certainly figure out what ground you'll be covering. So let the poor, half-asleep guy in the Corsica tag along. Let him do his job. Otherwise, he loses you and has to go back to the office to report it. And he gets his ass in a sling over it. Remember those days?

In a number of ways, the motherhouse at Mt. Alvernia could be thought of as the opposite number of St. Paul's retreat house. At least that's how Dorsey thought of it as he drove through the main gates, trying to convince the Buick to take on the steep, cobbled incline. Just beyond the city's northern edge, commanding the high ground, it was another compound of the religious life, this time female.

Dorsey moved the Buick upward through manicured lawns, passing several gray-stone sculptures, one of the Virgin and another he couldn't place. He parked where the ground leveled out in front of the main building. Dressed again in his lightweight suit, Dorsey stepped out of the car and admired the structure, one built in a style he could only think of as Classic Catholic.

Larger than any barracks Dorsey could remember from his hitch in the army, the building housed a girl's high school along with a convent. Perhaps only three-stories high, its size was in its length, occupying most of the hill's crest. The walls were dark brick with arched doorways and ornate trim at the windows. Dorsey climbed the slate steps at the main entrance and depressed the chime button mounted to the left of the double wooden doors.

After stating his business to a young nun in full habit, Dorsey was escorted down a long, wide corridor to a rather plain-looking wooden door that displayed no sign suggesting the room's purpose or inhabitant. The young sister asked him to wait a moment and gently rapped a knuckle at the door before opening it just enough to slip her head and one shoulder past the doorjamb.

"Sister Loretta said you may go in now," the young nun announced, stepping back from the door. "Would you care for tea or maybe coffee? Sister Loretta has tea everyday about now. Perhaps some tea, then?"

"Sure, tea would be nice." Dorsey wondered if the next time he met with a member of a religious order it could be held in a booth in Al's back room, with appropriate beverages. He smiled at the young nun as she went off for tea and then he stepped through the doorway.

Sister Loretta was not the nun that Dorsey had expected. After meeting the sister who was now chasing down his tea, dressed in full habit, including the tight-fitting wimple, he had this figured as a conservative order. But seated behind a polished desk that any executive would drool over, Sister Loretta had the look of a college dean. She wore a white blouse under a royal blue business suit and her gray hair was short and recently styled. With the exception of a small silver crucifix at her throat, she wore no jewelry. Dorsey figured her to be in her midfifties and was impressed. But he had to swallow a silent laugh as well. She almost pulls off the charade, he thought, but it's the lack of jewelry, and the lack of makeup, too. Plainclothes nun all the way. Easy to spot. Bet you that behind that desk she has on a pair of black shoes with laces.

"They tell me you want to talk about Sister Marie," Sister Loretta said as she rose to take Dorsey's hand. She invited him to take one of the guest chairs that faced her desk. "It's been awhile, but I remember something of her."

"Sister Marie?" Dorsey asked. "Maybe there's a mistake. I don't know any Sister Marie."

Sister Loretta laughed and gave her head a quick toss. "Sorry for the confusion, my mistake. That was the name Alice Sutton chose when she joined us. The name she used while she was here. For clarity, and maintaining sanity, we can call her Alice."

"Thanks," Dorsey said, settling back into the chair. "So tell me about her, about when she was with the order."

"You have a starting point in mind?" Sister Loretta asked.

"None in particular," Dorsey said. "I was hoping to get some background on her before you and I spoke, but, well, these things don't always go my way. And this is kind of a rush job, so I didn't want to miss the chance to speak to you. Just tell me what you know, what comes to mind. Maybe I'll hear something interesting and latch on to it."

"She was a trial. For everyone under this roof."

"Now that's interesting," Dorsey said. "This is starting to go awfully well already."

Sister Loretta spent a moment looking at the desktop and raised her eyes to Dorsey. "That was harsh, not what I should have said at all. You know I'd feel much better about this if I knew why we were having this talk."

Dorsey gave it just a second's worth of thought. "You're talking to me because your superiors told you to. That's all."

"How very true," the nun said. "I wouldn't have the likes of you in this building if I didn't appreciate the need for obedience within the religious community. Your past exploits have been well publicized and sometimes unappreciated by myself and others who live here. A few years back you didn't do the Catholic Church any favors."

"Believe me," Dorsey said, "I just might be doing it one now. Tell me why Alice Sutton was a thorn in your side."

"Because the vocation we follow here was not enough for her. Her problems were in her outlook, her attitude toward life and others."

"They haven't made a convent strong enough to hold the likes of her, right?"

Sister Loretta gave a rueful laugh. "We're not that restrictive, not that inhibiting. There is no formal vow of obedience as severe as that of the Jesuits."

Dorsey grinned. "You mean God's own Green Berets?"

"I didn't know that the laity was on to our in-house humor." Sister Loretta returned the grin. "No, we're nothing like that, but we do expect discipline in our ranks. In fact, I'm not sure as to why someone would seek us out if they weren't attracted to such an atmosphere."

"But your Sister Marie," Dorsey said, "she wasn't up for that?"

"We didn't realize it at first, although we should have." Sister Loretta straightened the cuff at her left wrist. "She came to us after college, which is unusual. She was fully trained as a teacher, with a year or so of classroom experience. Our Novitiates are traditionally much younger and our Order provides the education and training. But Alice Sutton had attended a Catholic institution, the College of Saint Rose as I recall, and her spirituality and faith remained unquestioned by any of her superiors. She was the most promising newcomer I can recall. And as a newcomer she was attentive, respectful, and observed our regulations. But, after a time, there came a change."

"A change or was it just that her true nature began to seep out through whatever cracks were available?"

Sister Loretta nodded. "You're right, of course. A change for us, revelation for her. She taught elementary school at several of our schools in the diocese and she started tinkering with the curriculum. Brought in some feminist themes at first, and that was okay, but it was taking up time meant for other matters. And then she moved on to sexuality issues, issues of sexual orientation and preference, that sort of thing, presented to the very young."

"And that," Dorsey asked, "proved to be intolerable?"

"Yes," Sister Loretta said, "but not a capital offense. She was ordered to stop and she did comply. But we soon found out that she complied with just our instructions, not the spirit of those instructions. Within weeks we began to get reports that she was leading classroom discussions challenging the supremacy of the priesthood and the Holy Father's confirmation of the priesthood's male-only membership. That settled matters."

"You showed her the gate?" Dorsey held a vision of two lines of nuns at the convent gates and a lone drummer rapping out a martial beat as Sister Marie took the Walk of Shame. Would have been something to see, he thought. Worth the price of admission.

"She was asked to leave; she was actively encouraged to do so."

"And she agreed to that?" Dorsey asked, still working up his daydream of religious court-martialing.

"I see you've never met Ms. Sutton," Sister Loretta said. "She most certainly did not leave on her own. To be absolutely honest, we had to force her out. And you may not believe this, but it took a police escort to get her off the grounds."

"I'll believe it," Dorsey said, straightening in his chair. "You just tell it."

Sister Loretta layed it out for him in detail and just as she completed her story, and before Dorsey could digest it all, there came a quiet knock at the door. Sister Loretta acknowledged it and when the door opened it was the young nun who had escorted Dorsey to the office. "Excuse me, Sister," she said, "but there are two young men at the front door asking for Mr. Dorsey. They look very official. In fact, they both showed me badges."

"Sorry," Dorsey said to Sister Loretta. "I mean about bringing the police down on you again. The neighbors might notice. You'll get a reputation."

7

Young men, Dorsey thought, she calls these guys young men? Christ, they look like a couple of prep-school boys trolling for prom dates. This is what the new DA sends out to bring in a guy?

The two of them looked to be half Dorsey's age, and he had them figured as recent law graduates with rich, connected families that had paid into the Douglas Turner campaign war chest. Both, despite the weather, wore dark business suits with the jackets buttoned. The blond one, wearing aviator sunglasses and slicked-back hair, leaned on the Buick's trunk. The second one, crew cut with his hands clasped at belt-buckle level in an officious manner, approached Dorsey. From his vantage point at the bottom step of the school's main entrance, Dorsey gave them each a playful grin. "So," he asked them both, "when did the DA start the summer internship program? He let you have the family car, tell you to give me a lift? Don't tell me, one of you two has a driver's license, the other has a learner's permit?"

The crew cut waved off the blonde, who looked insulted and held out a leather ID folder for Dorsey's inspection. "I'm Investigator Michaels," he said, barely working his facial muscles. "And he's Investigator Longley. DA's office."

"Like you guessed," Longley said, shoving himself away from the Buick and waving Dorsey forward. "C'mon, let's

40

get going. The man wants to see you. Time's wasting.''

"The man?'' Dorsey said, arching his brows and giving them each a chance to soak in his reaction. "They let you two run around talking like that? Hey, listen, guys. Really. If I give you two a hard time, will one of you call me a scumbag and tell me to assume the position?''

Longley slipped his shades into his jacket's breast pocket and moved forward, but Michaels proved more of a professional. "Mr. Turner would like a word with you. He asked us to bring you to him.''

Dorsey gave Michaels a courteous nod then looked at Longley, hanging his head and sighing. "Okay, kids,'' he said. "Fun's fun, but let's resolve this bullshit right here and now. Is this your idea of bringing me in for questioning, arresting me on some charge that you haven't even fucking mentioned, or are you just trying to be a pain in the ass at your boss's request? Tell me what this is about and make it at least semiofficial, or take a hike.''

Longley stewed while Michaels seemed to gather himself. Dorsey smiled, pleased to have a couple of kids on his hands. It was fun to kick around the authorities, for a change.

"Mr. Turner,'' Michaels said, hesitating and preparing his words carefully, "Mr. Turner requests that you accompany us to a meeting with him. He would like to have an informal and nonofficial discussion with you. Strictly off the record. It won't be at his office, and when it's finished we'll bring you back to your car. This won't take long.''

"Sounds good,'' Dorsey said. He followed the two of them past the Buick to a white Chevy Corsica with a municipal license plate and a whip of a radio antenna. Plainclothes nuns and unmarked police cars, Dorsey thought, folding himself into the backseat. It's like they come up and bite you in the ass.

Dorsey made his way through the revolving doors at the rear of the hotel, leaving the two delivery boys on the sidewalk with the parking valets and bellhops. There was one short flight of steps, a tiled landing, and then a choice between two winding staircases, both of which could deposit him in one of his favorite spots, the main lobby of the William Penn Hotel. One of Dorsey's favorites because it was an unintended history lesson, a reminder of the city's own Gilded Age. Large and multileveled, it was furnished with elegantly upholstered chairs and sofas gathered intimately around claw-footed coffee tables. Potted palms and soft lighting completed an ambiance of the solid wealth that had been enjoyed by the city's earliest industrialists and robber barons. Industrialists and robber barons, Dorsey thought, can anyone really tell the difference? Better yet, is there really a need to make that distinction?

Dorsey spotted Turner near the far end of the lobby, seated in a wingback chair. Dressed in a blue blazer and gray slacks, he rose from his seat and waved Dorsey forward, adding a welcoming smile to the gesture. For Dorsey, he looked like all his television appearances: slightly over six feet and less than one hundred and eighty pounds; his hair still dark, thick and, softly combed back; and metal rimmed glasses. The perfect suburbanite. Dorsey muffled a laugh as he approached, wondering if he had just called home and told his wife to light the charcoal.

"Doug Turner," the DA said, offering his hand to Dorsey and gesturing him into a chair beside his own. "Thanks for coming. You know, I really should apologize about this. I've been sitting here having second thoughts about the whole thing, especially about sending those two for you."

"Good," Dorsey said, half rising from his chair. "Then can I leave now? What with you feeling so bad and all?"

Turner snorted out a short laugh, steepled his fingers, and settled a little deeper into the chair cushion. "Well, we are both here and we should take advantage of the occasion. After all, it does seem that we have some business matters in common."

Dorsey rested his elbow on a chair arm and cupped his chin in hand. So, he thought, this is it. Doug Turner's version of an intimidating power setting. As if he were behind a huge oak desk with sunlight flooding in from the back window. You wrap yourself in this room, Doug, as if you were heir to the city's founding fathers. Christ, the old man, weakened with age and member of a passing era, he still has a better claim on this room.

"Have to tell you," Dorsey said, "this kind of bullshit is really lost on me. I like this place pretty well, but you don't fit in. You look like more a Sheraton-by-the-airport kind of guy. . . . Anyway, sorry I had to say that." Dorsey shifted in his seat. "Let's get to it, what do you want from me?"

Turner folded one leg over the other knee, checked the crease in his slacks, and appeared to examine Dorsey before responding. "You've had your say," he said. "That's good, it will make for better communication. So, now I think I'll have mine." He straightened his leg, both feet now on the floor. "You think I'm a smart-ass newcomer, maybe not up to the job. It's bad attitude you've inherited from your father, despite the fact that the two of you spend most of your time at odds with each other. And while we're on the subject of your father, his day, and that of the Big Democratic Machine, are over. All those loyal voters moved out to the suburbs and went Republican and cast their ballots for men like me. I'm sorry about his medical problems, but he's through as a power player. The man's a dinosaur. And you're little more than a private eye who gets lucky every now and again, especially when a few people die."

"Well," Dorsey said, shrugging his shoulders. "Fuck you, too. I guess."

"Yes," Turner said. "Fuck you, too. Now tell me what business you have with this priest Crimmins?"

"Can't help you there," Dorsey told him. "I could sit here and act like I don't know what you're talking about, but that's no good. After all, your tail on Crimmins spotted me and the priest together. And your having a tail on him, and now one on me, confirms your interest in him, so we're both in the same boat. Naw, I won't lie to you. I'm just not going to tell you shit."

Turner scratched at his nose and tried hiding a smile. "That's pretty much what I expected from you initially. And I expect you'll maintain that position for a while, but that is going to change. Reverend Crimmins has a murderous love triangle in his past and he's going to face charges on the death of Mr. Filus. And when I'm through, he's going to have a very long and involuntary assignment as a prison chaplain." Turner smiled again. "There, you see. All I want for the man is a life sentence, maybe even with a chance at parole. I'm not the type to chase after a death sentence for a priest."

"Makes me feel loads better," Dorsey said, "but I still think I'll keep a few things to myself. And that won't change. Besides, you don't need me. From what I understand you'll be making your move pretty soon."

"Of course I don't need your help," Turner told him. "What I mean to say is that yours is not an essential role in this case. But that doesn't change your assignment, which is one I can easily guess at. You've been hired by someone in the diocese to find problems with my case against Crimmins, as if there will be any. Or maybe you're supposed to come up with an alternate suspect."

"Like two young gang-bangers from Homewood?"

"You'll need to do better than that." Turner shook his head. "That's the stock answer that would have stood up pretty well if Crimmins wasn't laying his ordained wood to the widow. My concern is that you actually might come up with something better. After all, everybody has an imagination and you might use yours. I just don't want any surprises once charges are brought. Not from you."

Dorsey took in the room for a moment and thought, What the hell is this? The guy has you here to listen to his implied threats. He's a lawyer after all, and he knows he's tampering with a potential witness. Why take the chance if he's really got Crimmins in the crosshairs? And what's he have on you for leverage? What makes him think you'll cooperate?

"I'm leaving," Dorsey said, getting to his feet. "You don't have shit on me. You expect me to sit here and piss my pants in fear because some election official lost count because his shoes were tight and he couldn't get at his toes, so there's a miscount and you ended up getting elected DA. Well, you'll just have to do better.''

Turner rose to face him. He was an inch or so shorter than Dorsey, but he seemed to grow, like a frightened cat puffing out its fur. ''How about the old lady, the one from Lawrenceville who's up to her calcified hips in trouble? Things can go a lot of ways for her. The man I have on the case, he can push hard or he can ease up. He'll play it anyway I say. And you know I don't mind going after her on this one. I can't have members of the medical profession murdered in their examination rooms. They have rights, too.''

''Jesus,'' Dorsey said, ''that's pretty goddamned low. But you haven't got the balls.''

''I'm determined and I have my ways of making things happen.'' Turner shot him one last grin. ''Lucky, wasn't it? The judge getting sick, making you available for our conversation? Do you really think these things just happen?''

8

Stretched out in the backseat for the return trip to his car, Dorsey considered betrayal and all its many facets. Trading bodies, buying and selling information and confidences to keep one step ahead of the Grim Reaper. And in this particular case, inform on a priest you hardly know? Ruin his life and a few others in this process, and be a turncoat to your bosses? But the upside is that things go easily for an elderly woman who's been through hell these last few years. An elderly woman you've grown to care for an awful lot. Those are the options. Options? What a polite way to describe the process of determining right from wrong.

Dorsey looked out of the window as they crossed the Fortieth Street Bridge, watching coal barges being pushed up the Allegheny by workhorse towboats. The options mean nothing, he told himself. There are no options. Not when you're the one who's being asked to play the role of traitor. Because after it all goes down and someone gets hurt and another does just fine, you're stuck with yourself. Alone, frightfully alone. Shunned by others and, eventually, by yourself. You'll end up like Judas Iscariot, cut down from a tree after the truth set in.

Longley drove the Corsica through the front gates of Mt. Alvernia and climbed the brick roadway, pulling even with the Buick. Dorsey stepped out quietly and rounded the back of the car, digging his keys from his pants pocket. He heard Longley call out from the driver's seat.

46

"See how easy this went?" Longley said, a smart-assed grin showing beneath his sunglasses. "Not such bad guys after all, huh?"

Dorsey's shoulders sagged for a moment while he jiggled his keys against his hip. He loosened his neck with a twist and walked back to the Corsica, bending forward to face Longley.

"Nah, you're not really bad guys," he said. "You're just a couple of stupid guys. Young and stupid. Maybe that sounds better because the young bit gives a partial excuse for the stupidity. They give you badges, just like you've wanted since you were kids, back when you took the toy ones from the cereal boxes before your little brothers could get at them, and you think you're driving around town fighting crime. Think about it, what crime did you solve today? Did you prevent any crimes? As I see it, you two are political errand boys, hacks for the chief. Just a little more well-to-do than the ones I used to see as a kid. Cut yourself a break and get a new line of work."

Longley held on to his grin. "Anything else or are you through?"

"Just this," Dorsey said. "Go fuck yourself."

Dorsey climbed the front stoop of his Wharton Street home and found a fat manila envelope, doubled over with a thick rubber band crossing its midsection, sticking out of his mailbox. Slapping it under his left arm, he worked open the door lock, entered, and made for the office, where he flipped the envelope onto the desktop. He stripped off his tie and jacket, put the window screens and fans in place, and slipped a cassette into the tape player before settling himself into the swivel chair. A long dead Chet Baker, his arm no doubt freshly spiked, blew his horn and followed that with a little vocal work on "Let's Get Lost." Dorsey shared the sentiment.

Again he gave fleeting thoughts to Turner's proposition and again his only conclusion was a glimpse of himself dangling lifelessly from a biblical tree, silver pieces strewn about in the dirt. Just destroy the priest and save Mrs. Leneski, but not entirely. You also destroy yourself in the process. That's all Douglas Turner wants. And nothing less.

His answering machine had only one message; Father Crimmins telling him that he was to meet Louise Filus after eleven o'clock Mass on Sunday. He also suggested that Dorsey take the time to attend the service itself. Always the priest, Dorsey thought, saver of souls.

Ignoring for now the envelope on his desk, Dorsey decided to fight back and put in a call to Art Meeker's office. At least he should be warned, Dorsey thought, even if he can't come up with a defense. Again, he could only reach the secretary, just to be told the Mr. Meeker couldn't take his call at present. Like hell he can't, Dorsey thought.

"Are you saying he's not in or are you saying the guy doesn't have time to talk to the only viable witness he has in what is sure to be the only murder case he's ever likely to try?"

"Oh, he's in the office, all right," the secretary said, sounding put off by Dorsey's manner. "Mr. Meeker has a rather large and growing practice and he's with a new client right now. You'd be surprised how often potential new clients just walk through the door."

"No," Dorsey said, "I would not be surprised. I'd be absolutely amazed. And if these new clients catch wind of how little time and effort he's putting into Mrs. Leneski's case, and I'll make sure they do if it goes catshit because of him, he'll have to close down the law office and open a Seven-Eleven. So, get him to call me. Unless you want to go from filing legal papers to pouring Slurpies."

Dorsey hung up with a flick of the wrist, sending the receiver into its cradle on the hop. He shook the anger out of his shoulders and decided on another line of defense for Mrs. Leneski. Yeah, sure, fight fire with fire. He again lifted the receiver and dialed.

"I planned on seeing your father late Saturday afternoon," Mrs. Boyle said. "You should come along. As I mentioned, there is planning to be done."

Dorsey thought of Saturday and of Gretchen and the move. He didn't want to miss a moment with her, but the trial resumed on Monday and he was scheduled to take the stand. "How about Saturday evening, maybe around seven," he asked. "If that's good for you, I'll pick you up."

"Sounds like things have changed. You need . . . you need to see him, all of a sudden?" Mrs. Boyle held a tone of concern in her voice. "You must be careful not to overtax his reserves. He shouldn't be overstimulated."

"I'll keep it in mind," Dorsey said, thinking that his father would like nothing better that to go out by way of screwing a Republican district attorney.

They agreed to the evening visit and the phone rang as soon as Dorsey had replaced the receiver. It was Art Meeker's secretary asking Dorsey if he could come to the office at six that evening. Knowing that it was the best he could get from this shortsighted fool, he agreed.

Taking a cold Rolling Rock from the office refrigerator, Dorsey slid it across his sweaty forehead before cracking it open. He took a short sip and set the can aside, taking in hand the manila envelope he had retrieved from the mailbox. At the left corner were the multiple names of a law firm's masthead. Dorsey figured them to be Bill Meara's new employers. He worked a finger under the adhesive flap and tore across the top, jerking the envelope to its side and spilling two file folders onto the desktop blotter. So, Dorsey thought, the religious do keep employment records.

The top folder, and by far the much thicker of the two, had FATHER THOMAS CRIMMINS stenciled across the front followed by some type of serial number that was meaningless to Dorsey. Inside, the top page held a photograph that showed ten years of wear and a list of vital statistics such as date of birth, height and weight, and date of ordination. A few pages deeper and he ran into a short history of the priest's military career, something Dorsey had been totally unaware of.

From what he could gather from the documentation, it appeared to Dorsey that Crimmins had been drafted just weeks after his graduation from St. Bonaventure. And basic training and jungle-warfare school must have been accelerated because Crimmins was assigned in-country in plenty of time to partake in the invasion of Cambodia. Dorsey recalled the horrid accounts of that battle, and recalled that he was safely tucked away in New Jersey serving as an MP when those reports filled newspapers and television screens. As an infantry private, part of a weapons team, Crimmins would have been hip deep in North Vietnamese and Vietcong, and he sure as hell got through it alive by making sure that a few of the enemy *didn't* make it through alive. A Silver Star attested to that, along with an invitation to officer candidate school, an invitation that Crimmins declined. No reason given.

Well, Dorsey thought, isn't this bad news; the worst, actually. The holy man has a violent background, and who's really going to care if it happened to be in the service of his country? No one, not the way that DA Turner will portray it. And don't think for a second that Turner doesn't know about this. He has investigators, and they have connections, and those connections have computers that can pull down a fellow's military record. Turner knows, and he's ready to use it when the time comes. He'll play it just right, who cares if it's become fashionable to be a Vietnam vet? The priest has killed before.

It'll have impact, Dorsey told himself, because it's already made an impression on you. And you're working the other side of the street. Just keep your curiosities in check and remember the assignment. Don't solve the murder, clear the priest.

The rest of the file was mundane and swiftly gotten through. There were a string of assistant-pastor jobs in Baltimore, Philadelphia, and Buffalo, all of which resulted in glowing assessment reports from the supervising priest. Gives a good sermon, gets along well with the kids in the CYO, and runs an orderly bingo game. Dorsey wondered if those were the hallmarks of a man destined to be a spiritual leader.

But there was nothing negative in his religious career, and Dorsey was thankful for that. No trace of scandal, sexual or financial; no unexplained absences spent drying out from altar wine in the morning and Scotch through the night. And his present job, pastor at St. Anne's, that was a plum. It had to be a reward for jobs well done. A well-off parish filled with boat owners and golf-club members. The kind, Dorsey recalled from his talk with Father Crimmins, that really like to kiss ass.

Dorsey took a long pull on his beer, set aside the Crimmins file but not his worries about that hitch in the army, and prepared himself for the Alice Sutton story. Her folder was thinner and stamped INACTIVE across the front. Let's get to it, Dorsey told himself, let's find out how nuns are made and unmade.

A native of Erie, Pennsylvania, Alice Sutton had spent her high-school years under the thumb of the good sisters at the Villa Maria School. Her grades, discipline, and devotion were excellent, and her move on to the College of St. Rose seemed a natural. But once there, and Dorsey knew why, discipline went out the window. Smiling to himself, Dorsey thought back on the times, the late sixties and early seventies. Hippie priests who held Mass on picnic tables, nuns who went looking for a little action, and a young laity that urged them on. And Alice Sutton was in the thick of it. She managed to get a bachelor's degree and teaching certificate in three years, but the records also showed that she had found time to be arrested three times in antiwar rallies and once for leading a protest against the selective service policy of neither registering nor drafting women. Christ, Dorsey thought, reading the pages. Make up your mind.

Next was the Peace Corps, but that didn't last. Stationed in Honduras with the mission of building a school, Alice chose to invest her time in attempts to expose the connection between the CIA and several local chieftains. The Hondurans expelled her and the Peace Corps apparently did the same; she somehow landed in Pittsburgh, teaching at a parochial grade school, where, Dorsey figured, she heard the calling and approached the convent. Again, remembering the times, Dorsey concluded that the convent wasn't nearly as choosey as either the Hondurans or the Peace Corps. Recruits weren't knocking down the doors to get in.

Finishing his Rolling Rock, Dorsey skipped through the accounts of minor rebellions against convent rules and went straight to the final explosion that had been related to him earlier that day by Sister Loretta. Sanitized on paper, the file merely suggested that on a particular date Sister Marie Sutton had become unhinged, abusive and threatening, and had to be subdued. She was then escorted from the convent grounds by the local police.

Dorsey shifted back in his chair, laughing, picturing the mother superior's face as she blurted out the details. Sister Marie, nun with an attitude, has a little after-dinner debate with old Father Kelly, the convent chaplain and deeply entrenched member of the old school, over the position of women in the church. Sister Marie says that women should be ordained. Then she says that she, Sister Marie, should be ordained and should be saying mass and hearing confessions and getting her ass kissed like the rest of those who have been ordained. And in reply, Father Kelly of the old school calls her a blasphemer who isn't worthy of the title of Bride of Christ. Then Sister Marie really gets pissed and digs into the far reaches of her habit where only Kleenex and pitch pipes should be found and produces her little can of pepper gas and, relieving some long pent-up spiritual resentments, shoots a generous helping into Father Kelly's face. The paramedics come for Father Kelly and the local police, very discreetly, come for Sister Marie, who is involuntarily reverted to Alice Sutton, layperson. Dorsey decided the story was worth a second beer and reached back to the refrigerator.

Dorsey opened the fresh beer and thought of how he might approach Alice Sutton. Eventually he would have to find out what she knew and what she was prepared to say. He figured her for a talker. Everything he had read told him so. Yeah, she'll be pissed at first, and you better be ready to duck the pepper gas, but she'll say what's on her mind once she's pushed, and not pushed hard, either. According to the file, she hasn't shut her mouth since she left Villa Maria.

Making a mental note that his encounter with Alice Sutton had better be done early in the coming week and that he better be in the right frame of mind for it, Dorsey's gaze strayed to one of the front windows. What he saw startled him and sent him half out of his chair, spilling beer into his lap. Framed in one of the window screens was a round bald head with shining eyes and a broad toothy grin.

"One, two, three, calling on Dorsey!" Henry called through the screen, apparently enraptured with himself. "C'mon, Dorsey, remember? Like when you were a kid? Like when you went over to your friend's house, got'em to come out and play in the street? C'mon, get with it!"

"Just get the hell in here," Dorsey said, standing and wiping spilled beer from his trousers. He tried to suppress it, but Henry's laughter caught on with him, too. "Door's open. Have a beer and let's get the details on this vacation of yours."

Henry's entrance into the office was preceded by a flapping noise generated by the rubber thongs on his feet. Dressed in cutoff jeans and a T-shirt adorned with Bob Marley, dreadlocks to the hemline, Henry dropped into a chair across from Dorsey and accepted a Rolling Rock. What little hair he had was stretched back and bound in a pigtail. Al's wandering brother-in-law, he who held an on-again, off-again job as the afternoon bartender and lived in the bar's second-floor apartment. The man who misspent his post-army years in San Francisco running to the liquor store for Kerouac's and Ginsburg's wine jugs.

Dorsey shook his head and smiled. "Before you start in about how you just came back from having the time of your life, there's one question that must be asked and answered. How do you, of all people, rate a vacation? A vacation from what? We're talking about a guy who runs off for months at a time, on some sort of adventure I suppose, only to return and pick up where he left off. Working as a bartender for your brother-in-law is not rated after demolition expert as the world's most stressful occupation. This demands an explanation. Please, elaborate.''

Henry took a long hit on his beer and ran the back of his hand across his lips. ''I was born for this life,'' he said, grinning again. ''It's true. It's Karma. A lot of it's of my own making, but it's Karma nonetheless. You must be who you are, and I, thank God, must be who I am. You question the order of the universe. That's bad. It'll give you a sour stomach. Maybe even hives.''

''What a line of shit.'' Dorsey raised his beer can, saluting his friend.

''And it's mine, all mine,'' Henry said. ''It's important to have a line of shit at the ready. People are critical, and some of them are always looking to make a guy feel small. So don't get caught out there without your line of shit.''

How true, Dorsey told himself, how true. Having his own line of shit got him through the last twenty years with his old man. ''So let's hear about the trip.''

Legs stretched and with his ankles crossed, Henry rested in his chair and recounted ten days of hiking and loafing in West Virginia. ''Beautiful little cabin, great place. Just outside of Blackwater Falls, you know, the state park? Great place, great time.''

''Vacation's over,'' Dorsey said. ''Ready for tomorrow? You remember about tomorrow, right?''

''I'm ready, don't worry.'' Henry pointed his beer can at Dorsey. ''Question is, are you ready? She's coming back to stay.''

Dorsey thought it over and wondered if he *was* ready. What's worse, he reminded himself, is that you aren't even sure what it is you're supposed to get ready for.

Dorsey drove crosstown through the remnants of a Friday-night rush hour and parked the Buick just short of the intersection of Butler and Forty-Second streets. Stepping out of the car, he hung on the open door and peered two short blocks down the street. The scene of the crime, Dorsey thought, the former offices of the late Anton Novotny, M.D. Scene of the crime, he thought again. Well, a scene, anyways.

Closing the car door, he crossed the sidewalk and entered the freshly painted storefront that housed Artie Meeker's law practice. All of the glass was overlayed with steel bars, and entrance was gained only after ringing a doorbell and announcing yourself to the secretary through an intercom. Once the door's lock was released, Dorsey was ushered through a sparsely furnished and empty waiting room by a dark-haired woman in her late forties and into the inner office of Artie Meeker.

"Arthur Quinten Meeker," Dorsey mumbled, reading the diploma mounted at the far wall as he took the client's chair. Across a desk cluttered with legal papers, pink while-you-were-out messages, and empty Pepsi cans sat a very thin and nervous-looking man in his early thirties. He wore a floral tie and short-sleeved shirt, and his glasses slipped to the middle of his nose as he read one or another of the items on his desk. Dorsey waited a moment, then asked where in the hell the Quinten had come from.

"An uncle on my mother's side," Meeker replied, concentrating on the work on his desk, not looking up. "My mother's favorite brother, I think. Don't know why, supposed to have been something of a boozehound."

Dorsey gave him a few more moments, glancing about the office, again reading the law-school diploma along with the ABA membership certificate. Arthur Q. Meeker... sounds like a character out of that Rocky and Bullwinkle show, he thought, then went on to examine the Rotary meeting photos, a few of the family, and one of Meeker in a ball cap surrounded by a Little League team. A Mr. Coffee, the carafe nearly empty, rested on the credenza behind Meeker's chair. Enough already, Dorsey decided, and used both hands to beat out a drumroll at the desk's edge.

"Artie," Dorsey said a little loudly. "Let's go fella, important shit to talk about here. Murder charge, remember? Dead doctor with his finger up some poor guy's asshole, elderly and somewhat endearing lady on trial for it? Put that shit away, whatever it is, and talk to me. Now. Please?''

Meeker dropped his elbows onto the desktop, let out a deep sigh, and looked up at Dorsey. ''Jesus, you really are a pain in the ass.'' He took a moment to adjust his glasses. ''I know how serious Mrs. Leneski's case is, you don't have to remind me. But maybe I should remind you of how simple it is as well. She killed the guy, she's confessed to killing the guy, and thereby she's guilty. So that question is settled, and we don't have to bother fighting about it. So now my job is to get her the lightest sentence I can by putting her in the best light possible. Which shouldn't be hard. She's old as the hills and has a thousand friends who want to testify on her behalf. She has one of the world's saddest stories to tell about her granddaughter, which is where you can be of the most help. Besides, what prosecutor in his right mind wants to put away a little old lady?''

''Douglas Turner, he's one for sure. Whether he happens to be in his right mind or not.''

''Ah, that's bullshit,'' Meeker said, waving off the idea.

Dorsey gave it to him sharp and quick, all that had gone on between him and Turner that afternoon, leaving out Father Crimmins's name but not the deal that Turner had intimated. ''And even before that there was a problem with my testimony that you were either ignoring or were too goddamned stupid to see. The woman asked me to kill Novotny. Long, long before she did it herself. And when I talk about that on the stand, and you can believe that the prosecution will insist that I do just that, Mrs. Leneski might just go from grief-stricken to cold-hearted in the eyes of the court. So, counselor, after many attempts to do so, I'm here to ask you just how in the fuck you plan on handling these problems?''

''Turner really said these things to you?'' Meeker asked. Visibly shaken, he removed his glasses, polishing the lenses with the tip of his floral necktie. "You're not just being emotional about this?"

"My right hand to God," Dorsey told him.

Meeker held his gaze on his lap. "Well, then we've got problems."

Dorsey threw his arms in the air and spoke to the ceiling. "Finally! Thank you Lord! Now show this learned man the way. What path shall we follow?"

Meeker placed his glasses on his face and looked at Dorsey. "Okay, okay, you've made your point. Hope you're happy. But this is a bad one. I just don't know off-hand how to play this."

"Well, who are you going to ask?"

"I gotta think on this, talk to a few people, make some calls." Meeker was silent for a moment, apparently studying Dorsey. "Just for the sake of argument, how important is this other case, this other guy, to you? Any room for compromise? Maybe Turner will deal for just a little of what you can tell him, not everything. Just enough to get him off of Mrs. Leneski's back."

"You can do better than that," Dorsey said, wondering how many more tempters he would meet that night before he was safely in bed. "You have to do better, for Christ's sake. There's this weekend and that's it. Better cancel your plans, if any, and get your legal-eagle thinking cap on. I'll be around, you want to talk about my testimony and all the rest. You just call. But this idea about kissing Turner's ass is for the birds. It's out, no discussion, that's it."

"Well, this is difficult." Meeker looked at Dorsey for a moment, shrugged his shoulders, and held out his hands, palms up. Lost.

Dorsey got to his feet and left the room, deciding that help would have to come from a higher level. The next night's meeting with his father had just taken on new importance.

9

The rental truck was a thirty-footer loaded with the possessions that Gretchen had refused to entrust to the professional movers, who, Dorsey had to admit to himself, didn't look all that professional when they dropped a sofa off of the end of the van. Dorsey suggested that things might go smoother if they used the tailgate's hydraulic lift. The crew chief agreed, saying that he'd forgotten all about that damned thing.

Henry was behind the wheel, grinding and chopping at the standard transmission, a look of unabashed joy on his face. Dorsey rode shotgun, and Gretchen in her Acura was in the lead, out of sight since the climb up U.S. 62 out of Franklin. Forty minutes into the trip, they were emerging from farmland into the village of Polk, passing by that infamous state hospital that looked to Dorsey more like a religious complex—school and church, all brick and gables, and only a modest sign at the head of the driveway. Dorsey recalled his single visit to the facility. He had been sent by a patient's family to talk to the patient and a staff orderly about abuses at the hospital. The patient had said he was happy there. The orderly said sure, who wouldn't be? After twenty years of ice-water baths and being hung by your feet, you'd start to like it too. Everybody needs structure, a daily routine.

"You really dig driving a truck?" Dorsey asked, turning back to Henry. "What's it been, twenty, twenty-five years?"

"Somewhere in there." Henry geared down, getting into compliance with the village's thirty-five-mile-an-hour speed limit. "I just hope this run doesn't end like the last one. A year at one of California's state honor farms is okay when you're young, but those days are long behind me. And another thing. Furniture is a lot different than a load of illegal Chinese out of Vancouver. Think about it, you don't speak their language, they don't speak yours for the most part, and they're always asking or complaining after something. One guy has to piss, the other is car sick. And there you are in the middle of the night trying to stay on the road and get them from Canada to maybe San Francisco without getting stopped. Furniture is better, even if it takes more care to load and unload. Quieter, too."

Once on the interstate, heading south toward the city, Dorsey fell silent again, thinking how the demands of his business had taken the gloss from the day. It was supposed to be a homecoming, he thought, a day set aside. A full twenty-four-hour pass to spend with Gretchen, celebrating her return. But not after yesterday. Not after Turner had his say and after he had his say with Meeker. And found out that Meeker had shit to offer on how to get around this thing. Now the only hope was the old man and that he had a few more moves in him. Oh, hell. Home again, home again.

"So, when do you have to pick up Ironbox?" Henry asked, referring to Irene Boyle, as if reading his thoughts. Like Dorsey, he was dressed in shorts and T-shirt, already damp at the neckline from the morning's exertions. "Just wonderin', figured you had to get away early enough to shower and change for the royal audience."

"Early evening," Dorsey said. "Should be able to get all the heavy stuff in place by then. The other stuff we can do over the next couple of days." Shit, Dorsey thought, you get to move furniture all day. And tomorrow you spend the afternoon with the widow Filus. He recalled a time when Mrs. Leneski had complained that he didn't work weekends. Well, at least you're living up to her expectations.

The house that Gretchen had purchased was on a side street in Aspinwall, one of the river towns just north of the city that had won the struggle to retain its dignity and elegance. The streets were tree-lined and the homes were the solid-looking type: Pennsylvania brick, bay windows on all floors, and wide front porches for catching the last light of a summer evening. A few blocks away was a small, personalized merchant's row, and Dorsey recalled walking through it when Gretchen was considering the house. A quiet restaurant that served a hefty breakfast, full-service gas station, and a family-owned grocery that delivered. Now, if Al could just move the bar up here.

Henry pulled the truck to the curb, directly behind the moving van, and Dorsey hopped out into the street. Gretchen was on the sidewalk talking to the crew chief and signing a piece of paper he held on his clipboard. She was wearing shorts and Dorsey admired her legs, that strange mix of femininity and athleticism that he found so attractive, the results of long days and nights prowling the ER. Her hair held its natural curl but was a little long for her, trailing a few extra inches down her neck and showing a hint of gray at the tips. Dorsey gave her a squeeze on the shoulder and asked if the sofa was any worse for being dropped.

"It'll take a cleaning," she said, looking at the crew chief who gave her a shrug of submission, apparently willing to cover the cost. "Other than that, their part of the move was a success. Now"—she gave him her soft smile—"let's see how you and your free-spirited assistant make out."

The movers cleared out and Dorsey and Henry went to work, very slowly and cautiously. What they had been entrusted with were antiques from the Keller farmhouse in Lancaster, Pennsylvania. First off of the truck was a pine schoolteacher's desk with a four-inch pillared railing along the desktop. Then came a cornered secretary, armoire, and pie safe. Each piece was taken across the walkway that divided the front lawn, up and over the porch, and inside the house, where a maze of cartons waited to be unpacked. Gretchen supervised and shadowed their every move, taking a deep breath each time a piece had to be tilted to get through a doorway, covering her eyes when Henry's grip on the armoire momentarily gave out. Once the antiques were in their proper places, they turned their efforts to arranging the other furniture. Finished with that, Gretchen began to unload the cartons. Dorsey slipped Henry a couple of fives and sent him for beer.

"Take your time," Dorsey said. "Shop around, make sure to get the best price. Make your money go as far as you can."

"I take pride in being a comparative shopper." Henry took the money and started out the door. "I'll be sure to read each label, get all the prices and ingredients. But before I go, just what in the hell is a riboflavin?"

"Get," Dorsey said, shooing him out the door and firmly closing it. Pausing for a moment, he ran a hand through the tuft of hair at his forehead, then went from the front alcove to the living room. Gretchen was on her knees, working away at the masking tape that secured the top of a shipping carton. Dorsey leaned into a wall and allowed himself to slide into a sitting position on the floor. "He's gone for a while. Henry, I mean."

Gretchen sat back, haunches on heels, and closed the blade on the safety knife she had been using on the tape. "How'd you work it?" She asked, smiling. "Tell him to get lost for an hour or so, or did you give him bus fare and send him home? If he's coming back, I'll set the alarm clock for thirty minutes."

"Just a run down the street for beer," Dorsey said. He hung his arms over his knees, the wrists and hands dangling. "Welcome home. Or maybe just welcome back. Either way, welcome. I missed you. Even when it was for just a day. Sometimes only five minutes after we talked on the phone. Sometimes while I was hanging up, still had the receiver in my hand."

"It's good to be back," Gretchen said. "To really be back, here on a full-time basis." She held her thoughts for a moment before speaking. "And I want to be all the way back. Here, with you. I want to try this thing with you all over again. Me and my career and you and whatever it is you call what you do. I really want to give this a try." She was silent for another moment. "Oh boy, was that a lot to say at once. You okay with that?"

"I love you," Dorsey said, working up a sloppy grin. "But I can't do a thing about it today. Shoot me if you want, but I have to be somewhere else this evening. Now about later tonight, if you're not worn to a frazzle from this move, I could find my way back here. Just for the sake of keeping you company. I mean, if that's what you really want."

Gretchen shook her head and laughed, then crossed the hardwood floors an all fours. She took Dorsey's hands in hers, awkwardly wiped at the corner of her eye with her shoulder, and told him she was in love again. With him. "Maybe I wasn't for a while there. Maybe I just forgot that I was in love with you. It makes no difference."

"Not to me." Dorsey shifted about and pulled her close. "Not to me it doesn't."

"Well, then. I'll expect you in the late hours, won't I?"

Dorsey maneuvered the Buick left off of Forbes Avenue and drove a block up Craig Street to the redbrick and stone tower that held the apartment of Ironbox Boyle. It was one of several that held the city's wealthiest survivors, men and women of old money who maintained the fixtures and comforts of their past. Including, Dorsey thought, the liveried black doorman who strode out to meet him as he pulled into the short, curved driveway. He knew it for what it was, a racial anachronism, but it fell in so well with his overwhelming admiration of things aged and well kept. Of times passed, good and bad.

The doorman peaked from under the brim of his cap and dug into his dark, double-breasted jacket. He came out with a slip of paper, checked it and nodded to Dorsey, and returned to his station. Irene Boyle exited the building moments later, as the result of an intercom call from the doorman, Dorsey presumed, and helped herself into the Buick's passenger seat. In her lap was a thickly stuffed manila envelope.

She had on a cotton dress against the evening heat, and her white hair was done much more tightly to her scalp than the last time Dorsey had seen her. Dressing herself up, he thought, trying to distract attention from the damage left from her breakdown and hospitalization, result of the past that she never could shake. The weaker, softer eyes and the jowls that had developed from laxity brought on by medication told the true story. Her hands slowly wandered over the envelope, feeling the edges, testing the corners.

"So what's packed up in there?" Dorsey asked, thinking the hand motion was an invitation. "The old man's complete memoirs or the last will and testament, in which I get the house and perpetual care thereof by the county public works department?"

"Try not to be cruel, please?" Mrs. Boyle looked straight ahead, avoiding Dorsey by watching the traffic. "These are just some papers your father wants to look over. He called this afternoon, asked me to bring them along."

"Sounds like he's doing rather well."

"Certainly he is," Mrs. Boyle said. "Actually, he spends most of his day up on his feet or in a chair. Things have been improving. He's still weak, and fatigue seems to come over him suddenly, but he is better and better. Might even come home someday, with the right help. And he asks after you quite often."

It all sounded good, Dorsey thought, working his way through traffic onto Washington Boulevard, heading for the nursing home where his father's room overlooked the Allegheny River. He's strong, he'll listen to what I have to tell him about Turner and Leneski. And he'll know what to do and how it needs to be done. Never fear, there's always something that can be done, that he alone can make happen. And he'll be more than willing to do it because he owes that woman for removing Novotny, his blackmailer, the long-time millstone tied so firmly around his neck. He owes that old woman, Dorsey told himself, and that's the one thing your father understands.

"The last time we talked," Dorsey said, "you seemed pretty sure my father was not long for this earth, what with all the talk about getting ready for life without him. I take it you're seeing things in a different light these days?"

"Not at all." Mrs. Boyle shifted in her seat, facing him. "No, no, I still think we need to prepare. And so does your father. These papers have to do with some of his holdings, things he may want to move around to avoid inheritance taxes for you. And me, too. I'm following his lead."

Just as always, Dorsey thought, just as always. "But there's nothing, nothing medically, that you've kept from me about my father, right? And you don't suspect that there might be something that he's keeping you in the dark about, am I right?"

"No, that's impossible." Mrs. Boyle shook her head and turned her gaze outward through the windshield. "He would never do that. Even if it was his wish to keep secrets from me, it would be impossible. I would know. Yes, I'm sure I would know."

"Sounds about right."

Martin Dorsey was in the patient's lounge when they arrived, seated in a corner easy chair. Through the picture window was a wide view of the river, and it appeared to Dorsey that his father was watching the pleasure craft flirt with disaster at the edge of the Highland Locks. You've taken those chances in the past. Right, Pop? But never without the fix having been put in way, way ahead of time.

Ironbox Boyle lightly kissed his cheek and asked if he'd prefer to return to his room for their visit. Martin Dorsey rejected the suggestion.

"We can talk here just as well," Dorsey's father said, and motioned for his son to pull over two chairs. "The three of us, we're the only ones in the room with any hearing left." He swung out an arm, indicating the other patients, mostly in wheelchairs, who were scattered about the lounge.

"I wish I had known of such places earlier in life. It's the perfect place to hold a meeting. I could've run the whole county out of this place, done as I pleased, without a single secret leaked. No worries about the papers, the public, or the Republicans. Republicans in Allegheny County, that's a hell of a note."

Glad you feel that way, Dorsey thought. Please, get pissed off and stay that way.

Martin Dorsey tightened the belt on his navy blue robe and gestured for Mrs. Boyle to hand over the envelope. On a lamp stand to his right he found his silver wire-rimmed reading glasses and managed with only one hand, his still healthy right one, to hook them about his ears. He slipped his thumb under the envelope's flap, cleanly ripped through it, and began his review of the contents. "You two are going to be well-off in the very near future. And no death vigil over dear old Martin will be necessary. Inheritances will be received before the dearly departed departs. Now that's really rigging the game." He held out an empty palm for Mrs. Boyle. "Pen, please."

"I fail to see the humor." Ironbox dug into her handbag and produced a silver Cross pen. "You act as though no one cares about you, personally I mean. As though all either of us cared for was your estate and how it's to be divvied up."

Martin Dorsey affixed his signature to three documents before resting the pen and his hand on his lap. "I always have to explain myself to you," he said to Mrs. Boyle and then turned to Dorsey. "Sometimes you get it, but not always. You're getting better, but you may have reached your potential." He turned his attention back to Mrs. Boyle. "Irene, you, on the other hand, have to be spoon fed at times."

Mrs. Boyle gave him an allowance-for-the-sick sigh and invited him to continue.

"Part of running things, of really being in charge, is taking care of people." Martin Dorsey fiddled with the pen, and it was apparent to Dorsey that he was taking great care in his word choice. "Oh, let's be clear. Rank has its privileges and I loved every one of them. The respect of some, the groveling of others, and sometimes feeling as if rules only applied to those out of office. But there is also great personal reward in using your power to look after the few that you do choose to look after. Simply because you are in a position to do so. Not because it's a debt you incurred on an agreement or handshake years ago, not because it will further your career in the near future. So this is what I do. It's what I have to offer the world. For now, it's my calling.''

''There's something we have to talk about,'' Dorsey said, anxious to discuss Leneski and Turner and not sure if he wanted Ironbox to hear it. ''Something important that will further your calling.''

''Then that makes two important things we have to discuss,'' Martin Dorsey said. ''And yours can wait. As I said, I still run things.''

For an agonizing forty minutes, his father slowly walked Ironbox and him through the stack of papers. There were two documents that transferred stock to Mrs. Boyle, and Martin Dorsey urged her to get to a notary public as quickly as she could. Dorsey was presented with several treasury bonds, which he initially refused, causing an argument with his father. But he soon caved in, not out of greed or frustration but out of concern for an old woman on trial for killing a piece of shit that had it coming.

Martin Dorsey was tiring quickly and noticeably. So much so that Dorsey thought he could time the process, measure it and set an estimate for an average visit's duration. Circles grew below his eyes and darkened as if sight itself were slipping away. The tremor in his hand, mild at first, was now making the pen a burden instead of a tool. And words seemed harder to find. C'mon, man, he pleaded silently. Hold on, keep yourself together. You've got to hear about Mrs. Leneski and you've got to figure out what's to be done. Then you have to put it in motion. C'mon, hold on.

Martin Dorsey asked Mrs. Boyle to see one of the nurses

about getting him a glass of juice. He also asked her to take her time about doing it. Dorsey quickly began to tell his father about the Leneski trial, but he was abruptly cut off.

"I've arranged for you to meet someone," Martin Dorsey said, pinching at the bridge of his nose. "It's someone you need to know. A good friend."

What is this? Dorsey was about to ask before he caught himself. "Not now, Pop. There's something more important. We can talk about this somebody later. Mrs. Leneski, she's in hotter water than we realized. That prick Turner wants to really stick it to her. He plans on pushing this thing as far as it can go, make sure the old woman does time. We've got to do something about it. You've got to do something. You say you like to take care of people, well, look after her. Besides, you owe her."

Martin sighed and then shook his head. "This man I want you to meet, he'll be here for you after I'm gone. He's on the inside, he's on the inside of any number of things. When you, you or Irene, have any troubles, any kind at all, you can call on him. See? It'll be as if I never left. The two of you will be looked after."

Dorsey couldn't believe what he was hearing, perpetual care for the living. It's insane, he thought, as if his father was trying to beat the rap on death, putting in one last big fix. Martin Dorsey goes on forever, the politician who never retired. But Dorsey had to pull back from his father's latest and possibly last outrage; he had to get back to Mrs. Leneski.

"Are you listening?" Dorsey asked his father. "You have got to hear this. It's been one hell of an afternoon." He started in on a full replay of the meetings with Turner and Meeker but quickly started to edit out the extraneous parts. The story was getting too long and Martin Dorsey's fatigue process began to accelerate. His head began to droop, and each time he caught himself the recovery time lengthened.

"Let's save this for another time," Martin Dorsey said, his finger massaging the corner of his eye. "They give me these pills sometimes. They make me tired. I suppose they help me rest, but how much rest can one person stand?''

"What other time are you talking about?'' Dorsey took his father's good arm and gave it a rattle. "For Christ's sake, the old woman is going to jail and come Monday morning I get to start sending her there. You have power, goddamned sneaky-assed power. Just what we need for the job. You're the one who offered to cover the woman's defense costs. Well, my man, the bill has come due. And it has to be paid with the kind of currency you've stuffed in your mattress all your life. C'mon, Pop. What in the hell are we gonna do?''

"I better get in bed,'' Martin Dorsey said, turning his head in confusion and apparently looking about for an attendant. "You just wouldn't believe how tired I get. And so quickly, too.''

10

With his left arm dangling over the side molding, Dorsey took up the last pew in St. Anne's Church, doing his best to appear interested in the eleven o'clock Mass. He wore a light sport jacket and a broadcloth shirt without a tie and felt horribly overdressed. All of the young men he saw between him and the altar wore T-shirts and athletic shorts or slacks, and Dorsey had the feeling that Sunday Mass had become the launching pad for an afternoon in the park. You've been away a long time, he reminded himself. And even if Father Crimmins hasn't captured your attention, you've come to the right place, the right place to consider perjury. Yesterday it was betrayal, today it's perjury. What unholy temptation will Monday bring?

Dorsey had never lied under oath. Never. Not in a hundred court appearances, not in depositions too numerous to count or remember. And he knew more than his share of others who did it often. Men and women who saw a sworn lie as a convenience, one employed so often to help Lady Justice get her job done despite herself. Tempted? Sure, he thought, plenty of times. But never like this.

But what's left? Dorsey thought, watching the congregation queue up to receive Communion, two lines formed in the center aisle, terminating with the eucharistic ministers standing at the altar steps. And who else was there? Not the old man. Dorsey had called the nursing home that morning and had been told that his father wouldn't feel up to having visitors for another twenty-four hours, at his own request. So the old man didn't have it in him. He either couldn't get up the muscle or couldn't get up the enthusiasm to get up the muscle. So it's up to you. It's up to you to lie. Not so Mrs. Leneski gets off completely, but just so she doesn't have to shoulder more than her share. Not bad. As rationalization goes, not bad at all.

Father Crimmins dismissed the congregation and marched down the center aisle, flanked by altar boys dressed in black cassocks and white surplice. Dorsey rose as he passed and they exchanged quick nods, and Dorsey knew she was here. In his telephone message the day before, Father Crimmins wasn't sure if she would be attending Mass. She might be out of town, he had said. No way to be sure. Well, Dorsey told himself, let's see if we can pick her out of the crowd.

It was easy, because she stood out in that crowd. The sun was bright and strong on the church's granite front steps, and when Dorsey stepped outside she caught his eye the way strangers recognize each other when they first meet on a blind date. She wore a silken print dress and flat shoes, apparently to deflect attention from her height, Dorsey thought. Her hair, a darkly rich brown, was expertly but simply cut in a style that Dorsey admired but couldn't name, a style that put him in mind of Jean Tierney in *Laura*. What priest could be expected to resist all that?

"You must be him," Louise Filus said as Dorsey approached, extending her hand. "Mr. Dorsey, I mean. Father Crimmins described you well. He said you were around his height, with a little extra beef." She gave him a playful smile. "His words, not mine."

Her manner was so lighthearted that Dorsey wondered if she knew the reason for their meeting. Of course she did, he told himself. Lovers can't keep those kind of secrets. "Sounds like Tom's way of putting things," he said. "And please, let's leave the Mr. Dorsey behind. Call me Carroll, or maybe just Dorsey. That seems to be the popular choice."

"Let's go with Dorsey," she said, arching her eyebrows. "And Dorsey, let's get going."

Leaving the parish grounds, they walked along the cemetery's iron-fenced boundary just as Dorsey and the priest had done several evenings before. "This hasn't come up too fast for you, has it?" Dorsey asked. "Time is short. That's what they tell me, and I'm starting to believe it. But still, this must have come up quickly for you. I know it did for me."

"I prefer it this way," Louise Filus said, still showing no sign that she was distressed by the subject that would soon be at hand. "That's why I suggested to Father Crimmins that he have you come here this afternoon. Now we can sit, have a little lunch, and talk this out. Do you like chicken salad? I made it yesterday. I like for it to chill overnight. How's that sound?"

Sounds like you're either nuts or one hell of a hostess, Dorsey thought. "That's very nice of you. I cook some, but it's mostly basic stuff. Chicken salad sounds like work; all that chopping and mixing."

They crossed the street, Sunday empty, and then stepped up onto a wide front porch with carefully arranged white wicker furniture. Louise Filus found her key in her handbag and worked the front-door lock, gesturing with a jerk of her head for Dorsey to follow her. They entered immediately into a formal living room done in white paint and furnished in French provincial. Without stopping they continued on beneath an arching doorway to the dining room, where two settings had been arranged on the table's near corner. Against the papered walls were a matching sideboard, silver tea set centered on top, and an older console stereo. Louise Filus dropped her handbag on the edge of the sideboard, invited Dorsey to take his place at the setting on the table's side, then toyed with the stereo until she found a station that played classical music.

"Iced tea?" she asked, passing through a swinging door that Dorsey assumed led to the kitchen.

"Sure, fine," he said, settling into his chair. The plate before him had a green and gold print of a village in winter and his glass was cut crystal. This is getting ridiculous, he told himself. You're here to ask her how she likes sleeping with the neighborhood priest and what she knows about her dear husband's murder, and she plays the dutiful hostess. Hell, maybe Emily Post does cover this situation.

Louise Filus returned to the dining room with an ice bucket and tongs and distributed three cubes each into their glasses. Then it was back to the kitchen from which she produced two smaller plates, each with a stuffed tomato sitting perfectly at the center. On her final trip she brought a pitcher of tea.

"Is that going to be it for a while?" Dorsey asked, smiling and watching her pour the tea. "You can get a person nervous with all this back and forth. C'mon, sit down. It's your house after all. We can eat and talk about what there is to talk about."

"You mean Father Crimmins, right?"

Dorsey had started to pick at his food but set his fork down. "That's another thing. We need to talk about some serious and, for you, uncomfortably personal matters. So what say we call him Tom instead of Father Crimmins. We both know him well enough."

Louise Filus dug a small bite of chicken from the tomato on her plate and then touched her lips with her napkin. "You're here to be cruel?" she asked. "That's not what I expected, not from the way that Tom described you."

"No, no," Dorsey said, chewing on his food. "I'm not here to make things tougher than they already are. And you're right, I don't always put things as diplomatically as I should. But, Louise, we need to have some straight talk. And not just for the sake of Father Tom. If the DA makes his move, and it sure looks like he will, you're in for a lot of heartache yourself." He explained to her his feelings that she would be implicated in any accusations against the priest.

Dorsey watched her calmly place her fork at the edge of her plate, take a sip of iced tea, and leave again for the kitchen. Jesus, he thought, she must have to replace the carpet between the two rooms every couple of months, what with the way she beats a path across it. But this could get rough and it was best for him to show his fangs early. When Louise returned and took her seat, Dorsey could see that she had wiped her eyes and had done some repairs on her makeup.

"Listen," Dorsey said softly. "You're a very lovely woman, for a lot of reasons. And Tom, well, he's got a lot going for him. What's gone on between you two doesn't surprise me. And it sure as hell doesn't shock me." Dorsey took a pull on his ice tea before continuing. "Now, I need you to tell me about it all. With any luck you'll never have to talk about it again. With no luck, this'll be good practice."

Louise smiled at the last of it, had a little tea, and said, "Okay."

If you learn anything from this, Louise told him, never volunteer it. "I've heard men say that about the army, but I'm speaking of the church. If you give the pastor or the parish council the slightest inkling that you have some spare time, well, then you are sunk. Through my friend Helen, I agreed to help out at the parish summer street fair. It was supposed to be for one evening behind the baked-goods table. In that one evening, Mrs. Fechter of the altar committee, Mrs. Olivo of the youth committee, and Mrs. Oaster of the education committee, all learned that my boys were headed off to college and that there was only my husband, a minor consideration to most of the parish wives, holding me back from having nothing but free time in my future. So, unable to say no to these representatives of Holy Mother Church, I became an integral part of the parish machinery."

"This was what?" Dorsey asked. "Three years ago?

"More like four." Louise was silent for a moment, as if catching her breath before a long soliloquy. Dorsey took a hit from his tea, reminding himself how difficult this was on the woman. Let her lead the way. "The boys, Greg and Mark, they're going to be seniors this year. At Brooke College, that's in West Virginia. Both of them play linebacker for the football team. That's why they're not at home now.

The football team has to report early for training camp."

She rose from her seat and went to the mantel on the far wall, where she retrieved two photos, each framed in gold. Dorsey wondered how pure the gold was before he realized that he didn't give a shit. "Here they are," Louise said, standing the portraits on the table. "These were taken just before they left for school."

Dorsey compared his memories of those news-clipping photos to the pictures sitting in front of him. Both of them, obviously twins, something he hadn't gathered from the clippings, had their mother's features and coloring. Each had close-cropped hair and the bull necks and humped shoulders that are the trademarks of small college football players. "Fine-looking boys. How'd they deal with what happened to their father?"

"They were strong," Louise said. "For me they were strong. There was some game-facing you might say, but that cracked after awhile, so they experienced some delayed rough times. Their grades suffered; and Greg took a few courses over at community college during the summer. But, all in all, with everything that happened, they've done fine. And they were a help to me and others during those tough times."

It was Dorsey's turn for a silent moment over his tea. Setting down the glass, he folded his hands on the table, waiting.

"Yes," Louise said, "we need to get on with my tale of corruption. As I said, I was suddenly a full-fledged church lady. On an average of three nights a week I was at a meeting. Or I was working the telephone to organize a meeting. Or writing up the minutes of the last meeting. I became an officer on two committees, secretary of youth activities and president of the finance committee. That must have looked like a natural for me, what with David being a CPA and the parish hoping for his services without charge." She shook her head and shrugged. "Poor man. You know I don't even have a photo of him to show you. After his death, and with Tom and me still together, the thought of looking at his picture scared me. Guilt, I suppose. I didn't think much of myself at the time. Well, regardless, to save myself the anguish, I packed away all the photos of him, and of the two of us together. Isn't that a horrible thing?''

Dorsey thought of all the ass-backward ways he had coped with low points in his life, losses he had suffered and injuries he had endured. It's not a horrible thing, he wanted to tell her. It was something that worked, that got you through and is still getting you through. You, Louise, you want to feel horrible? Okay, then you be the one who stepped off the bus on a chilly evening, looking forward to a hot meal and maybe to listening to some guy who's more actor than journalist read the news at eleven. Take your husband's place. You be the one who never got to eat that hot meal. You be the guy who had his brain stem obliterated just a block away from home. Now that's horrible.

"In this instance, I say take care of yourself," Dorsey told her. "Don't think twice about it."

Louise Filus smiled and for a moment laid a hand on Dorsey's wrist. "Thanks. But back to our little story."

The finance committee was what finally put her together with Tom Crimmins. No surprise there, Dorsey thought. A pastor was judged by the size of the parish bank account, and no priest he had ever known had given a parish finance committee much room to maneuver. Louise told him how it had started, with innocent planning meetings with her and the priest.

"But then again," she said, "there never was an innocent meeting. Not after the first time we talked. Nothing happened, but for months it was nothing except delay and control on both our parts. Meetings where we smiled way too much at each other and then the friendly hug or an arm around the shoulders that we hoped would be sufficient to hold the rest at bay. And then one day we talked and agreed that we both knew what was going on and that we should avoid each other. A week passed and then we planned . . . for when we could see each other.

"You're probably wondering where a wayward housewife and a fallen priest can go and be together. Well, it's not easy. The only thing that made it less difficult is the ease in which a priest can slip into civilian clothes nowadays. That and the fact that with the exception of Sundays, a pastor can set his own schedule for the daytime hours. While David was alive we met in restaurants out in the suburbs, maybe as far away as the airport. There are motels all over the place. Nice places, really. Then, after David was gone, we started coming here. I couldn't do that before. It was David's house, too. I refused to meet Tom here, just refused. Partially out of respect and partially out of fear. I was afraid he'd come home and pick up on the smell of afternoon sex. I wasn't ready to tell him the truth, and I just didn't want to get caught.''

"Who knows about this?" Dorsey asked. He jammed his fork at the chicken salad and snared a hunk of meat. "Anyone? A friend you confided in? Does anyone in the parish suspect? Rumors?''

"The rumors start before anything else." Louise Filus grabbed the ice tongs and dropped an extra cube in each of their glasses. "Even before the affair or relationship or whatever. When the two of us were just friends, people could see that we were drawn to each other. Rumors are always there, and I say the hell with them. But to answer your question, there's no one. Maybe if Tom was just another guy, maybe I would have taken someone into my confidence. Lord knows I wanted to a million times. But with Tom's position, I was too frightened. I didn't dare.''

Well, that's a relief, Dorsey thought. If she's telling the truth. The fewer who know, the better. Fewer to refute if it comes to that. Now for the one that knows for sure. Dorsey chewed, swallowed his food, then spoke. "So what about Alice Sutton?''

"I knew her name would crop up in this conversation," Louise said, sighing. "Tom said you're one of the direct ones. Very direct, but in your own damned sneaky way.''

"Sorry," Dorsey said, "but it seemed like the time had come. You look like you're ready for this part. Any pain you suffer now, in private, just might save you from going through it all over again with a million thrill-seekers looking on. So tell me. How's Alice Sutton fit in?''

"Alice Sutton," Louise said, her gaze hard on Dorsey, "is a monstrous, obsessive bitch. She wraps herself up in this image of the tragically unfulfilled servant of God, the woman who only wants to do God's work but is misunderstood. She's half crazy, if you ask me. And the other half is just pure cruelty.''

Dorsey returned the stare, adding a slight, encouraging nod. He thought back over all he had learned about the Sutton woman. The willfulness, and a sense beyond that, a sense that she took all things to the extreme. And then he thought of the encounter to come. He'd have to speak to her, that was assured. If only out of an overwhelming curiosity.

"So it's more than what she knows," Dorsey said. "It's what she does with the knowledge. Tell me about both."

Louise began by recounting several finance committee meetings in which Alice Sutton had squared off with Father Crimmins. Not on major issues, she explained, not even minor ones. She kept bringing up old matters, ones that had been voted on and resolved. "Things, decisions that she had disagreed with from the start," Louise said. "She could never let go of anything. It could've been a vote on where to buy a basketball for the CYO, who had the best price. As if she couldn't stand to be disagreed with, that disagreement was the same as her being wrong. At the beginning of the next meeting she'd ask that the question be reopened. Even if the damned basketball had already been bought!''

Dorsey shook his head and shrugged, thinking of all the others he had met that matched the description of Alice Sutton. The blindly self-righteous emphasis on the self. But, no, he thought. There hadn't been that many. And they never stayed long in his life. They just did their damage and moved on to the next person they'd wound while conducting another crusade. Louise broke into his thoughts.

"She has this obnoxious aggressiveness," she said. "In

your face stuff, literally. She'd be right up in front of you, leaning in, just inches from your face. It was almost nose to nose, even across a table. Her eyes seemed to get wider and sort of take over her face. And each response from her was more and more forceful.'' Louise squared her shoulders as if those ice tongs had been played along her spine. ''Frightening, really frightening. I made a practice of sitting as far away from her as possible at meetings. I've even switched seats halfway through to keep her at a distance.''

Dorsey ate a little and then set down his fork. ''So, you hate her and from all accounts she hates you back. If only in the sense that you are an impediment to her zeal. Now, here's a gentle nudge back on track. How much does she know about you and Tom and how does she know it?''

''She used to follow us.''

''Come again?''

''She followed us,'' Louise said. ''Tailed us, conducted a surveillance, however you wish to put it. We didn't realize it at first, of course. We were a good distance from here, and we didn't bother to look over our shoulders. The places we chose seemed safe. And we always traveled separately.''

''Well, then, who was she following?'' Dorsey asked. ''You or Tom? I don't care how religious she is, even she can't be in two places at the same time.''

''Must've been Tom,'' Louise said. ''She hated him more. And she hated him first. You could tell in the committee meetings.''

''Okay,'' Dorsey said, lifting his fork and toying with it. ''Even with all you've told me about her, dear old Alice would have needed a good reason to play private eye. I assume she has some kind of job that could let her get away to do this. All in all, this was a big undertaking. Why?''

Louise took her napkin and carefully dabbed at the corners of her mouth. ''Yes,'' she said, ''the woman has a job. She's the manager of this food co-op by McPherson Boulevard, or maybe it's on Penn Avenue, somewhere in between. And of course she had a reason. She saw Tom and me sitting in my car after a meeting. You see, to travel from the church hall to the rectory, the distance of half a city block, seldom calls for a ride. We saw her walk by and stare. And then run off.''

Dorsey couldn't help but wonder what Alice Sutton had found in that car. Hand holding? An out of place caress? God help them all if there was more. If this went public, lurid testimony was damaging testimony. ''I suppose,'' Dorsey said, ''we can take it as an article of faith that Sutton has kept a log of your travels. Times, dates, places. And neither you nor Tom have any believable defense for these meetings?''

''Just that Tom and I are in love.'' Louise Filus moved about in her chair, squaring her shoulders. ''I'll take all the scorn that's to be parceled out concerning my relationship with Tom. I realized long ago that would be the price to be paid if people found out. But I didn't play any part in my husband's death, and I won't be made to suffer for it. I can't speak for Tom, but I'm sure he feels the same way.''

''If Tom's willing to pay that price, why hasn't he?'' Dorsey squared his own shoulders, mimicking her movements. ''This thing between you two has been going on for years. When's he gonna come clean, leave the priesthood, and marry you?''

''That's a question that you'll have to ask him,'' Louise said. ''Maybe he doesn't want tongues wagging over David's death. But my guess is his sense of commitment to the priesthood, to his vows, and all the confusion they've caused for him, internally. You have no idea of it all and you'll have to discuss it with Tom. If that sort of thing interests you.''

It does, Dorsey thought, it does. It had the sound of a challenge to Dorsey, as if she wouldn't mind his lighting a fire under the priest. Great, he thought, that's all this tale needs. A spat between the prime suspects. Boy, would Douglas Turner eat that up.

Dorsey leaned forward and propped his chin in the cup of his hands. ''That's not all there is, right? From what you're telling me, all that Alice the wild woman can prove is that you two have been running around together. That's enough to wet the DA's interest, but it's nothing for him to start making noise about, even inside his office. So what is it? If you don't know, tell me what you think.''

Louise Filus didn't let a beat go by. ''I suppose it has to do with the money.''

''The money?''

''Yes,'' Louise said. ''The money.''

11

Sitting on the edge of the wooden back porch, Dorsey tugged on a can of Rolling Rock. The yard that stretched out in front him needed an overhaul, as did the wooden fence, and Gretchen was walking about with a small sketch pad, planning for the next Spring. Dressed in shorts and a Pitt T-shirt, she drew angled plots for vegetable gardens, flower patches, and a central location for a patio table with umbrella. Dorsey thought it sounded like a lot of work and told her so.

"You'll just have to take your time," Gretchen said, continuing at her work. "Just spread the job out over two, maybe three, weekends."

"Oh."

"Relax," she said, turning to him with a smile. "There's a whole winter to get through first. During which the interior of the house will provide more than enough challenges, I'm sure. Meanwhile, tell me more about your afternoon."

"Money," Dorsey said, staring past his beer can. "That's the worst thing you can throw into the mix. Add some cash to an illicit love affair, and you've got a lot of explaining to do."

Gretchen climbed the three wooden steps and sat next to Dorsey, helping herself to a sip of his beer. "This whole porch would look a lot better in a dark green," she said. "How much money are we talking about?"

"A few hundred thousand worth of David Filus's life

insurance." Dorsey took back the can and had a drink. "It covered the loss, and surely saved Tom Crimmins his pastorship on the next inspection by the bishop. Old Dave might've been a hell of a CPA, but he sure couldn't pick an investment to save his ass."

The story had flattened Dorsey. Over a second iced tea, Louise Filus had run through it all. How Tom Crimmins, on his own without the help of the parish finance committee, had been looking for an investment for some surplus cash and had called on David Filus for advice. Tom Crimmins had taken him up on that advice, commodity futures, and the advice had been rotten. Two hundred thousand dollars worth of rotten. And after her husband's death, Louise had given just about that same amount to her lover to cover the loss. "Then worst of all," he told Gretchen, "it seems that Alice Sutton was just as adept at following a paper trail as she was at following the ones left by humans. Louise Filus figures she's been through the books and has all the transaction dates and amounts of the loss as well as the anonymous contribution, which can be easily traced back to Louise."

"So it's bad," Gretchen said. "How bad?"

"To be honest," Dorsey said, "I don't know what the DA is waiting for. He's got two motives. If this didn't involve a priest, he'd have his people sweating answers out of those two, I can promise you that. He wants more; he's looking for something that seals the case. Maybe something strong enough for a plea bargain." Dorsey took a sip of beer. "Now, that would be perfect, for DA Turner, I mean. That way, he shows how fearlessly he tracks down crime, wherever it happens to lurk. And then he shows mercy, saving the community from a trial that can only cause it pain. He'd look like one hell of a guy."

Gretchen studied her sketch pad. "Carroll, did these two kill that man?"

"How the hell do I know? What am I, some kind of detective?"

"Seriously," Gretchen said, setting the pad aside and taking his hand.

"That's not what I'm being paid to find out," Dorsey told her. "That was pretty easy to keep in mind before this afternoon. There was some idle speculation, sure. And then with you moving back here, I had other matters on my mind. Better things to think about. But now, if I were still working out of that office at the courthouse and drawing a county salary, I'd like the odds on the two of them for the killing. I'd be checking out the priest's war record, where he was that night, and I'd be searching for the gun, which I assume no one has found or Tom and Louise would've had their pictures in the paper by now. Iron bars in front."

"And your next step?" Gretchen asked. "If you were some kind of detective, I mean."

"Get another beer, at least." Dorsey drained the bottom of the can. "Spend a few blissful hours with you, get through tomorrow's court appearance, and then face off with Tom Crimmins and have the talk we didn't have the last time."

"Things will be fine for Mrs. Leneski, you'll see." Gretchen got to her feet and pulled Dorsey along with her. "I'll be at the hospital until late tomorrow, but call and have me paged. I really want to know what happens."

No you don't, Dorsey thought, following her through the screen door, mudroom, and into the kitchen. He hadn't told her how it was playing out, about what he had in mind for tomorrow, because he'd figured she was his confessor. Like all those times in the past, when his job had called on him to get ugly, violent; all the things that he regretted and that were against his nature. She was his confessor, so he hadn't told her, because you don't go to confession until after the sin is committed. When you really need it. "I'll call as soon as it's over."

He took a fresh Rolling Rock from the refrigerator and they went into the living room. The bay windows were screened and open, allowing a breeze to push through from three angles, flapping the temporary sheer curtains. Earlier that evening Dorsey had wired together her component stereo and Gretchen searched through her CD collection. She settled for one that Dorsey had given her several years before, Ella Fitzgerald's *Gershwin Song Book.*

"Feel at home?" she asked, settling next to him on the couch, her right hand massaging his neck. "Given any thought to staying the night?"

Dorsey patted his pockets and sighed. "Sorry, no tooth-brush."

"Get dentures. I'll keep a glass on the night stand."

Dorsey moved about in the darkened bedroom, using only the moonlight to guide him as he gathered his belongings. Like those on the first floor, this room was large, oversized with a twelve-foot ceiling. The furniture suite consisted of the treasured armoire, a writing desk and chair, dresser, and an ageless four-poster bed. Supporting himself with an arm propped against the top of the armoire, Dorsey had just managed to slip into his shorts from a standing position when Gretchen stirred.

"Two nights in a row," she said, pulling herself to a sitting position and adjusting the pillows behind her.

"I stayed over last night." Dorsey searched the floor for a second sock. "You forgot already? Well, I'm meeting my past sexual standard, I suppose."

"No, no," Gretchen said, "my memory's fine, both short- and long-term. I was referring to your distracted attitude." Gretchen's smile was caught in the moonglow. "Seems like your heart just hasn't been in it, know what I mean? You've got that irritating I'm-locked-into-a-big-case-or-nasty-situation preoccupation of yours that just doesn't go well with a homecoming celebration."

Dorsey gave up on finding the other sock, dropped the one he had in hand, and settled into the writing table's chair. "I thought I was covering it pretty well. Really. I don't want to be this way; I didn't want things to be this way for the weekend. It was my original plan to have Henry's help in moving you, then find a way to ditch him for thirty-six hours that would be spent at your side. That was the plan. But several attorneys, my father and Ironbox, a priest, a good-looking middle-aged widow, and an elderly woman in big trouble all conspired against me.''

''Is there more than you've told me?''

''Yes,'' Dorsey said, ''there certainly is. And I'm not going to tell you, not yet. Tomorrow evening would be a much better time. I'll need to tell you then. That's when you can help me with it.''

Gretchen folded her arms across her small breasts, stared at the windows, and for a moment Dorsey thought he had angered her. ''I know where this is headed,'' she said, turning her gaze to him. ''The general direction, at least. And it's okay. And you knew it would be okay, didn't you?''

''Hoped it would be,'' Dorsey said. ''I don't always have your confidence.''

''My confidence comes from putting in a lot of thought. An awful lot of thought.''

''Sorry, but I suppose that life with me can be thought provoking.''

Gretchen reached behind her head, took hold of a pillow, and flung it at Dorsey. He could see that it wasn't a completely playful act. ''Don't push it,'' Gretchen told him. ''I was being serious, and I'm about to get even more so. All of this thought that I've put in has brought me to the conclusion that I'm completely comfortable with you. Completely. I know you so well, and I've allowed you to get to know me so well that there are no pretensions between us. Surprises, yes; disagreements, of course. But I accept all of it, all of you. Just like now. I know something's pestering you and that whatever it is, you're not ready to tell me. You will, though. Soon. Because you'll have to. It will make you physically ill if you don't. And I'll help you when that time comes. And you knew all that before I said it.''

''I'll tell you everything,'' Dorsey said. ''Tomorrow, first opportunity.''

''Sure you will,'' Gretchen replied. ''That's why I came back.''

12

The next morning, staring into the bathroom mirror, Dorsey
conducted the longest shave of his life. The shaving lather
was applied carefully, rolled along the chin line and then
spread out onto his cheeks in waves that bridged below his
nose. He held the safety razor in a firm grip, not the hap-
hazard way he did most mornings when shaving was an
annoyance to be tolerated, and each stroke was carefully laid
to slightly overlap the previous one. Ah, he thought, the
classic delay tactic of your youth. What would an analyst
have to say about this?

There had been a time, Dorsey remembered, when he had
gone completely overboard. It was during second grade at
Sacred Heart School. He had so hated his teacher, Sister
Angelica, that each evening was filled with a dread of the
next school day. Then young Dorsey came upon a scheme
to delay tomorrows—by fighting sleep, staring at the ceiling
from his bed and counting off the moments, making the
freedom last. The scheme lasted until one Thursday morning
when he collapsed on the sidewalk, running to answer the
school bell. Then the delay lasted for an additional three
days of hospital observation. A politician's kid got pretty
good care back then, he remembered.

Forgetting his apprehension, Dorsey dressed quickly in a
dark business suit and went down to the kitchen to make
coffee. He switched on the counter radio, and while he
worked at the filter, molding the paper against the walls of

the coffeemaker's basket, Benny Carter played "Joy Spring." For a while Dorsey lost himself in a bygone world that he had been born too late to ever see. Then the office phone rang.

"Let's have an update," Bill Meara said before Dorsey could get in a hello. "How'd you spend your weekend and what do you have that's gonna make this all go away for us?"

Dorsey had to gather himself for a moment, recalling which of two pressing matters he had to address. "How about two black junkies from Homewood who, between the two of them, managed to kill one white CPA?"

"If you can support it, great."

"I can't," Dorsey said. "So it isn't."

"Then try a lot fucking harder," Meara said, his voice leveling. "Tell me every goddamned thing that has transpired since Friday."

Dorsey built his time line and filled it in: Crimmins the war hero and combat veteran, Crimmins the piss-poor financial manager, Crimmins who reaped a windfall benefit from the Filus murder, Crimmins as the number three man in a love triangle. And then there was Alice Sutton, amateur snoop and full-time obsessive-compulsive and keeper of the record for the Crimmins-Filus love affair. Most importantly of all, he recounted his meeting with Douglas Turner.

"The money stinks," Meara said. "That hurts and you better look into it."

"Thanks," Dorsey replied. "The thought never crossed my mind."

Meara either ignored or missed the sarcasm. "The Turner business has me thinking a couple of ways. What's he bothering with you for if this thing is almost sewed up? You figure, he has to know what you're just finding out, so he must know a hell of a lot. But he's not making any moves. Except to try to get your help. He's taking his time with this case, but then he jumps all over you, not twenty-four hours after he learns of your involvement. This guy is anything but evenhanded. And sometimes not being evenhanded translates into being off-balance, which, I told you once before, is good for us.''

"Sometimes," Dorsey said, "I'm not sure if you hired me to build an alternate case or just to be a pain in the ass for the DA."

"Same difference."

"Same difference?"

"Hell, yes," Meara replied. "I want the guy to fail. However you help in the effort, you help in the effort."

"And on that inspiring note," Dorsey said, "we can bring this conversation to an end. I've got to get my ass over to the courthouse and stop an attorney from losing a case despite his best efforts."

"Leneski?" Meara asked.

"Yeah."

"Go get'em," Meara said. "Look at it as just another opportunity to be a pain in the ass."

Dorsey left the Buick in the lot at Grant and Forbes avenue and, dodging rush hour traffic, jogged diagonally through the intersection to the granite steps of the county courthouse. A stone-and-mortar affair that dated from the previous century, it had a connecting archway to a jail built of similar materials, and together they formed several acres of anachronism within a modern and continually renewing business district. Anachronism, Dorsey thought. What a lovely word.

Inside, he climbed several flights of wide marble steps to the courtroom of Judge Thomas Malloy, who from all reports had made a full recovery from the twenty-four-hour-plus weekend flu. The hallway was littered with small groups: attorneys, defendants, frightened families and lovers; all a little lost, Dorsey knew, all waiting for uncertain outcomes. Dorsey checked his wristwatch and found an empty piece of wall to lean against, steeling himself one last time for the crime to come, joining the rest as they waited for that unknown outcome.

Perjury is a lie, Dorsey thought, a lie that's material to the case. A lie that has some bearing on the case. And that, he reminded himself, is always open to argument; the meat and drink of being an attorney. Look at something in the proper light, and it might take on a whole new meaning. Up can be down, day can be night, left can be right. This whole thing might not be relevant.

Dorsey crossed the hall and watched his reflection in one of the windows that looked down on a central courtyard with a fountain. Up is down, night is day, left is right. But, he thought, bullshit is always bullshit. Chickenshit can't be chicken salad. And when you tell that lie, it will be perjury. You will commit a crime. Yeah, sure, it's fire against fire. Your lie versus Turner's blackmail and your father's indifference. But so what? Face up to what you are and what you're doing, and then go have a long heart to heart with Gretchen. Oh, hell, at least you get to be a pain in the ass. Thanks for that, Meara.

Slipping through a tall wooden door, Dorsey found himself in a familiar and anxious spot, a courtroom waiting on a judge. The room was deep and wide with high windows, ancient, dangling light fixtures, and very little in the way of furniture. The gallery consisted of two rows of unmatched plastic and wooden chairs, and the expected railing between the gallery and the trial area was missing. To the left was a jury box devoid of seats for this non-jury matter; and the judge's bench was a multitiered structure that had always reminded Dorsey of an elaborate playground jungle gym. Integrated into the first levels were pockets for the court reporter, a judge's secretary, and witness chair. Ranging across the top was the judge's compartment, long with plenty of work space, and placed at a height that might inspire a modern-day Kafka. And milling about were a few uniformed policeman, county workers, and attorneys, all hoping to convince the judge's secretary that they just needed to steal a few moments of the great man's time before the day's work began.

Mrs. Leneski, dressed in her black dress that gathered at the neckline and wrists, was seated at the defendant's table with her attorney. Meeker spotted Dorsey, made a quick remark to his client, and met him at the door. Leading him to one of the gallery chairs, he asked Dorsey if he was ready to deliver his testimony.

"Ready," Dorsey said, as Meeker sat next to him. "How about you? Come up with anything new over the weekend?"

Meeker shrugged and turned his palms skyward. "We have to go with what we have."

"What's that?"

Meeker got to his feet and mumbled something about getting back to his client. "Don't worry," he said, walking away. "You're experienced. Just relax and it'll be fine."

Ah, Christ, Dorsey thought, another empty well. It's just you, buddy. Prepare to lie.

Dorsey watched as Meeker settled back into his seat at the defendant's table and gave Mrs. Leneski a comforting pat on the shoulder. She returned the gesture with a glare and then left her seat and came toward Dorsey. "You've had your breakfast?" she asked, taking the chair that Meeker had just occupied. "You should eat. You look bad."

"I feel it," Dorsey told her. "This morning, anyway. Could've stayed in the sack, sheet pulled over my head."

"You," Mrs. Leneski said, "you worry about all this." She shot a glance toward Meeker. "You worry about him. He doesn't help, but he can't hurt things too bad. Wanna know why?"

Yes, Dorsey thought, I desperately want to know. Tell me something good, get me off the hook.

"They call this the justice system, that's what I keep hearin' from these people. All of 'em." Mrs. Leneski fussed at her neckline and played a finger across her chin. "But it's a system, just a goddamned system. It's how this bunch does stuff, the way they get their work done for the day. The justice part is all over with. I took care of that back when I shot that sumbitch Novotny. The justice is done and these goddamned fancies didn't do shit to help. So, it's all okay. I'm old and they can have me. But they can't make me shut up. That lawyer, that Meeker, he tells me to say

I'm sorry for what I done. That way, when this is all over, the judge will feel sorry for me. For me? Bullshit. Feel sorry for my granddaughter. The judge should feel sorry because he's a big shot and he couldn't help her. Don't feel sorry for me because I ain't sorry. I kill that sumbitch again, right now, you give me a chance.''

"Would it hurt to be contrite?'' Dorsey asked her. "Just put it on a little bit for the judge, that's all you'd have to do. What good would it serve, if he had to punish you now, at your age?''

Mrs. Leneski turned in her seat, facing Dorsey, sending him a look that was heavy with disappointment. "You should learn from old people. You should learn how to be old from old people. How to be all grown-up. I thought maybe you learn from me, a little.''

Dorsey thought of all the things he valued, and with the exception of Gretchen, he found them all to have cobwebs clinging at the edges. The music he loved, the city buildings, Ironbox and his father, Al and his bar, the woman sitting next to him, the row house that held his home and business. All had the grace of age, the dignity of maturity and having survived over the long haul.

And, he asked himself, what would a mature man give to save the things he treasured? He'd give it all. Perhaps painfully, but he'd give it all.

"I'll try to do better,'' Dorsey told her. "In some cases, most cases, I can be a slow study.''

"After this is over,'' Mrs. Leneski said, leveraging herself onto her feet, "you come visit me. I feed you good. You should eat more.''

A thin gray-haired man poked his head in from a door to the left of the judge's bench and gave one of the sheriff's deputies the high sign. The police officers who had been milling about found seats in the gallery, and a few attorneys made for the hallway where Dorsey assumed they would work the ground for cases. The court reporter checked her store of paper rolls and seemed to take on a much more serious air while the deputy straightened into a military stance. Without announcement, Judge Thomas Malloy made a brisk entrance, waved everyone back into the seats they were just getting out of, settled into his chair, and flipped open the file on his desktop.

"We're still on the Leneski matter?" Judge Malloy addressed the room at large. "That's right, isn't it?"

To Dorsey, Thomas Malloy had the look of a man who could fill in for any one of the Clancy Brothers at a moment's notice. He wasn't very tall, but he was large with a boxy look made up of large shoulders atop a body without contours. His beard was shaggy and red, and what little hair he had on his head seemed to call for a tweed cap. He needs a brick-and-mortar wall behind him, Dorsey thought, and before him should be cabaret tables topped with pints of black ale. And to each side there would be a family member decked out in wool slacks and an oversized sweater, asking the audience if they had any favorites they'd like to hear. Born to be a Harp, Dorsey thought, that's the lot of Tommy Malloy.

"And, Mr. Meeker," the judge continued, "with whom shall we begin the week?"

Artie Meeker pushed his chair back against the tile floor with a shriek, gathered his dignity despite the smirks and giggles that earned a glare from Judge Malloy, and announced that he was calling Carroll Dorsey to the stand. Dorsey got his feet, flexed his arms to straighten the lay of his jacket, and went toward the bench where he was met by a Bible-toting tipstaff-secretary. With a hand on the Good Book, Dorsey agreed to tell the truth before God, to whom he would answer on that last great day, and took the witness chair.

Moving nervously before the defense table, Meeker took Dorsey through the basics. They covered his full name and address, education, work history, and state licenses; and while doing so Dorsey got his first good look at the assistant DA handling the case. Dorsey figured him for a Turner clone: early forties, well-placed streaks of gray in his dark hair, and dressed in a suit that Artie Meeker could never afford, even for the day he was named president of the local Kiwanis. Dorsey watched the assistant DA scribble notes and he had to wonder what interest the man might have in the date of his college graduation. Or maybe it was the day he dropped out of law school that captured his interest.

Meeker picked up the pace, at Judge Malloy's urging, and asked some open-ended questions that allowed Dorsey to recount his full involvement with Mrs. Leneski. How she had hired him to find her missing granddaughter and, sadly, what he had finally found. In the telling, he was able to discuss Dr. Novotny's taste in young girls, the private conversation he had had with the doctor, when Novotny had freely admitted to these predilections, and how he had hoped to get a shot at Mrs. Leneski's granddaughter. All of which helped him rest after a long and difficult day of writing illegal prescriptions for neighborhood druggies.

Dorsey was painting a ten-gallon black hat and the wings of death on Novotny, and the assistant DA sat still through it all. Even the note-taking had stopped, and that scared the shit out of Dorsey. His meeting with Novotny had been private and Novotny's words, as Dorsey restated them, were hearsay, totally uncorroborated. But the assistant DA was content to sit on his hands. And then Dorsey saw why.

A blond young man left his gallery seat and went to the courtroom door as Meeker ended his questioning and returned to his chair. It was Longley, the boy detective, Dorsey realized, and wondered when it was that he had slipped into the room. He stepped into the hall momentarily and returned on the heels of his boss, Douglas Turner. So this is it, Dorsey told himself, this is where Turner shows you how big his balls are. This is where he sees to it that you get your ass kicked in public. Something you're unlikely to forget and which just might convince you to see things his way. Now, my friend, let's see where deception takes you.

The assistant DA, who introduced himself to Dorsey as John Rasher, came to his feet and consulted a few sheets of papers he had on the table before him. ''There's just a few matters I'd like to review,'' he said, stepping around the table and looking at Judge Malloy as if for approval. The judge raised his head, nodded his assent, and went back to scribbling some notes.

Dorsey's spine instinctively went rigid, like a startled cat. Just a few matters to review, he thought. Why doesn't Rasher just ask you to drop your guard while he winds up a haymaker aimed at your jawline? A few matters, sure, like hell. He's got something planned and you can bet your ass that Turner was in on the planning. Dorsey rolled his shoulders and sucked in a little extra air. Stay composed, he warned himself, at least outwardly. You've been through this before. So, so many times.

"Your employment by the defendant," Rasher asked, "began in the spring of last year?"

"That's correct." Dorsey's reply came slowly, softly, as if each word had undergone close scrutiny before being uttered. "It was in mid to late May as I recall. The exact date is in my office records."

"Your recollection is sufficient; it's fine really." Rasher made a show of returning to the prosecution table for just a moment, where he checked his notes and then turned his attention back to Dorsey. "And the purpose for which she employed you was to find her granddaughter. Is that so?"

"Yes, that's correct."

"And for no other reason?"

"None." Dorsey itched, trying to anticipate where he was being led.

"This employment arrangement with the defendant, it ended when?"

"After the young girl was found," Dorsey said, looking toward Mrs. Leneski. "After her identity was confirmed by the coroner's office."

"You did nothing more?"

"No," Dorsey said. "That was the end of our business relationship."

"In the matter of the defendant's granddaughter, Maritsa Durant," Rasher said. "In that matter, did you give a deposition to the district attorney's office? During the previous D.A.'s administration?''

''Yes,'' Dorsey said, sensing something but not yet seeing it form. ''Yes, I did.''

''That deposition, it was given after your investigation was completed? After your work for Mrs. Leneski was completed?''

''Correct. The deposition was my account of that investigation.''

''And once again,'' Rasher said, looking quickly to Judge Malloy, as if to assure himself of having the judge's attention, ''once again I have to ask if you have conducted any other investigations for the defendant, Mrs. Leneski?''

''I've maintained a personal relationship with her,'' Dorsey said, ''but all of our business was concluded when the young girl's body was found.''

John Rasher spread his arms, his palms out, the pleading supplicant. ''Then for whom was it that you conducted the investigation of Dr. Novotny?''

Dorsey turned and looked upward at Judge Malloy. ''Your honor, I'm sorry. I just don't understand the question.''

''I think,'' Judge Malloy said, leveling his gaze at Rasher, ''that the assistant district attorney is about to enlighten us all as to where he's headed. At least he'd better.''

John Rasher went back to his chair and lifted the briefcase that rested against the back legs. Opening it on the tabletop, he extracted three inches worth of bound legal-sized documents and approached Dorsey. ''This is the deposition given by Mr. Dorsey to the office of the former DA. I'd like him to examine it for a few moments, and I'd like to direct his attention to the six tabbed pages.''

Artie Meeker hopped to his feet with an objection. Finally, Dorsey thought, a moment to think. He thumbed open the deposition at the first tabbed page and then quickly went to the second and third. Novotny, goddamn him, he's having the last laugh. Maybe the joke is on your father, but he's getting to him through you. You're the ass.

Rasher met Artie Meeker's objection by providing him with a second copy of the deposition and a third was given to Judge Malloy, who gave the matter some apparently brief thoughts before giving Rasher the go ahead. And now Dorsey knew where he was being taken. The deposition, he thought, that simple compromise with the truth to protect his father. Martin Dorsey, the consummate political black operator, had long ago left himself open to extortion by Dr. Novotny. Extortion that the doctor had used to procure Martin Dorsey's intercession against drug charges, tax evasion, and twenty years of illegal abortions. One of which resolved a difficult situation for Dorsey's father. And so, under oath, Dorsey had told the authorities the tale of Maritsa Durant's last few months on this earth with certain omissions. One of which was Dr. Novotny's having prescribed the drugs that had killed her.

Dorsey let the deposition drop into his lap and looked out across the room to Turner. The DA was stone-faced, a purposeful blank that carried much more malevolence than any evil grin could. But Longley, sitting next to the DA, was a different story. You little prick, Dorsey thought, watching the investigator surreptitiously throw him the bird by appearing to scratch the side of his nose. Have your day, Dorsey wanted to tell him. Because another one's coming, you little pissant.

"Mr. Dorsey," Rasher asked, his voice even, "you agree that this is the deposition which you gave in the matter of Maritsa Durant's death?"

"Yes," Dorsey said, just as evenly. "This is the statement I gave at that time."

"And this is the only one you gave? There are no others?"

"None," Dorsey told him.

Rasher walked in front of the bench for a moment, as if in thought. "In your business, your profession, is it not customary for the client to receive a final report of an investigation?"

"That's correct." Jesus, Dorsey thought, this guy even

knows about that. Dorsey had begun to prepare his report at the time of the granddaughter's funeral, but Mrs. Leneski had refused to accept one. "You already told me how it happened," she had said. "I don't need more goddamned bad news from you." How did Rasher know about it? Meeker, that silly-ass, he must've let it out somehow. The guy's a mess, Dorsey concluded. Leave him in charge of the cash register, and he'll give away the store.

"Did you prepare such a report for Mrs. Leneski?" Rasher asked.

Dorsey hoped to jump a step ahead. "No, I didn't. I had intended to, but Mrs. Leneski was emotionally distraught and asked that we merely drop the matter, being as the investigation was over and the report would serve little purpose."

"Very understandable," Rasher commented and continued his questioning. "So again, this is the only account on record of your investigation and the role played by Dr. Novotny in that young girl's death?"

"I suppose it is."

"May I take that as an affirmative response?" Rasher asked the judge.

"It's the best you'll get from Mr. Dorsey without a protracted duel of words," Judge Malloy said. "Let's take it for what it is and move along."

"Now, Mr. Dorsey," Rasher said, waving his copy of the deposition. "We can go through this rather long document page by page or the two of us can come to an agreement. That agreement being that the six tabbed pages contain the only mentions made of Dr. Novotny in your deposition. Would you agree to that?"

Maintaining a neutral manner, Dorsey conceded that this was the case.

"And would you further agree, that these six entries in no way, directly or indirectly, establish any liability on the part of the late doctor in Maritsa Durant's death?"

"Indirectly, I'm not so sure," Dorsey said. "But no, the deposition does not establish any direct liability."

Again Rasher appealed to Judge Malloy. "Just settle for what you've gotten," the judge told him. "There's no jury to convince, and I get the picture quite clearly."

"Very well." Rasher returned his attention to Dorsey. "So, the question remains as to where and when you either gathered or obtained all of this supposedly damning information about the late doctor?"

"During the investigation I conducted for Mrs. Leneski." With difficulty, Dorsey was maintaining an unaffected appearance.

"But you didn't report this information to her, correct? You issued no written report, isn't that so?"

"I provided a complete report, verbally," Dorsey said. "That verbal report contained all of the details concerning the doctor."

"Other than yourself and Mrs. Leneski," Rasher asked, "did anyone else partake in this discussion? Any witnesses at all?"

"It was a private conversation," Dorsey responded, feeling his credibility with the judge slipping away. The purpose of his taking the stand, of his court appearance, was to establish mitigating circumstances for Mrs. Leneski's actions. And now all that he had said was being brought into serious doubt. All the evil that was Dr. Novotny was unsubstantiated. Nothing in print, no one to back up his story, and nothing he could do to save it all, other than bring his father's name into the discussion. And that wasn't going to happen. Doug Turner and Rasher, his monkey on a leash; they can have you for lunch, but they don't get the old man.

Rasher returned to the prosecution table and consulted the notes on his yellow legal pad. Dorsey wondered what portion of his story and character would be attacked next. You already look like a lousy detective who forgets to write down his notes on a case. Maybe they'll completely run you out of the business before it's over. Carroll Dorsey, displaced worker.

"So," Rasher said, approaching the witness box. "Let's

assume that this unwitnessed debriefing between yourself and Mrs. Leneski did take place.''

''It did take place,'' Dorsey insisted.

''Agreed, for the purposes of our discussion it did take place.'' Rasher said. ''What was Mrs. Leneski's reaction?''

''Extreme sadness,'' Dorsey said. ''And, understandably, anger.''

''How did she express this anger?''

So this is it, Dorsey told himself. You can tell the truth, recount Mrs. Leneski's request that you kill the doctor, and sink her completely. Now, on the other hand, your credibility has been destroyed and nothing you say can be of any help. Jesus Lord, what the hell are you going to do?

''Mr. Dorsey?'' Rasher asked again. ''How did Mrs. Leneski express her anger?''

''Let me stop you right there,'' Judge Malloy said, shaking Dorsey out of his conflicted thoughts and dramatically shifting the room's attention. ''Mr. Rasher, I'll see you, Mr. Meeker, and his client in my chamber. You can have your boss tag along, too, if he wants.'' Judge Malloy lifted himself from his seat and then hesitated. ''Mr. Dorsey,'' he said. ''Let's have you in there, too.''

13

Only Mrs. Leneski was offered a seat, and once Judge Malloy was satisfied with her comfort he undid the zipper of his robes and hung the garment on a clothes tree. Beneath that he wore an oxford cloth shirt and tie with geometric designs. He combed out his red beard, slipped into a padded leather chair behind his mahogany desk, and looked at each of the men arrayed before him. "For the good of the county," the judge said, "and for the sake of justice and the court's time, I'm bringing this matter to an end."

Douglas Turner pushed John Rasher aside and took center stage before the judge's desk. "Before we get started on whatever it is we're doing here, I have to protest this man's presence." With a wave of his arm he indicated Dorsey, who had taken up a position against the wall in the far-right corner. "Mr. Dorsey is not an officer of the court and has no standing in the case at hand. I think it would be best if he was excluded from our discussions."

What the hell's going on? Dorsey wondered. Though, he couldn't blame him; the man was right. From a legal stand-point, you have no business being in this room. And if things didn't go well for Turner, and it sure as hell looked like they might not, Turner would be embarrassed in front of the man he was trying to intimidate. Well, Dorsey, Turner's gonna be pissed at you. . . . And more to deal with.

"As always," Judge Malloy told the DA, "I give your suggestions careful consideration. But this time I think you're wrong. Mr. Dorsey has a close relationship with Mrs. Leneski, and I think it would be for the best that he stay. Unless he would rather leave?'' Judge Malloy shifted his attention to Dorsey. ''I hope he doesn't.''

''I'd be glad to stay.'' Dorsey returned the judge's stare. ''If I can be of any help.''

Turner glared at Dorsey, but at the same time he seemed to shrink backward, his hands thrust into his hip pockets, his spine taking on a slump. Getting set to take a beating, Dorsey thought.

''Now,'' Judge Malloy said, benignly concentrating on Mrs. Leneski, ''I would never be so impolite as to ask a lady her age. But I think it's fair to say you are of an advanced age. Agreed?''

''I could've changed your father's diapers,'' Mrs. Leneski said. ''And powdered his ass with Johnson and Johnson's.''

''No doubt.'' Judge Malloy smiled and looked about the room, as if encouraging the others to share his response. ''And tell me if I'm correct in understanding that you in no way deny having shot and killed Dr. Anton Novotny?''

Artie Meeker leaned forward to speak into Mrs. Leneski's ear, but she shrugged him off. ''I shoot him.'' Mrs. Leneski said. ''No one else, not the police or this fella here, this DA, would do a goddamned thing to stop the bastard. Dope and little girls. He'd do just like he pleased. Nobody stop him.''

That's right, Dorsey thought, shrinking a bit farther into the corner. No one could do a thing, thanks to Martin Dorsey, who still hasn't done a thing to help out this woman.

''We could play out the rest of this trial, and I could send you to jail,'' Judge Malloy said. ''I could do that, you know. The law says so. But I'm supposed to seek and ensure justice in that law. There's no jail for you, no geriatric cell block for women. However you killed a man and that can't be excused. So this is how it's going to be.'' The judge allowed a dramatic moment for the attorneys to draw closer. ''It's my intention to find you guilty of voluntary manslaughter. And you're to be sentenced to six years of house arrest, which means you're going to be supervised by the county probation office and you'll be wearing one of these.''

Judge Malloy slipped open one of the desk's side drawers and produced a metallic ring with a diameter of approximately three to four inches. He worked at the ring for a moment and undid a latch. ''What I have here is a detection anklet. Once around you're ankle and activated, your probation officer will be able to monitor your movements electronically.'' He handed the ring to Mrs. Leneski for her examination. ''The probation office will explain all the particulars of house arrest.''

Mrs. Leneski held the ring in her hand, weighing it. ''Maybe,'' she said, ''maybe it'll be good for the arthritis.''

Standing over Mrs. Leneski, Turner planted both feet, unbuttoned his suitcoat, and dug his thumbs into his waistband. ''Not for a moment, madam,'' he told Mrs. Leneski, ''will I stand for this. You planned a murder for revenge, carried out that murder, and you've shown not an ounce of remorse. I'm not agreeing to any of this. As far as I'm concerned, we can all get back out into the courtroom and continue Mr. Rasher's examination of Mr. Dorsey.''

Artie Meeker set himself to respond, but Judge Malloy cut him off with the wave of a hand. ''No need, Mr. Meeker. And, Mr. Turner, you will address me with your objections. Not the defendant.''

''Your Honor, this is way over the line.'' DA Turner faced Judge Malloy. ''This is blatant interference with the prosecution of a felony case. If you push this through, I'll file a complaint with the judicial board, State Supreme Court, or anybody else who'll listen. There's going to be nothing but trouble if you force this down our throats.''

Judge Malloy held his silence, tugging softly at his beard. Turning to Dorsey, the corner of his mouth seemed to twist sharply and then quickly relax, as if signaling that an inside joke was about to be sprung. And Dorsey suddenly realized why he had been asked into the room.

''Mr. Turner,'' the judge asked, ''how long have you been on the job? A year, a year and a half maybe? You don't have to accept my proposition. And we can go out and continue this trial, which has no jury. All there is, is me. And I am giving strong consideration to recusing myself from this case.''

"How?'' Turner asked. ''On what grounds? And at this late date?''

''The time factor is irrelevant.'' The judge looked down at his desktop and rubbed a finger at a blemish in the polish. ''New information has been brought to my attention, something that I had not been aware of.''

Dorsey watched as Turner shot a quick look at Rasher, who responded with a mystified shrug. This is gonna be good, he thought. Smart-assed bastard, Turner, it must've been the old man who had Friday's court session canceled. Maybe they even had you thinking that you had finagled it. Okay, let's see how the old man put in the fix this time. This has to be his doing.

''You're threatening a mistrial if I don't agree to this arrangement?'' Turner asked. ''Let's hear the basis for why you can't continue in this trial.''

Judge Malloy gathered himself in his seat, pushing back the chair and folding his hands on his lap. ''This isn't the proudest moment for my family, and it's something that I've been able to keep secret, with the help of a few people.'' The judge shot a fast glance at Dorsey that couldn't have gone unnoticed by the others in the room. ''Some of you are aware that I have a son, Sean, who's in his early twenties. Well, if you do know him, you might have noticed that he hasn't been around lately. That's because he's doing a twenty-eight-day dry-out and rehab program. Ever hear of a place called Gateway Rehabilitation?''

''Sure,'' Artie Meeker said as if thinking aloud. ''That's the place that was founded by the rabbi who's on TV once in a while.''

''That's the place,'' Judge Malloy gave Meeker a look that Dorsey could only translate as shut up and let me get through this so I can save your case for you. Please, Dorsey thought, let the man finish.

''My wife and I visited Sean over the weekend,'' Judge

Malloy continued. "It was the first time we were permitted to do so. And he told us a few things we hadn't realized. We knew far too well that he liked to drink beer and wine like there was no tomorrow. What we didn't know was that he especially liked to do that when he was washing down a handful of pills. Painkillers, of course, and Valium and Librium. This was pretty difficult for him to tell us, and I can assure that it was tougher to hear for his mother and me. But what was a lot worse for me, professionally, was when he told me that he had been taking the pills for years. And that he had to find a new source for the pills just after the beginning of the year because his old source had died. Dr. Anton Novotny."

Jesus Christ, Dorsey thought, wondering how much of it was true. The boy being in rehab would be easy to confirm, so that must be straight. But the Novotny connection was up for grabs. If it wasn't true, then no wonder court was canceled on Friday. It would take three days to cook up a story like this one. And to talk Judge Malloy into hanging out the dirty laundry for all the legal community to see.

"You'd go public about your son?" Turner asked. "If you recuse yourself, the reason becomes public record."

"That I know far too well." Judge Malloy pulled his chair closer to the desk, concentrating on Turner. "This matter is all up to you. You accept the deal I've outlined for you or I recuse and you get a mistrial. I'm sure Mr. Meeker will demand that."

He damned well better, Dorsey thought, but he knew it wouldn't come to that. Turner couldn't say no. If he stands firm, calls Malloy's bluff and loses, he'll end up with a mistrial. And he'll be that young and tough DA who couldn't even put away a little old grandmother. A new trial would be a joke, especially when the new judge hears about the deal he refused. A deal that would move the court's calendar nicely along and save a fellow member of the judiciary's family from public embarrassment. Mrs. Leneski walks now or she walks later. Get the point, Turner? You're screwed. Learn to play the game before you take on the big boys. The rest of us had to.

Turner looked at Rasher, who shrank away from his boss, shoulders knotted together and eyes downcast. The DA next looked at Dorsey, grunted a laugh, and through up his hands. "You've got it," he told Judge Malloy. He took Rasher by the arm and pulled him along as he left the room.

Dorsey moved from his spot in the corner, feeling the judge's eyes on him as he made for the door. He turned to him for a moment and nodded. Don't worry, Dorsey thought, my father will get a full and glowing report.

Mrs. Leneski left her chair and reached across the desk and took Judge Malloy's hand. "Sorry about your boy," she told him. "I should've shot that Novotny bastard a lot sooner."

14

Dorsey rushed down to the ground floor of the courthouse and found a bank of three pay phones. He dialed the number Gretchen had given him at the hospital and left a message on her voice mail that all had gone well and that he would explain everything that night. He also told her that he was headed for a meeting with the man who had made sure that all had gone well.

Martin Dorsey was in the same position in which his son had left him three days earlier, seated near the nursing home's visiting-room window, watching boat traffic on the Allegheny River. This time, Dorsey noticed, he was resting in an easy chair, and instead of pajamas he was dressed in a sport shirt and slacks, as if he were in a clubhouse awaiting his tee-off. Only the tripod cane gave him away.

"Looks like you've improved since our last meeting." Dorsey pulled a plastic scoop chair next to his father, following his gaze out the window. "Maybe even go home soon, I'll bet."

"Sure, I'll be home soon." Martin Dorsey turned to his son. "But not because I've improved. It's just that I'm sick of this place. If I'm to be a weakling physically, I'll do it at home. At least, then, if I'm flat on my back, I can stare at my own ceiling. Besides, I can afford it. Just a little less for you and Irene to inherit."

"Spend it all, old fella. We've been through this conversation before."

"Please," Martin Dorsey told him, "don't take that so lightly. What with the price of competent private care these days, I may leave you with debts to be paid. But not to worry, there's plenty to be had, and I've been a thrifty sort. Maybe I'll hire back that weightlifter of a physical therapist. He was a fine chauffeur besides."

Dorsey tugged his necktie loose and unbuttoned his collar. "So, how much of what Judge Malloy had to say was true?"

Martin Dorsey's eyes returned to the window. "That boy of his has troubles, drinking and the pills, from what they tell me. Salvageable, but in great need of help. And some of that help should come in an effort not to sully his name or impair his future. Young people may make early mistakes and then grow to do great things. I believe that."

"And Sean Malloy, he's one of these misled who might be a future giant?" Dorsey asked. "Was his connection with Novotny for real?"

"Tom Malloy came to visit me, here, last Friday," Dorsey's father said, still looking out at the water. "He came here to thank me for helping with his son. For helping in the arrangement of the commitment, which was not a voluntary one, and in keeping that commitment out of the public eye. While he was here, I mentioned to him my debt to Mrs. Leneski. And as a friend chatting to a friend, I wondered aloud if he could help me in return."

Dorsey bent forward in his chair, his chin propped up by his palms, and watched a towboat aim a barge into the Highland Locks. Tom Malloy, Dorsey now realized, had been called here for an audience with the great man, an event so important that it called for a day's postponement of court business. So once here, he gets the word: save Mrs. Leneski or your kid goes through life with one hell of a blemish on his reputation. And, Dorsey knew, there had to be a carrot with that stick. That's how this business was conducted. Corruption was always in everyone's best interest. Judge Malloy was surely told he'd experience an upswing in his fortunes if he played along. So he played along.

"But the kid," Dorsey asked, "he got his pills from Novotny?"

"Sean Malloy found an illegal way to get pills," Martin Dorsey said. "Dr. Novotny, an evil dead man who can in no way be damaged further, provided pills to those who sought them. Illegally. And I had been made fully aware, by others, that Mrs. Leneski, an elderly woman who worked hard all her life and never really saw a thing for it, was being maliciously overprosecuted by an upstart of a district attorney, who I believe is not long for that job. I have neither the time nor the strength to consider questions without consequence."

"So why not let me in on things?" Dorsey asked. He stood and walked to the window, turning to face his father. "Believe me, I didn't need to know the details and I realize that it was best that I be kept in the dark about them. But you could've let me know that something was in the works. I had a hell of a weekend, preparing to lie if I had to, to save that woman. Last Friday night I sat in this room and pleaded with you to help the woman, and all you kept talking about was some guy you wanted me to meet. You talked about how important it is that I get together with him. And you could have easily taken a moment to tell me that Mrs. Leneski was taken care of. Now, what the hell was that?"

"I just told you, I don't have the time or strength to go over things that have already been resolved."

Dorsey remained silent and motionless, clearly unsatisfied with his father's response. "Look," his father said, motioning toward the chair next to his own. "Please, sit. I'll explain. Hopefully you'll understand."

Angered, Dorsey held his position while his father again gestured toward the chair. But the anger faded as curiosity replaced it. The old man, he reminded himself, always has a reason for his actions, or inactions. You may not understand them, they may make you wretch, but the reasoning is always there. Slowly, Dorsey eased himself into the chair.

"It's apparent to anyone who has known me in the past that my capabilities are greatly diminished." Martin Dorsey gripped the tripod cane and shifted in his seat, facing his son. "But my situation is much worse than any non-medically trained observer could realize. I have no residual strength, no reserves at all. I use what I have, deplete the battery so to speak, and then I rest. Sleep. And I fall asleep with very serious doubts about waking up again."

Dorsey settled deeper into the chair, his eyes leveled at his father. Okay, he was saying, go ahead. Tell me more.

"There is still business for me to conduct and I can't waste precious time. On Friday, when you were here, the matter of Mrs. Leneski had been settled. And this other matter, the arrangement of your meeting with a most important man, was foremost on my mind. And I didn't get through it. I couldn't; I didn't have the power. So I drifted off with the fear that we would never finish the conversation. That's how it is for me. That's why I'm returning to my own home. I don't want my last sight on this earth to be that of some decrepit old stranger sitting across the room and drooling. If there is going to be drool, it'll be my own, staining my own carpet."

It wasn't enough, Dorsey thought, studying his father, watching him sink even deeper into his easy chair. But, it was never enough. You never lived up to his expectations and he's always fallen way short of yours. And now he doesn't even have the strength to try. You can be pissed-off about the past, when outrageous things were done with leisure time calculated in as part of the equation. But if what he's telling you now is true, then there's no reason for anger, no justification. What you have here is a very old lion who's closely rationing his roars.

"Who is it?" Dorsey asked, his voice even. "The man you want me to meet. What's this all about?"

Martin Dorsey seemed to rise to the question, sitting a bit taller, as if parceling out a measure of his power. "A number of years ago, when you had made it abundantly clear that you wanted nothing to do with politics and little to do with me, I started to groom someone I would call a junior partner. With any accommodation I made, with any favor or forgiveness I dispensed, I made it absolutely clear that as far as I was concerned, the recipient was as beholden to my partner as he was to me. And I'll tell you now, there were several who didn't take me seriously. To say the least, they had short and undistinguished careers in public service. The names might surprise you.''

''No more surprises.'' Dorsey waved off his father. ''Anymore and I'll be on the waiting list for this place. Concentrate your strength on getting through this.''

''I developed this protege for two reasons,'' Martin Dorsey said. ''Firstly, I wanted my work to last, and that meant having someone to turn it over to. You and I have had that conversation before.''

''And we're not going to have it again,'' Dorsey told him.

''So, then, let's get on to the second reason.'' Martin Dorsey lifted the cane as if to point it at his son, but he only got it a few inches off the floor before giving up. ''Even if you don't acknowledge it, as long as I've been around, you've had something to fall back on. That was me. And Irene Boyle had the same thing. Of course, in her case, she realizes the situation. Well, I want that security to continue for the both of you after my demise. That's the deal I struck with this fellow. Anytime there's trouble, anytime you or Irene need anything, you are to get in touch with Ed Shearing. And if he let's you down, I'll make it back here and drag him into hell along with me.''

The name meant nothing, at first, as Dorsey searched the seemingly unending list of names he had stored over the years. Men he had seen while still a boy, arriving early to have a tea and toast breakfast with his father, or perhaps one of those he had overheard leaving the house long after midnight. Then the image started to form. A short man with dark hair and rumpled suit. Eddie Shearing. ''If I've got the right guy,'' Dorsey told him, ''Eddie Shearing ran the county road maintenance department. But not all of it, just the division that handled the area in the west, by the airport.''

''Yes, he did that,'' Martin Dorsey said. ''Think of it. He

controlled a road, the main road, for many years the only real road, to a major international airport. That control included power over the maintenance contracts for that road, the most heavily traveled one in a three-state area. Then along came federal grant money, and the old CETA jobs program, and I can't remember what else. Airports and planes are very important things to have, but you've got to drive awhile in your car to get to them. And when there is money and jobs to be distributed, there are votes and loyalties to be gathered. I created a very powerful man, who, once I am gone, will be at the disposal of you and Irene Boyle. And, to an extent, a few other loyal followers.''

"You know what my reaction is to this, right?" Dorsey asked him.

"I don't care what your reaction is," Martin Dorsey said, "because it is your initial one and, as always, a foolish one. I could try to be eloquent and go the route of no man being an island, but you and I have traveled far beyond that in our lives. Irene Boyle is old, frail in both mind and body, and will need help very soon. You . . . you want independence, especially from me; and you want your girlfriend. I would like you to have both, and I think you will. But in pursuing those two goals, you leave a great many things unattended. There are areas that are left unsecured, blindspots for others to exploit. Face it, Carroll, you've never learned to watch your back.''

"True," Dorsey said, "I can't seem to get that one down pat. Although you've tried to teach it to me. Personally.''

"Hate me tomorrow." Martin Dorsey shook his head as if warding off fatigue and frustration. "Or maybe in just a few hours when I'm in bed, dead to the world. Temporarily, let's hope. But this I did for your future. Think of it as an option, for yourself, I mean. For Irene, it's going to be a necessity. And I fully expect you to make sure she takes advantage of it. In a number of ways, I'm leaving her in your charge." Martin Dorsey threw up his hands. "There is no one else.''

Dorsey held his silence, slumped down into his seat, and

considered the facts. Ironbox Boyle was going to be his responsibility. He had always known that, reluctantly, but that didn't change things. Like the elderly uncle who is really only a third cousin to your father and who takes up residence on your second floor. Because he is some kind of kin, because he is old and alone, and because you must pay your debt to the generation who came before and managed to keep the place in one piece for your use. Eddie Shearing would lighten that load. In that way, thank God for him. But as your father's latest temptation, the hell with him. Because that's what he is, your father's last best shot at buying you. You, Carroll Dorsey, the big one that always got away from him. He'd love to go into the next world with the bragging rights on how he finally landed you.

"Rest assured," Dorsey told him, "I'll play conduit between Shearing and Irene. But that's it. Besides, you'll never die. You'll talk about it, make plans for it. But, shit, it'll be like everything else you've ever done. Somewhere behind the curtains there's a second set of plans. The ones you really hope to put in place. With which demon are you negotiating for eternal life on earth?'

"Just be sure Irene is looked after," Martin Dorsey said. "I'll arrange for you to meet with Eddie very soon." With that, Martin Dorsey closed his eyes and his breathing changed into a gentle snore.

Dorsey was halfway across the parking lot to his car when a nursing aid shouted from the front door, calling him to the telephone. He took the call at the nurse's station and Bill Meara sounded pissed.

"Congratulations on whatever kind of bullshit that got pulled in court today," Meara told him. "But it just came back to fucking haunt you."

"Let's hear it." Dorsey looked around the lobby, instinctively worried that Meara had been overheard.

"That Sargent guy from the church just called me. Two of Turner's men just picked up Father Crimmins for questioning. You must have really pissed him off this time."

15

Following Meara's instructions, Dorsey drove crosstown and again forced the Buick to take on South 18th Street. Leaving the South Side flats and passing under the railroad trestle that seemed to serve as the gatepost for a suddenly steep and winding incline away from the river basin, he considered the possible greeting that might await him. Meara would be pissed and looking to blame him and the old man and the Mrs. Leneski business for this latest development. But then again, Dorsey thought, trying to console himself, it was Meara who had said that it might be beneficial to the priest's cause if Turner moved too fast. If Turner acted rashly, made statements he couldn't back up, it would all be to the good. It would be like having the DA undercutting his own case. This could be good. Things might be okay.

The Buick bucked in hesitation as Dorsey turned off of South 18th toward the retreat house, then seemed to catch its breath on the level hilltop. Dorsey slipped into the parking lot, turned off the ignition, and listened for a few moments as the engine chugged and pinged its way into repose. No, he told himself, looking out beyond the fencing to the cityscape, this is not going to go well. Father Crimmins has been hauled in for questioning, and he may be foolish enough to answer some of those questions—without the possible answers that you were hired to find. Yeah, Dorsey, this is gonna be bad for you.

The brother on front-desk duty sent Dorsey back to the

conference room, where he found Monsignor Gallard in his
wheelchair at the window, looking out to the city. Perhaps,
Dorsey thought, he had the Duquesne campus in his sights,
wishing he still had that cluttered professor's office. To hide
in, this time. Dorsey wondered about the connections between old men, strokes and wheelchairs, and well-placed
windows.

"Bill Meara and Father Crimmins should be here
shortly," Monsignor Gallard said, addressing Dorsey's reflection in the window. "Bill's a pretty sharp lawyer,
shouldn't come as a surprise to any of us that he has secured
Father Crimmins's release so soon."

Of course it shouldn't, Dorsey thought. The man has half
of Turner's staff leaking him information. Hell, the call from
Bill Sargent most likely came after two or three calls from
the DA's office itself, while the boys were on their way to
pick up Crimmins. Poor dumb-assed Turner. Hope he enjoys
his four years. They'll be coming to an end. Fast.

"So, you're angry with me." Dorsey slipped into one of
the chairs surrounding the conference table. "So pissed off
you can't stand the sight of me, just my image smeared
across your favorite pane of glass. Can't really blame you.
But get this straight; I don't care. I made a decision, and I
guess my father did too, that I'd do my best for Mrs. Leneski. And that decision was made long before anyone realized that Father Crimmins had gone and gotten himself a
girlfriend."

"The basketball player is now a prizefighter." Monsignor
Gallard kept his eyes on the window. "That is the strategy,
correct? Always land the first blow? I agree with you. I
never cared for counterpunchers, always taking the damage
first. Sometimes the first is best. Sometimes it's all. But not
this time."

The elderly monsignor executed an about-face with his
wheelchair, navigating his way to the table. "So, as you
suggested, let's get a few things straight. I'm happy for the
old woman but I'm madder than hell that her business
spilled over into that of the church. And it did so because

it was my idea, originally, to bring you in on this. But let's be clear on this; I'm angry with you and not myself. So you just figure out a way to earn the money we're paying you and get Father Crimmins off the hook.''

It was difficult, almost painful, but Dorsey held the monsignor's gaze with his own. Ah, shit, why argue? The man was right, the Dorsey family just cleaned up one of its own messes and in doing so tracked mud all over some else's floor. "Okay," he said, "be pissed at me, I won't fight you about it.''

Monsignor Gallard's chin dropped and he pursed his lips. "All right, then," he said, again lifting his eyes to Dorsey. "We need to get on with things. No charges have been filed; Mr. Turner just wanted to rattle his saber with a few questions. That's what Bill told me by phone just a few minutes ago. When they get here, the three of you can plan your next moves.''

"You're not staying?"

"Bill, as my lawyer, will give me a full update. In the meanwhile, I expect Father Ambrose to come through that door any time and force me into a nap.''

"Have an extra cot for me?" Dorsey asked.

"You stay," Monsignor Gallard said, allowing the thinnest of smiles to escape. "Young men should fight the good fight. Myself, I've run my good race.''

As if on queue, Father Ambrose quietly slipped through a side door and leaned down to Monsignor Gallard's left ear. The monsignor nodded an acknowledgment as Father Ambrose took control of the wheelchair and turned him about. "Bill and Father Crimmins just pulled into the parking lot," the monsignor said over his shoulder as he left the room. "Do try to keep the discussion in the lower decibel levels. I know Bill can become verbose, but this is a retreat house after all.''

Father Ambrose reached backward, closing the door behind him, and Dorsey laid his head against the chair's ladderback and closed his eyes. He speculated on how the picking up of Father Crimmins and his detention might have been handled. Hopefully, it had been a discreet knock at the parish residence door, a few quiet words on the front porch, and then a friendly walk to a waiting car. But, on the other hand, it could have been a hard-assed public display. It was conceivable that Turner had remained as pissed as he was when he had stormed out of Judge Malloy's chambers. Maybe he had sent word for his people to pick up the priest and suggested that they throw in a little embarrassment for the hell of it. Hopefully, the truth fell somewhere in the middle; prayerfully, it landed much closer to the side of discretion.

Hurried footsteps approached down the corridor and Dorsey pulled himself back to the business at hand. Meara was first through the door, his suit coat draped over his forearm and his briefcase in hand. Next, closing the door behind him, was Father Crimmins wearing khaki shorts, collared sport shirt with grass stains, and a ragged pair of sneakers. He slipped Dorsey a grin. "They grabbed me while I was doing the gardening. Just finished the mowing and had moved on to pruning the hedges. If the clippers had been motorized, they'd have never taken me alive."

"Hilarious." Meara tossed his jacket across one of the chairs and jerked loose his necktie. From his briefcase he took a yellow legal pad and pen, then settled in at the head of the table. "C'mon," he gestured at Father Crimmins to take a seat. "There's a lot to go over, and I left my sense of humor at the office." He turned to Dorsey. "And you, thanks for nothing."

"You want to be pissed-off," Dorsey said, "don't bring it in my direction. I'm not taking your shit on this one. You want to be pissed off, be pissed off at all those high-minded voters who thought they had to change the district attorney's office, save the county from itself. The idiots who elected this hot-head Turner."

Meara grumbled a bit at the tabletop, scribbling on the legal pad. Father Crimmins picked up the slack, cracking the tension. "So where do we start?"

"At the beginning, where else?" Dorsey said, then turned

to Meara who nodded his agreement. "From the moment they picked you up, tell me how that was handled."

"As I said, I was cutting the hedges, at the far corners of the grounds, across the street from the cemetery fence."

"Anyone with you at the time?" Meara asked, looking up from his notes.

"I was on my own," Father Crimmins said. "I think there may have been some folks sitting out on their front porches at the time, but I can't really say if they took any notice."

Dorsey looked at Meara and returned the stare. Yeah, he thought, they noticed. Kids, or maybe older parishioners, out on the front porch. Especially the elderly, who examine every car that passes by or dares to pull up to the curb. Hell, yeah, they noticed.

"Go on, tell us about the pick-up," Dorsey said. Again Meara nodded his consent.

"It was the Chevy Corsica, remember that from the other night?" Father Crimmins smoothed back his hair at the temples and continued. "I knew who it was, who it had to be, when they pulled up in front of me. They flashed their badges and said I was to come along. I said I'd like to get a few things from the house, make a few calls, at least let somebody know what was going on. They made it pretty clear that wasn't permitted."

Dorsey asked him to describe the DA's men.

"Young," Father Crimmins said, "awfully young for their jobs, I thought. Well-dressed in suits, and they talked like they were all business. One wore a crew cut, the other was a blonde with sunglasses."

"The blond guy," Dorsey asked, "did he do the talking or did he just seem to hang around, like a cool guy asshole? Making tough-guy gestures, those don't-give-me-a-hard-time looks?"

"Cool guy . . . what you said," Father Crimmins said. "Definitely that."

"Know the guy?" Meara asked Dorsey.

"The next generation of politically connected law enforcement. Daddy ponies up enough during the campaign, and the son gets a pay check for running around town pretending he's in the movies. His being sent was more of a message to me than anything else.''

''That's good news,'' Meara said, rolling his eyeballs, switching his attention to the priest. ''Keep going.''

''Well, they didn't handcuff me or anything, and they didn't say I was under arrest, but they seemed supremely confident that what they were doing was legal, so I went along with just a minimum of argument. Luckily Bill Sargent pulled up just then. Soccer practice was scheduled for about a half an hour later. Good thing he was there. Otherwise I might still be at the courthouse being asked questions.''

Again Dorsey looked to Meara. The courthouse, where they've never met a secret that could be kept. If Turner had wanted more in the way of confidentiality, he could have conducted the interview anywhere, even the lobby of the William Penn. Could the newspapers and TV stations be far behind? Please, Dorsey thought, not this shit again.

''So they asked questions,'' Meara said to the priest. ''How about answers? How'd you handle that?''

''Name, rank, and crucifix number.'' Father Crimmins smiled again. ''I confirmed my identity, when they asked, just as a formality, I think. Otherwise, I told them that I knew I had the right to remain silent, which they didn't care for. In turn, I was told that I could stay silent but they could just go on asking questions anyways. So that's all that happened.''

Meara shot Dorsey a fast look and the glint in his eye told him they were both on the same page. Downtown, they had asked questions and gotten nothing in return. But they had lost something in the process because the questions revealed what they didn't know. Maybe Turner's little scare tactic would come back and bite him in the ass.

His pen poised above his notepad, Meara asked Father Crimmins to name everyone who had been present. ''I don't have all the names,'' the priest said, ''but I should be able to do you some good. The two guys who picked me up, they stayed in the room. The crew cut was taking notes and the blonde kept curling his lip at me. When he wasn't cracking his knuckles.''

The guy lives out the role, Dorsey told himself. And that silly-assed Turner lets it go on. That blonde's family must have one hell of a bankroll. Dorsey gave Father Crimmins a general description of Rasher.

''No,'' Father Crimmins said, ''that doesn't match. Mr. Turner was there. In fact, he made quite a production out of introducing himself. As if to let me somehow know that I had met my intellectual match. And there were two more, both gray-haired, thin on top. One of those two asked most of the questions.''

''Stenographer?'' Meara asked. ''Anyone keeping an official record?''

''Not that I could see.'' Father Crimmins thought for a moment. ''I suppose the discussion could have been taped. There's really no way of telling.''

Meara shook his head. ''That's unlikely. If the talk had been in a police station, maybe. But I don't see that happening in the DA's official chambers.''

''I'd have to agree with that,'' Dorsey said, ''from my own experience. Tell us what went on.''

Father Crimmins described how Turner, and then his gray-haired assistant, tried at first to bait him, asking him if he knew why he had been brought in for questioning. ''I just told them that I wasn't sure,'' Father Crimmins said. ''I also told them that I thought it would be unwise of me to speculate in front of law enforcement officials. After awhile that tennis match got boring, and they started to ask me about my relationship with David Filus and his wife.''

Dorsey pulled a little closer to the table. ''And what was it that you said?''

''That they were my parishioners. And then I declined to give any other answers.''

Dorsey relaxed his hunched shoulders, letting the tension flow down along his spine. Thank God for your good sense in not volunteering information. The truth would have sealed the motive portion of Turner's case. Dorsey looked at Meara and found himself being closely studied. After a moment, he gestured for Meara to continue.

"But," Meara said, turning his attention away from Dorsey and addressing the priest, "they kept asking questions. Let's hear what they were."

"They asked about Alice Sutton."

"I'd like to ask you about her myself," Dorsey said.

"You two are going to have plenty of time to confer," Meara said. "Tell me what else they wanted to know."

They had asked about his war record, Father Crimmins told them. Then they asked if he owned a gun. Next, they asked him a load of questions about his financial responsibilities at the parish. The final questions had to do with his whereabouts at the time of David Filus's shooting.

"And you declined to answer?" Meara asked.

"First I asked them to give me the time and date," Father Crimmins said, smiling. "Then I declined."

"So Turner is even more pissed-off now." Meara had his head lowered, jotting down his notes. "Be careful, nobody likes a smart-ass, priest or not. Now that you're out of their clutches, put a little more Bing Crosby in your act."

Dorsey massaged the bridge of his nose with thumb and forefinger and figured, What the hell, he'd ask the same question. "You know, Tom my friend, that's an area we've never covered. Exactly where were you when the guy got himself shot? And you already know the time and date."

Father Crimmins took on a serious manner. "I was hearing confessions. All that evening, like I do at that time each week. Check the church bulletin for the schedule."

"Ah, for Christ's sake." Dorsey dropped his chin to his chest. There's a murder taking place, and this guy is under suspicion. So where was he at the time? Sitting in a blacked-out confessional, a sealed box. And when someone comes in to tell their sins, all they can see, if anything, is the shadow of a man's profile through a screen. As far as hearing goes, Dorsey couldn't remember a priest who spoke in anything but a reverent whisper while granting absolution. Why couldn't Filus have died on bingo night?

Meara capped his pen and pushed away his notepad. "That's not good, but I'm not ready to worry about that yet. And I don't want the answers to any other questions, not until the time comes when I have to. And Mr. Dorsey is going to make sure that never happens."

"Yeah," Dorsey said. "I forgot. I'd better do that."

"The work's tough but the pay is good." Meara looked over the priest, apparently taking a moment to consider matters. "You can't go back to the parish house tonight."

"Sure I can," Father Crimmins. "Besides, I have the six-thirty Mass tomorrow morning."

"No, you can't," Meara said. "Monsignor Gallard will place a few calls and another priest can fill in for you. Just for one day. Anybody who gets roped into the DA's office for questioning gets noticed. Maybe we can't keep you out of the newspapers, but TV doesn't run anything without film. They can mention your name, but I don't want to see your face at six and eleven. One day to let the dust settle, maybe two. I can talk to the bishop and make it an order, if that's what it takes."

"No need," Father Crimmins said. "I get the picture."

"Besides, it'll be fun. Dorsey can put you up at his place."

"What the hell," Dorsey said. "You know you're always welcome." He thought of Gretchen and the work he had to do, but mostly about Gretchen and seeing her that night. "You priests, you still go in for that solitude stuff, right? Not much for running around at night? Happy to stay home on your own?"

16

After circling his block twice to be sure that no one was on watch, Dorsey parked the Buick in front of his row house and hustled Father Crimmins inside. He propped open the office windows, put the box fans in place, and told the priest to make himself comfortable. After securing the paperwork on his desk with a ruler and dirty coffee cup, Dorsey went back to the fans and clicked them on to their highest setting. "Beer?" he asked, stripping off his suit coat and dropping it limply atop the room's filing cabinet. "All out of altar wine. Had a bunch of Jesuits in last weekend and they cleaned me out."

"Beer sounds good." Father Crimmins seemed to look over the room and then settled onto the chaise, stretching out and letting his feet dangle over the edge.

"No," Dorsey said, bringing the priest a can of Rolling Rock and then fetching one for himself. "No, after a day like this, a beer, maybe several, sounds great." He fell into the swivel chair behind his desk and dug through a side drawer, looking for the tape cassette, the one of many that he had in mind. Moments later, after the pushing of several buttons on the office tape player, Johnny Hodges competed with the fan noise, playing "Going Out the Back Way."

Dorsey pulled loose his necktie and let it crumble onto the desktop blotter. "You want to stick with that I-was-in-the-confessional-all-the-while story? May sound good to you, but it doesn't help the cause."

Father Crimmins slowly sipped at his beer, then turned his face to Dorsey. "That's were I was. I can't identify anyone who's confession I heard that night, you know, seal of the confessional? But that is where I was. That's all there is to it and I don't foresee any change, reality being what it is."

"Ah, what the hell," Dorsey said, "it was worth a try. One of those things I have to put you through. Just to double-check things, right?"

"I suppose." Father Crimmins rested his head on the cushions of the chaise.

"There're a few other things we should cover while we have the time." Dorsey lifted his legs and dropped them onto the desktop corner. "Just us two guys, one under suspicion of murder, having a few beers. A little conversation wouldn't be bad, pass the time."

Father Crimmins gave him no response, pulling on his beer and looking toward the windows.

"Good," Dorsey said, "I'm glad you agree. So, did Turner and his people ever get around to asking you about your military record, your war record?"

"No, but I had the feeling that it would have come up." The priest shifted onto his side, propped on one elbow, facing Dorsey. "Bill Meara's arrival cut things short. But they were heading that way."

"The Cambodian invasion, right?" Again, Dorsey thought back to the newspaper and TV reports of the fighting. He even recalled Nixon's evening on television, showing Vietcong weapons seized in the invasion and trying once again to explain himself to America. "You were in on that?"

"As a lance corporal, sort of a squad leader," Father Crimmins told him. "Just me and the boys, walking through the weeds, a few of us getting knocked off every few hours, firefight to firefight. Day after day of being scared to death, until the helicopters took us home."

"Knocked off or death by fear," Dorsey said, "you fell victim to neither. How come?"

Father Crimmins hesitated for a moment. "I was pretty good at it," he said finally. "At warfare, I mean. Tactics, foresight as to the enemy's movements, pretty sharp with a weapon. I suppose you could say I got them first. And I got a lot of them first."

"Yeah, I read about the decorations," Dorsey said. "About the weapon, I take it you mean an M-16. How about sidearms, did you ever qualify at the range?"

"Oh yeah," the priest told him. "I didn't get much chance to shoot from the outside at St. Bonnie's, but I developed a pretty good eye in practice, when a guy can have some fun. Remember?"

"Hell, yes." Dorsey recalled his afternoons at Duquesne, in the practice gym without the screaming fans and coaches that populated the Civic Arena at game time. The crowds are supposed to get you psyched, he had been told again and again. Bullshit, let me play the game in peace. "As far as sidearms go, you don't own one, do you?"

"No, no. Not at the parish rectory."

"Ever borrow one from a parishioner, one of those back-slappers you told me about? Ever been invited out to the firing range for the afternoon?"

"Sure I've been invited," Father Crimmins told him. "And I've accepted a few times."

"Well, I can't say any of that helps your cause." Dorsey slipped his legs from the desk and turned to the midget refrigerator. Ready for another?" He asked, taking a Rolling Rock in hand.

"Not ready, not yet." Father Crimmins said. "While we're on the subject of my military time, Turner also asked some questions about my LBJ time. He seemed to know about that, too."

"What the hell is that?" Dorsey asked. "LBJ? You knew the president?"

"Not the president," the priest said. "LBJ, Long Binh Jail. It was an army stockade. Horrible, horrible place. Army stockades, those are the places you learn all there is to learn about discipline. Army discipline. I was there for ninety days.''

Dorsey hung his head. Things just kept getting worse. ''How'd you manage to get yourself locked up?''

Father Crimmins finished his beer. ''It was right after they pulled us back from Cambodia. We were back on patrol, with a green lieutenant who thought that walking down the middle of a road was a smart thing to do. Figured that we'd draw enemy fire and thereby engage them. I told him that no way would I be a part of that. Then he grabbed my arm, shoved me forward, and I punched out his lights. So three months in LBJ.''

Dorsey shuddered. Tommy Crimmins had just gone from a likely military hero to a man convicted of striking a superior officer. ''When the hell did you get around to finding religion and a vocation for the priesthood?'' Dorsey asked.

''In LBJ, where else?'' Father Crimmins asked. ''Do you think I'm the first guy to find Christ in a jail cell? There was a chaplain, Methodist. He wasn't much, but when he teamed up with this other inmate, Billy Karkis, the two of them made God come alive. Billy was awaiting sentencing for killing a whore. I don't know what ever happened to him, but somehow while he was locked up, he found God and he found a way to pass on his discovery. He got through to me.''

''Let's move on.'' Dorsey wondered if finding God and the priesthood in jail would cancel out the reason for being in jail in the first place. If it ever came to light, like at a trial. ''Tell me about the money deal with Dave Filus. The one his life insurance helped you make good on.''

''Louise said you two had touched on that.'' Father Crimmins shifted into a sitting position, facing Dorsey, both feet on the floor. ''David was a bright fellow. He was no salesman, but he didn't try to be one. Just very bright and confident. The position he held at Lambert Associates spoke for itself. He knew money.''

''So what did he talk you into?''

''He didn't talk me into anything,'' Father Crimmins said.

"He let me in on something. That's how they say it. He played it close to the vest, but the deal had to do with buying up property right around here, in South Side, and over in North Side, too. But it fell through."

"That's all he told you?" Dorsey asked. "The money gets flushed down some unknown crapper and you get no explanation? Sorry, fella. The deal just fell through?"

"I was dealing with Lambert Associates, remember?" The priest said. "Have you ever been to the office, had the full treatment? The place reeks of old money. Hell, I half expected to bump into Frick and Carnegie in the hallway."

"And sleeping with his wife, you felt a special bond."

Father Crimmins placed his beer can on the floor. "Just when I thought I was starting to like you, you insult me, try to hurt me. Care to explain? I'm getting tired of answering all the questions."

"Ah, it's part professional tactic to keep you off guard," Dorsey said, shaking his head. "And some of it has to do with me being an uncontrollable wiseass. Sorry. But on the other hand, you've been awfully free with information about your relationship with Louise Filus. And she was the same way when we spoke. Considering the clash of vows, marriage, and ordination, it's not the first area I thought you two would come clean on. By the way, she's a very beautiful woman. You're very fortunate."

"Thanks," Father Crimmins said. "Considering the stakes, a murder investigation, I came to the conclusion that my secret love life wasn't such a potential scandal. Louise agreed. And, well, she and I have discussed the future together. We're going to have one, so the truth comes out now or later."

"You'll have to go looking for work." Dorsey took a pull on his beer. "Face it, the bishop will insist."

"I'm resigned to that, but I don't care for it."

"Pushing for married priests?"

"Not necessarily," Father Crimmins said. "A priest should have a total commitment to his parish, and I guess I'm talking strictly parish priests when I say this. Total commitment is called for, but is a life time's commitment absolutely necessary? Think about this. You train a priest, man or woman, pretty much as they do now. But the commitment to the priesthood is only for six or seven years.''

"Sort of like the service academies?" Dorsey asked. "Get out of West Point, complete your military hitch, then move on to the world of business or academia.''

"Not a bad analogy," Father Crimmins said, his face brightening with the conversation's turn. "During a person's term as a parish priest, they have to follow all the rules, celibacy included. By the way, that's really not such a tough thing in the short run, especially if other parts of your life are going well. And it's only temporary. The term comes to a close and a person can make a decision to leave or make the commitment for another term. Just like re-upping for a second hitch in the army. Works pretty well, I think. You have a laity filled with former, experienced priests. And the present clergymen feel a little more in command of their lives. They have decisions to make, important ones. Just like their parishioners.''

"But what about once a priest always a priest?''

"I agree," Father Crimmins said. "You'd always be a priest, you'll never lose that quality, I guess you could call it that. You just wouldn't hold the office any longer. Like a former president.''

"That's a way to go, a direction for the church to take," Dorsey said. "But let's face it, we don't live on an historic time line. All of us, you included, we live in the here and now. The immediate, for the most part. So temporary, married, male or female priests may be a comfort for the twenty-first or-second century. But that sort of leaves you out. You plan on having a life with Louise, and I sure can't blame you for wanting it, but how are you gonna pull it off and stay within the faithful?''

Father Crimmins rose to his feet and moved about the room, stopping at one of the windows as if to inspect Wharton Street. Turning back to Dorsey, seemingly satisfied with what he had found outdoors, Father Crimmins crossed the room and slumped into one of the visitor's chairs, facing Dorsey across the desk. "I suppose I'll do what so many others have done, both the famous and anonymous," he said. "I'll expand the faithful, by one. Or by two if you include Louise. Historically, it's what's always been done. In a number of ways, that's what the Reformation was based on. The reformers wanted to serve God and Christ, but they couldn't do it within what the Church had to offer at the time. They couldn't serve God's will, which is one hell of a complicated matter. I want to serve a God who has given me the ability and a strong inclination to love a woman, a mate. And then, to really make it tough, he puts the woman that I can truly love in a house just a few blocks away from where I live. She sits a few rows back from the altar every Sunday as I say mass. In a pew on the left hand side of the center aisle. She works with me on the various parish councils. C'mon, Dorsey. God does test people, I don't doubt that. But he surely doesn't set out to torture them."

"So," Dorsey said, finishing off his beer. "So you'll find your own way."

"Yes, I will. I'll find my own way. I have my faith and part of that is a faith in God's presentation of reality. I'm a priest who plans on living with the woman I love, that's what I am. That's what the Creator created. Maybe it's something I shouldn't argue with. Perhaps it's something I have to accommodate, to develop on my own."

Dorsey gave some thought to another beer but held off, planted in his swivel chair, eyes on this priest who seemed so ready for a rite of Confession in reverse. He's opened his soul, Dorsey thought, revealing his motivations, which is okay in the abstract, but do you want to know what those motivations have led to? Hell, yes you do. But that doesn't mean shit, because you better not know. Guilty knowledge is a clear concept, even for a guy like you with barely a year of law school. But it's tempting. Father Crimmins can intellectualize away his ordination vows, and you can't argue very well with what he has to say. But can he go all the way for what he wants? C'mon, Tommy. Did you blow away the husband to get the wife? Not to mention the money that would keep you from being just another ex-priest running some underfunded social service? Man, wouldn't you just love to put the question to him now, while he looks to have his guard down? It's the moment that investigators live for.

The phone rang, interrupting the silence, and he lifted the receiver just before the third ring was completed. Dorsey kept his eyes on Father Crimmins, said hello, and listened to what he was told.

"No shit? He's at the bar?" Dorsey asked. "What's he want? Did he say anything?" He listened a few seconds more, his eyes flicking from the priest to a spot on the far wall, giving matters some thought. "How about you coming down and keeping the Father company? Okay? Good, bring some beer along, we're running low. Tell Al I'll pay him when I get there."

Dorsey returned the receiver to its cradle. "Well, I'm not so sure about myself," he said, getting to his feet, "but it looks like you're in luck. You get to while away part of the afternoon sipping beer with my friend Henry Antosz. Interesting is only one of the many things he is. You'll have a good time, I think. As for me, well, I have an appointment with a guy I've only met once before. And that time didn't go so well in the end."

17

Dorsey walked the several blocks to the bar. At Carson Street, waiting for a break in traffic, he saw Henry coming his way, toting a brown paper bag under his arm. Henry waved for him to stay put and then ran broken-field style through moving cars, meeting Dorsey at the curb, his lungs heaving for air as he wiped sweat away from his bald crown and into his pigtail. "He's got this guy with him," he told Dorsey. "Tall and skinny. Has gold caps on some of his teeth, like a lot of black guys do. Al's got them in a booth in back."

Him, too, Dorsey thought. But then a shadow only leaves you at night. He almost asked Henry if he thought the guy had a gun on him. Stupid question, deserves only a wiseass response.

"Have a good time with the priest," Dorsey told him. "Toss back a few and tell some lies. He's in the mood to talk. And to listen, I think."

Once across Carson, covering the last block and a half, Dorsey was sickened as he thought about his last encounter with these two. Dexter, the long and deadly gunman who had stood by as Dorsey's friend had his head caved in with a tire iron. Smart-assed son of a bitch, too; talked like he swallowed a copy of "Cotton Comes to Harlem." And then there was his boss, the state senator. The one who directed you to a-know-it-all jailbird of a witness who never lived long enough to retell his story. What did these pricks want now?

The barroom held only a few of the regular patrons and
Al was stationed near the taps, his right hand held below
counter level. He jerked his head to the side, gesturing for
Dorsey to stop by before heading for the backroom.

"How much trouble should I get ready for?" Al's right
hand drifted into sight, his grip firmly about the thin end of
a Louisville Slugger, Bill Mazeroski signature model. "This
is all I keep on the premises; my level of violence hasn't
kept up with the times. But I could make some calls, if you
want."

"I think we'll be safe," Dorsey told him. "The guy's an
elected official, and with any luck the tall one is just window
dressing. But if you see me being led out of here at gun-
point, put up a fuss, okay? You'll do that?"

Al slipped the bat under the bar. "You're always safe in
here."

Dorsey ordered a Rolling Rock, paid Al for the beer
Henry had carried to his place, and made for the back room.
Descending the three steps to the red-and-white-checked tile
floor, he spotted Dexter sprawled in one of the red Leatherette booths, his feet dangling over the edge, encased in a
pair of Air Jordans. In the second to last booth was a stouter
black man dressed in a tan, lightweight suit and print tie.
Louis Preach, presently the state senator for most of the
city's black population. Dorsey came even with Dexter and
stopped.

"Good seeing you," Dorsey said. "Watch anybody die
lately?"

"Just watched." Dexter gave him a smile that showed his
gold caps. "Lately, I mean."

"Don't mess with him right now," Louis Preach said
from his booth. "Bring your beer over and take a seat. We
should talk."

"Ah, fuck him anyways," Dorsey said, slipping into the
booth and setting his Rolling Rock on the Formica-topped
table. Preach lifted a can of Diet Coke and poured some into
a glass with ice. "You're a big man again," he said to
Dorsey. "Big man on a big case is what I hear. Just like

the last time we met. Sounds like you've bounced back the last year or so.''

''I get by.'' Dorsey took a pull on his beer. ''Now, as I remember, in that last meeting you just mentioned, you had your sights set on a congressional seat. Ah, what the hell, state senator isn't bad. Right?''

''Absolutely.'' Preach shrugged his shoulders. ''I suppose I should admit to a little disappointment when the nomination didn't come through. In fact, I was kind of pissed-off at your father. Never did figure out where he stood on the whole thing. But this Harrisburg job, state senator I mean, this may be the one for me. Keeps me real close to the home folks.''

''To both constituents and contributors, I'd imagine.''

Preach rattled the ice cubes in his drink. ''Save your cynical bullshit for another time, okay? We both know the score; there's no sense in going over the obvious. Besides, I want to discuss your business, not mine.''

''You're here to help me,'' Dorsey said, ''just like last time. I'm a lucky son of a bitch.''

''I came here to help you avoid trouble,'' Preach said. ''And I also want to prevent you from making any trouble for me.''

Dorsey sipped his beer and looked about the room, taking in the other booths, the unplugged jukebox, the now dark electric beer signs that graced the walls. With a quick look over his shoulder he saw that Dexter hadn't moved from his position of repose and that Al was keeping watch by way of the backbar mirror. You're going to hear him out, he told himself, that's why you came in the first place, not just to get in a few wisecracks with Dexter. Hear what he has to say, just be sure you hear why he's saying it. ''Okay,'' he said, ''nobody hates trouble and problems worse than me. No bullshit, tell me how we can avoid both.''

Preach hunched his shoulders and leaned into the table. ''First, let me tell you that I know all about the shit going on with Filus, the priest, and tight-ass white boy Turner. He's got this thing all wrong. He's looking in the wrong place. And I'll bet a truck of that green bottled beer you're always slurping down that you're looking in the wrong place, too.''

Dorsey laughed. ''Sorry, I know this isn't funny, and I'm glad to hear that Turner has fucked up. But how would you know where I'm looking? I don't even know where I'm looking. I'm just trying to get a handle on things.''

''It's where you're headed that bothers me,'' Preach said. ''It's where you want to go because it's the easiest place to get to. Hell, Father Crimmins didn't kill nobody, right? Because this rich white Filus guy got hisself killed by a nigger junkie or two. Shot him for what was in his pockets and hauled ass back to Homewood. That's what you want to hear. That's what people are gonna want to hear, and you and your people are gonna say just that when the time is right. And that's shit I just don't need.''

''What shit's that?''

''Blame it on the niggers shit.'' Preach fell back against the Leatherette seat and ran his hand across his temple, lingering at the first sprigs of gray. ''Young black men. No-good, drug-eatin' niggers. I get enough of that kind of talk in Harrisburg every time I rub up against any of my fellow senators who hail from the rural districts. Seriously, do you have any idea how rural, how absolutely covered with woods this state is? You live here in Pittsburgh, or maybe Philly, you think the state is two cities with three hundred miles of suburbs between them. I'm telling you, it's nothing but trees and bushes out there.''

''I've seen it, on occasion,'' Dorsey said. ''Thought it was kind of pretty.''

''Missing the point,'' Preach said. ''These small-town and country boys in the legislature, the only time they see a black face is on TV. And then it's some young black man in manacles being led into an arraignment hearing. Or some guy being led from jail to his sentencing. Shit, they must think we all dress in orange overalls issued by the state corrections department. Like that stuff is fashionable. And because of it, I can't get a goddamned thing accomplished.''

This is good, Dorsey thought. He was getting the motivation first. It made sense. And who could say, it might be the truth. Dorsey nodded for Preach to continue.

"I try to do something, maybe introduce a jobs training bill, get some money for education, and I can't get jack shit. While I'm talking about those things, my colleagues from out in the wilderness are fighting it out to see where the next maximum security prison is gonna be built. It's as if they were telling me, sure, we'll educate your niggers for you. But let's get them safely behind bars first. That'll give 'em a quiet place to study. And the goobers who vote for us can work as guards, enforcing quiet hours during study hall."

"And who would want to vote for you if you never manage to come through for them?"

"Hey, fuck you, Dorsey," Preach said. "I'm no saint, but things aren't always just about me. I got a sense of community, of who my people are, no matter what you think. And when the time is right, the defenders of Father Crimmins are going to dredge up the image of a few more black villains. The boys in Harrisburg will eat it up and I'll be in shit shape even worse than I am now."

"So," Dorsey said, "how do we go about avoiding all this heartache?"

Again Preach came forward into the table, gesturing for Dorsey to do the same. "There's another option for you. Another direction for you to take in your investigation. Killers come in all shapes and sizes. Regardless of color, creed, or national origin."

"Is this an option," Dorsey asked, "or is this the path to the truth?"

"It's a lead," Preach said, his voice low, conspiratorial. "You're a detective, you follow leads, right? And every case has more than one lead, am I right? Not to follow up on one would be unethical in your profession."

"Very," Dorsey said. "And it wouldn't be any good for business."

"Now the last time I came through for you," Preach said, "a few years back, I gave you the straight shit. How am I supposed to know if a guy is ready to die? Yeah, yeah, he looked like hell, but I see worse than him everyday, stumbling along the sidewalk, nodded off in doorways. But I pointed you in the right direction.''

"The right direction,'' Dorsey said, "in one hell of a roundabout way.'' He never did figure out how much Preach had really known about the conspiracy that led him about by the nose.

Preach again shrugged his shoulders, as if dismissing the point. "Make up your own mind on this one. All I have to say is that everybody's running around investigating the suspected murderer without giving a thought to the victim. Maybe you should spend a little time looking his way.''

Dorsey looked Preach over, watching the sly smile etch its way across his face. Sure, Dorsey thought, last time Preach did give up the guy who had the answers. Ninety percent of the answers. And that missing ten percent came as a hell of a shock. So, do what you're supposed to do. Hear the man out, put what he has to tell you through a sifter, and see what ends up on the kitchen table.

"So," Dorsey said, "you want to kick around the idea that Filus had something going on in his life that led to his killing? Be my guest. Let's see how you narrow down the possibilities.''

Preach worked himself into the corner of the booth, extending his legs across the seat. "From what I can see, everybody has been concentrating their efforts on the man's personal life. What's his wife up to with that priest friend of hers? That's where you guys are poking around. But, shit, there was more than that to the man's life. He had a job, pretty good one. He was going somewhere with an employer who could take a guy places. Nobody bothers to snoop around in that section of his life.''

"Are you suggesting that all isn't what it's supposed to be at Lambert and Associates?''

"Well," Preach said, "I'm sure that if you asked Mr. Lambert, or whoever, if things are going well, you'd be told that things couldn't be better.'' Preach rearranged himself, putting his feet on the tile floor and crowding in on Dorsey. "A company like Lambert handles other folks' money. A lot of other folks. The money comes in from separate places, but it all gets mixed together along the line. Just like you were mixing a cocktail. Once all the ingredients are in the glass, and the bartender has given them a good stir, ain't no way they can be separated out. Same with money. Once it goes through a few filters, it could be anyone's money and could have come from anywhere."

"Money laundering?" Dorsey asked. "For who?"

Preach's grin reappeared. "You've been around, and your old man, now he's been there and back. How's Chick Rosenthal sound to you? That's what I hear. The Italian boys, the Larimer Avenue people, they must have arrangements of their own, with someone else. But Chick's people deal with Lambert."

Chick Rosenthal. In his mind's eye, Dorsey could still see the file photos he once reviewed while still on staff with a long-gone DA. Short, no more than five feet, three inches, and not an ounce of fat or muscle hanging from his bones. The shirts were always too big and the tail of his necktie had to be tucked into his shirt to keep it from flapping about his knees. Yet despite that, he ran the numbers business and sports books in every mill town in the eastern end of the county. The Clean Jew, they had called him. No dope, no girls, nothing but betting. He drew a moral line. But then again, he had ways of enforcing that line and even more ways of keeping himself on the top of the heap. If he was dealing with Lambert, and Filus had done something to seriously get on the man's bad side, well, then Filus would have found out what it was like to be in serious trouble.

"What else?" Dorsey asked. "You have anything else, anything specific? Like Filus cleaned out the Rosenthal money and had one-way tickets to Mexico for both him and a beautiful blond secretary?"

"You like it easy, don't you?"

"It helps," Dorsey told him.

Preach laughed. "You're looking for another explanation

for the man's death, here's some information that might lead you to one. Best I can do. But I'm pretty sure you'll find something that'll make people take notice.''

It could work, Dorsey thought. If Preach was being straight, it would work. Instead of the love triangle that ended badly, you now have the unsolvable underworld hit. The romantic underworld hit of a smart-assed CPA who thought he could outsmart the bad guys. Filus becomes the guy who tragically got what he asked for. It would kill Turner. But this was an area Dorsey was not ready to jump into. Because a victory, a happy ending, was so unlikely. Swift and sure justice, the hallmarks of Turner's beliefs, just weren't going to happen. Although, it could work. ''Okay,'' Dorsey said, ''let's see how it goes.''

''So who are you going to talk to?'' Preach asked, laughing. ''Chick Rosenthal or the top boys at Lambert?'' He worked his way out of the booth and got to his feet. Behind him, Dorsey could hear the scuffing of Dexter's feet on the tile floor as he followed suit.

''Ah,'' Dorsey said, looking up at Preach, ''I'll probably just get Chick on the phone and ask him if he's knocked off any CPA's lately. Sound like a plan to you?''

''Sounds like an ass-backward approach.''

''I think you're right.''

Preach hesitated for a moment, gesturing for Dexter to wait. ''Let's get straight on this,'' Preach said. ''If you people push this nigger-junkie business, it's gonna cause me some problems. But I'll return the favor, count on it. I'll do whatever I have to do to make that priest look like shit. Put him on the cross, burn him at the stake, however the public would like it. I'm not letting my people down on this one. I'll use my office and have my say. I'll find a way.''

''Sounds fair,'' Dorsey said. ''I'll pass the word along.''

18

Dorsey found Father Crimmins on the office chaise, flat on his back with his mouth open. His snores were deep and wet sounding, as if they gathered strength in the bottom of his lungs before picking up moisture on the journey out into the air. Henry was in the swivel chair, his feet propped on the desk's edge, flipping his way through a dogeared paper edition of Farrell's *Studs Lonigan*. He looked up at Dorsey and then inclined his head toward the chaise. "It doesn't take much to put him away," Henry said.

"He's had a full day," Dorsey said, pulling his sweaty shirttails out of his waistband. His fingers started at the buttons. "Mine was chock full of excitement, too. But then again, I didn't have that dip-shit of a DA asking me questions and letting me know that he figures me for killing my girlfriend's husband. Now that would really sap your energy."

Henry pushed away from the desk, tossing the paperback onto the desk blotter. "As much as I like that particular book, I'd just as soon hear the rest of that story you just started." He took two cans of Rolling Rock from the office refrigerator, handing one over to Dorsey. "C'mon, tell me the rest. With Father Crimmins sawing logs like he is, you've got time to kill. C'mon, gimme the dirt."

"Sure," Dorsey said, running the beer can across his chin and throat, letting the chill do its work. "But not just this

minute. I have to get changed and then work the telephone
a little bit.''

Dorsey climbed the hallway steps to the second floor,
passing his beer from hand to hand as he worked his way
out of his shirt. Once in the bedroom he sent it hook-shot
style toward the hamper but was off target to the left. Mentally, he jotted down his list of calls and then shuffled them
into priorities. There was Gretchen, of course, and then a
call to Meara, and then who knows how many calls to Lambert and Associates to convince, cajole, or frighten the right
person into talking with him.

He stripped off his suit pants, considered the possibility
of hanging them up and getting another day's wear before
sending them to the cleaner, then recalled the day's events
and the 90 degree weather. Rolled up in a ball, they went
underhand across the room, this time hitting the target.
''Nothing but hamper,'' he mumbled.

The call to Meara, he said to himself, that'll get him off
your ass. Pass on to him what Preach had to say and play
it like the guy ought to be trusted this time, let the past be
the past. At least buy yourself some time to look into the
possibility. If you can play this like a Mob hit, throw in
Chick Rosenthal's name and maybe a few others for au-
thenticity, Doug Turner will never pursue the priest any further. What's the public want, bad guy priests or evil, but so
romantically portrayed, gangsters?

In an old pair of khaki shorts and T-shirt, Dorsey hustled
back down the steps, a pair of socks and his running shoes
in hand. In the office, Henry had returned to his book and
Father Crimmins had turned on his side, facing the windows. Just another restless sleeper fighting a semiconscious
battle with the heat. Dorsey sat in the visitor's chair and
pulled on his socks. ''Can you stick around for the evening?'' Dorsey asked Henry. ''He's supposed to stay put
and I may have to go out after a while.''

Henry looked up from his reading. ''This is my night to
be behind the bar, from about eight till closing. But let me
give Al a call. Just mentioning your name should spring me

loose. He thinks of you as his own. The son he always wanted.''

And maybe he's the father I never had, Dorsey thought, and immediately felt disloyal. ''Ah, I was a pain in the ass when I was kid. He should be glad it didn't work out.''

''Nah, nah,'' Henry said, shaking his head. ''Al's got a different picture. He doesn't feel bad about never having a little boy. Maybe he did long ago, but not now. He wants a grown-up son. Somebody who has a job and his own place. But the kind who never forgets the old man. Stops by to say hello, maybe have dinner, never waits for an invitation. And never calls ahead to make sure it's a good time to come by. Just takes the chance because the old man's time on earth might be short and he doesn't want to miss any of it.''

''It's a good thing, you not having steady work,'' Dorsey said, pulling his shoelaces taut. ''A mind like yours would be put to misuse with concerns like mere survival. Scientific observation can be time consuming, I'll bet. Philosophy takes brainpower, and an eight-hour shift would only leech that out of you.''

Henry smiled and went back to his reading. ''I don't tinker with the plans of God and his universe.''

''Then I won't, either.'' Dorsey got to his feet and took the telephone in hand. He released the wire from the baseboard wall jack and turned for the hall. ''Rather than disturb our guest, I'm going to set up in the kitchen, make my calls. Hand me the phone book, okay?''

Henry reached behind him and grabbed the directory from the top of the midget refrigerator. ''Hope you get your party,'' he said, handing it off to Dorsey.

In the kitchen, Dorsey hooked up the phone in a jack mounted above the counter and wondered why he had never purchased an extension, for either the kitchen or bedroom. Not being able to come up with a sensible answer, he settled into a chrome-legged chair that matched the kitchen table and got to work.

He caught Gretchen as she was leaving the hospital and

made arrangements to be at her place later, prepared to tell her all. The second call was to Meara. Despite the onset of evening, he was still at his office. "Okay," Dorsey said once Meara had picked up after six rings. "I've got ten bucks that says you can't describe your wife or tell me how many kids you have. Twenty says you can't get their ages right. Really, man, get home in time for dinner once in a while."

"I'll go home," Meara said. "But not for dinner, or any other meal for that matter. The kids I can name and I can guess at their ages based on the due dates of orthodontic and tuition bills. And my wife doesn't cook. Because she can't, and has the wisdom to accept that. So she dials instead. She dials Domino's, she dials the local Chinese delivery, she dials, she dials. No wonder all the kids want to go away for college. But none of them are willing to take me along. So, how's Crimmins?"

"Resting."

"But you're not, I'm assuming," Meara said. "Better fuckin' not be. I need good news from you."

"Let's try this," Dorsey said, "and you can judge for yourself." He gave Meara a rundown on his meeting with Louis Preach.

Meara was silent for a moment and Dorsey imagined gears and fan belts working together to produce human thought. "If it pans out," Meara eventually said, "it'll force Turner to shut this business down and go look for other bad guys to get famous on. He won't try to make a villain out of a priest when we have a real, live racketeer to toss in his face. Chasing after clergymen while the forces of evil run wild, maybe killing legitimate businessmen as they walk home. This can cinch things for us, but listen. . . ."

Meara told Dorsey what he needed of him. "Remember, like we talked about way back when, don't try to pin this thing on anyone at Lambert or, for God's sake, Chick Rosenthal. He wouldn't take it kindly, no matter who your old man is. We don't even need any written confirmation on anything. We just need to talk to somebody in the know.

Somebody who can give us the scoop. Then we go to Turner and tell him what we have. And then we poke around in the air and make a lot of suggestions about all the other things we might be able to find. Then he drops all this horse shit about Father Crimmins, and Father Crimmins can go back to saving souls and counting the Sunday collection.''

Dorsey thought back to his afternoon conversation with Father Crimmins. Well, he'd be free to go back or move on, as he chose. But there was no need to let Meara in on that. "So now that you've been brought up to date and are hopefully a little more pleased in my performance, I'm going to put some calls into the Lambert office, maybe catch somebody as dedicated as you. If not, I'll leave a few voice-mail messages and pick up on it in the morning. Once that's done, I still want to put the squeeze on this Sutton woman. She sounds like a bitch on wheels and I want to meet her, if only to satisfy my own curiosity.''

"Hell with your curiosity," Meara said. "I want to know as much about her as possible, I need you to get as much out of her as you can. If I get the chance to sit down with Turner and tell him all about the corruption at Lambert and the possibility that Rosenthal offed Filus, I don't want him pulling out this Sutton as a trump card. You find out all you can.'' Meara fell silent and again Dorsey imagined gears and fan belts. "Make your calls to Lambert. And I'll make a few of my own. Between the two of us, somebody will agree to meet with you.''

"Don't tell me," Dorsey said. "Lambert handles some of the diocese's money? Jesus Christ.''

"If they don't, they might like to.''

Dorsey said a quick good-bye, hung up the receiver, and dug into the phone book. After locating the number, he worked his way through a maze of recorded voices offering any number of options until he found what must have been the most junior of staff members, staying late to finish his work and, Dorsey assumed, save his ass. Dorsey laid it on thick, suggesting a possible scandal, the murder of a well-placed employee, and the shadow of a sinister investor. The young man at the other end swallowed the hook and became embarrassingly obsequious, making Dorsey a little ashamed of his own acting abilities.

"I'll be happy to pass on the message, sir," the young man told him again and again. "You can be sure that one of our partners will be returning your call at the beginning of business hours tomorrow." Finished with him, Dorsey redialed the main office number and left a few angry land-mines in some well-placed voice-mail boxes just for back up.

Dorsey unplugged the phone and lugged it and the tele-phone directory back to the office where he handed them over to Henry. Father Crimmins had turned himself over again but remained asleep, one arm hanging free with the back of the hand resting on the carpet. "Almost fell off," Henry said, gesturing toward the priest. "Just a few minutes ago. Almost went ass over tea kettle onto the floor but caught himself just in time. Passed-out guys are like kittens, most times. Perfect sense of balance. Always catch them-selves at the last minute."

"You'll be here?" Dorsey asked Henry.

"Sure, sure," he said. "You go do your stuff."

As always, trying to place things in his own version of a socio-historical perspective, Dorsey considered the express-way on which he drove to be the outside wing of three parallel transport systems that served the city and had per-mitted its growth. The earliest, inside lane was the Alle-gheny River, a watery pathway for settlers that became the foundation for a barge industry that could move coal, oil, and other resources on the cheap. On the riverbanks were the railroad right-of-ways, the next stage, the steel tracks that hugged the river for a time and then veered off , carting away finished goods made possible by the smoke-belching Industrial Revolution. And now for the post-industrial pres-ent, a highway that allowed workers from the northern com-munities and counties to get from their homes to the computer-equipped cloth and plastic cubicals where today's money was generated. Shit, Dorsey thought, and your old man doesn't think you understand cities and politics.

Dorsey left Route 28 at Delafield Road, entering Aspinwall at the northern end, nearest to Gretchen's home. The ramp was circular and dropped him onto the river flat on which the town had grown, just above the railroad tracks. After several blocks and a left-hand turn, he guided the Buick to the curb, parking a few doors up from Gretchen's. Sunset filled the river valley with reds, yellows, and long shadows as he crossed the front porch and depressed the doorbell.

"Are you ready to talk?" Gretchen asked through the screen door. "Last night was last night. But this is the day of atonement."

Dorsey nodded his agreement and Gretchen released the door's spring lock then headed back through the living room into the kitchen. She was still dressed in her work clothes, Oxford cloth shirt, khaki slacks, and running shoes; and Dorsey watched as she poured ice tea into glasses already set at the table. He sat at what he took to be his station while Gretchen set the pitcher on the table, ice cubes clacking inside, and took the chair across from Dorsey. She seemed to be waiting for him to start.

"I didn't care for what it would lead to," Dorsey said, "but I came to the conclusion that I had to save that old woman. And after talking to her attorney and my father, and then receiving a blackmail threat from the sitting district attorney, I sincerely thought that the job was all mine. And that meant denying a few things that actually happened. It never came to it, and I was sweating bullets over it, but I intended to perjure myself."

Dorsey laid it all out for her, every detail and every conversation with Turner, his father, Art Meeker, and Mrs. Leneski. And the feeling was unlike any other. Coming clean, saying the words as a purification process, the benefits of Confession without saying ten Hail Marys and the Apostle's Creed. Dorsey knew it was because he was telling her. She had a power over him, given willingly and readily, that neither Tom Crimmins nor any other priest could capture. He finished with a recounting of his visit with his father and Father Crimmins's increasing problems.

"Your heart was in the right place," Gretchen said, reaching back to massage her neck. "Although the subversion of the legal system scares the living hell out of me." She sipped her tea. "Your work seems to put you in some type of shadowland where justice gets lost in some dark corner. And you find yourself being the one with a flashlight. We've talked about this before, and we're destined to do it again."

"No doubt about it," Dorsey said. "Can you live with that?"

"Can I live with that?" Gretchen set her glass on the table and shook her head in amazement. "Listen, dummy, I do live with it. I made that decision when I came back to Pittsburgh, remember? We had a bit of a talk on moving day? For a detective, you seem a little slow at times. Picking up on the subtleties of life, I mean."

"I'm starting to agree." Dorsey smiled. Absolution had been granted.

Gretchen sipped her tea and spent a few moments with her gaze lingering at the window, apparently stuck on the last of the sunset. "Your father sort of left you hanging on this, but what would you say if I suggested that he was looking out for you?"

"You've just suggested it," Dorsey said. "Let's hear what's behind it."

"Okay, then. My theory." Gretchen made a show of finishing her tea. "Martin Dorsey is an elderly man who has been through an awful lot and survived. He's had to find a lot of strength, both in himself and others. He had to get from others what he couldn't supply on his own. So he knows himself pretty well. And he knows others pretty well, too. Including you."

"You'll get no argument here," Dorsey said.

"He knows your virtues and your weaknesses," Gretchen

said. "And he knows how the two of them can get together and get you into trouble."

"Are you saying that he knew how far I'd go for Mrs. Leneski?"

"That's exactly what I'm saying," Gretchen told him. "He knew that a fix had to be put in and he wanted to be sure that you weren't involved in it. He was looking after his son. He has a corrupt stain on him and he doesn't want it to spread to you. He kept you clean because he realized that you were tempted to get dirty. So thank him when next you see him."

"I guess I will," Dorsey said, smiling. "Unless he makes his usual best efforts to alienate me first."

At a quarter past eleven that evening, Gretchen smiled at him from her pillow, gave Dorsey a quick chuckle in exchange for the wisecrack he had just made, and told him to go home. "But I brought my own toothbrush," Dorsey said, propping himself up by the elbow, adjusting as his weight sunk into the mattress. "Thought it would please you. The last time I left you didn't take it very well."

Gretchen raised her eyebrows and sighed. "I've had time to think about it, that's all. And the more I thought about it, I realized that I like having my very own home. And I also like the idea that you have your own home. Separately."

"Are you switching gears on me?" Dorsey asked. "I thought we had things pretty well worked out."

"We do, we do." Gretchen pulled herself to a sitting position and lightly ran her fingertips along Dorsey's chin line. "And I think this should be part of it. It's just something I want right now. It doesn't mean I don't want you."

"Sure about that?" Dorsey pulled himself from the bed. "Things like this throw a scare into me."

Gretchen laughed. "If it will make you feel better, I can pay for the toothbrush."

19

Dorsey returned from his morning walk and found Father Crimmins awake and dragging himself up and off the office chaise. His hair was matted and cowlicked from a fitful night, and Dorsey could see the salt lines that ran along his neck and stained his collar. "Shower's upstairs," Dorsey told him, leaning against the desk and wiping the sweat from his own forehead with the hem of his T-shirt. "There's a towel up there, too. Possibly clean. I'll see about some coffee."

In the kitchen, Dorsey measured out coffee into the metal pot's basket, slowly added tap water, and lit one of the stove's front burners. Father Crimmins had followed him down the hall and settled in at the Formica-topped table. "Thanks for putting up with me," he told Dorsey. "I'll shower in a minute. I was wondering if you could give me a ride back to the parish house afterwards. I mean, after you get a chance to clean up, too."

"Can't help you," Dorsey said, digging into the refrigerator. "There's a very early appointment I have to keep. Maybe when I get back, but you better check it out with Meara first. He's head honcho, remember? He certainly does. Remember, I mean."

From the refrigerator, Dorsey came away with a tub of soft margarine, strawberry jam, milk, and tomato juice, lugging it all over to the tabletop. "There's a toaster over on the counter and there should be about half a loaf of bread

147

in the bin next to it. Help yourself when the coffee's ready.''
Dorsey opened the back door, checked that the screen was
locked, then stretched his arms out against the frame, letting
a weak morning breeze do what it could.

"Well," Father Crimmins said, "if you have to get going,
you better take the first shower.''

"No need," Dorsey said, turning from the door. "This is
one of your less than formal appointments. It's outdoor; al
fresco. And possibly of great of benefit to your cause.''

"Tell me.''

"I gotta go," Dorsey replied, heading for the hall. "You
slept through a hell of a telephone conversation last night.
Fill you in when I get back.''

"Are you about to save me?" Father Crimmins asked.
"It'd be nice having this done with. It sure felt good the
last time I thought that both the parish and myself had this
behind us.''

Without changing clothes, Dorsey drove the Buick out of
South Side, taking the Birmingham Bridge over the Monongahela River and into the city's Oakland section. He
took the boulevard into Schenley Park and saw that the early
morning haze had just begun to burn away, exposing the
top floors of the Cathedral of Learning on Pitt's campus.
Once in the park and circling past the swimming pool, he
parked near the mouth of several nature trails, just across
from a playground. There was only one other car parked in
the area, a green, richly colored Lexus. He said he was an
attorney, Dorsey reminded himself. A young successful one.
The kind of guy who can't keep it to himself.

Dorsey did a few leg stretches against the Buick and
started making his way along the nature trail, pitching
steeply downward into Panther Hollow. Heavily wooded on
both sides, the trail took Dorsey under the spans of a bridge
leading to the Pitt campus then momentarily tilted uphill
before taking a permanent slant, aiming down toward a
small man-made lake. He stopped at the first of several dark
stone-and-mortar foot bridges that straddled the hollow and

waited for his meeting, sitting on the wall, dangling his feet in front of a cornerstone that read WPA 1939.

When he had returned home the night before, Henry pressed a square of paper into his hand and said he was heading home. "Call this man," he had said. "No rest for you until you do. He hasn't given me a break all evening."

Dorsey read the name, noticed that the telephone number was a downtown exchange, and made the call. The party on the other end bitched him out for not being available for his earlier calls and for disturbing his office staff. "Sorry, Mr. Lambert," Dorsey had said. "And tough shit, too. Tell me what you want to tell me." Lambert told him when and where, and the meeting was set.

Dorsey heard the footfalls coming from the direction of the lake, the noise in competition with little else so early on a weekday morning. The rest of them, Dorsey thought, the weekend Olympians, were crammed into buses jockeying for elbow room. Or in a carpool with three guys who belch traces of their breakfast all the way to the office. He saw the jogger, a tall, bearded black man in matching Nike shorts and singlet, rounding a bend in the trail by the farthest bridge. As he neared Dorsey, he downshifted into a stiff-legged walk, panting with his hands at his hips.

"Dorsey, right?" the black man asked, slowing his pace further.

"Sure, sure," Dorsey told him. "Park's pretty empty this time of day."

"That's the plan."

"Good plan." Dorsey watched the man come to a rest against the bridge wall and dig into a zippered pouch strapped around his waist. From it, the black man produced two small snap-top cans of orange juice.

"A touch of civilization," the black man said, handing over one of the cans. "Jim Reeves is my name, in case you were wondering."

Dorsey took the juice can and then shook the extended hand. "Been with the Lambert people for a while?"

"Not very long." Reeves snapped open his juice and took

a long pull. "Good, stayed halfway cold," he said, and wiped the back of a hand across his lips. "I've been with them just long enough to be stuck with this kind of meeting. And to be trusted for this kind of meeting."

"We're going to talk about David Filus, right?" Dorsey held the juice away from his mouth, waiting on the answer before he drank.

"Sure," Reeves said, "but only in the roundabout never-pin-me-down way in which I've been trained. And with one very clear understanding."

"Depends on the nature of the understanding." Dorsey drank off the juice in one gulp. "I'm willing to listen."

Finished with his drink, Reeves shook the last few drops into the dirt and put the empty can in his pouch. He took Dorsey's and did the same. "From what I heard, last night set the record for after-hours phone calls at Lambert and Associates. You did your rantings on several lines and then a Mr. Meara did the same. The bishop followed that up, and both he and Meara mentioned your father's name for punctuation."

All the big guns, Dorsey thought, all to save Tommy Crimmins. Christ, he better be innocent or the heavens will fall. "The understanding?" he asked.

"I can give you a lot," Reeves said, "things I didn't know about till the middle of last night. And with what I give you, your Mr. Meara will have a long talk with the DA and nothing bad will ever be uttered about a certain priest again. Correct?"

"That's the hope," Dorsey said, "that's the plan."

"The plan better work and it better stay discreet." Reeves stood to his full height and rested a hand on Dorsey's shoulder. "Because everything I say here will later be denied, if need be. We never met, I'll say I don't know you from Adam. And anything you attribute to this conversation is a lie. That's if one word of what I tell you gets past the DA's office door. That's the understanding."

Out here in the midst of nature, Dorsey thought, where no one can hear the conversation. The two of us dressed for warm-weather exercise, allowing no secure place to wear a wire and microphone. And who the hell would ever believe that a lawyer and a detective held a high-level discussion out in the woods. No wonder Lambert had been so cranky, the guy had put a lot of work into this. Must've stayed up late along with Reeves.

"I'm in no position to make promises," Dorsey told him. "Maybe Mr. Meara and the bishop can do that, being a few rungs higher up the ladder. But not me." Dorsey hopped down from his seat on the wall and gave Reeves a grin. "But then again, I don't have to be. Because we never met, according to you. So let's get to it."

"You first." Reeves returned the grin.

That's how it's gonna be, Dorsey told himself. You tell a story that barely holds together and Mr. Reeves here will fill in the blanks. Maybe. And only if you take the story in the right direction. Dorsey turned from Reeves and looked down the hollow to the lake. "Okay, where to start?" he said returning his gaze to Reeves. "David Filus was a very successful handler of other people's money, the kind of person that does well at Lambert. Right?'

"No argument there."

"Other people," Dorsey said to Reeves. "Other people can be all kinds of people. Rich, poor, bankers, farmers, businessmen; regardless of the type of business they happen to be in. Chick Rosenthal fall into any of those categories?"

"Mr. Rosenthal is a distant client of ours," Reeves said slowly, as if recalling a practiced speech. "By distant, I am suggesting that he keeps his relationship with the firm very low key and most times prefers to maintain this relationship through any number of intermediaries."

"So I might not see his name on the portfolio. . . ." Dorsey thought for a moment. "Big-assed, high-powered investment firm, and you guys launder Rosenthal's gambling money?"

"We discreetly invest the man's money."

"And Dave Filus," Dorsey continued, "he handled Rosenthal's money while he was alive? And it is Rosenthal's gambling profits, right? Regardless of how you color it."

"Just up to a time slightly before his death," Reeves said. "Seems that Mr. Rosenthal's group lost confidence in him and demanded that their account be reassigned."

"He started losing the man's money?" Dorsey asked, then aswered his own question "Sure he did. Father Crimmins lost a tidy sum of the parish's money following his advice. Filus let the priest in on what he said was a sure thing, like a fixed horserace. Did he let Rosenthal down the same way?"

Reeves stayed silent for a moment, concentrating on the ground as he cut a line in the dirt with his sneaker. "Actually," Reeves said, looking up. "Actually, it was the same horse race. And that's not a bad analogy."

Crimmins had said the deal revolved around buying up property, cheaply, Dorsey reminded himself. Riverfront property on both sides of the city. Recreational use? he wondered. Boating, amusement parks? No way, the return would be too low. And throw Rosenthal into the mix with his expertise. Make money by renovating the river fronts. "Holy shit," Dorsey said aloud. "Filus bet their money on the state legislature and lost. Yeah, sure, it would have fallen apart that summer. And then Filus would have gotten it in November."

"Congratulations," Reeves said, softly clapping his hands. "Riverboat gambling, some people's idea of how to solve the woes of any city."

"And to get on the boat," Dorsey said, "you have to walk along the shore. Better yet, in most places, the boat never moves, just stays tied up at the dock. And things expand, build up, and you can't tell where the dock ends and the boat starts. So the land next to the water turns into a gold mine for those that own it, or lease it, or build on it. Pretty nice investment plan."

"If, and only if, the state government cooperates."

Which they did not, Dorsey thought. The state legislature had voted down the bill to allow riverboat gambling in Pittsburgh the year that Filus was killed. Months before. But Filus must've thought it would go the other way, maybe he even had an insider that was telling him that it was going through. So he convinced Rosenthal to put in his money, and then feeling generous, because he's a genius who had just invented a machine to make money, he let Father Crimmins have a little slice. And it all went to shit.

"Was all the land sold off?" Dorsey asked.

Reeves shrugged his shoulders. "They got what they could for it. There was depreciation and tax breaks, but a lot of money was flushed away. Along with some money to grease the palms of locals and to pay off the infallible insider that had told Filus that the bill was sure to pass."

"I suppose Rosenthal gave Filus some time to make good on his losses?" Dorsey looked into Reeves's eyes and wasn't sure he was getting through. "C'mon, Filus wasn't killed until November and Rosenthal isn't an unreasonable guy. He would have demanded that his money be guaranteed before the investment, there had to have been some kind of assurance. Maybe Filus gave him that assurance himself, feeling as cocky as he must've. So when the money was lost, Rosenthal, being reasonable, would've given the guy a few months to get the money together. But when Filus didn't, or couldn't, well, the marker was called due."

"That's one hell of a leap in logic," Reeves said. "And as far as myself or anyone at Lambert is concerned, totally without basis."

"But Rosenthal . . ." Dorsey asked, "Rosenthal was made whole on this thing?"

"He was reimbursed."

"When? Before or after those bullets lodged themselves in Filus's brainpan?"

Apparently uncomfortable, Reeves again worked his foot into the dirt. "You'd have to figure that out yourself."

Dorsey gave the attorney a slow and thorough examination, one that seemed to put Reeves even further ill at ease. He decided to ask a question with no relevance to his job. One that he was dying to ask.

"Hey Reeves, no shit, you think Rosenthal had this guy killed? Or are you like another guy I know who would simply prefer this explanation rather than one about a black addict who killed the guy for the contents of his pockets?"

"Shit, why'd they have to send me?" Reeves looked away as if studying the far bank of the hollow before turning back to Dorsey. "I don't know what, if anything, happened. Around ten last night the phone rang and I was told to haul ass over to Mr. Lambert's, where I've never been before. I just figured it as bad news. Maybe the worst, like I really screwed up and he was letting me go. But when I get there he tells me about these calls from members of the inner circle, you might say. The bishop, Mr. Meara, and your father by inference. And then we have hours of conversation about what might be going on in some accounts at Lambert and about a few things that just might've taken place. Then we end with poor Dave Filus and how this priest is being smeared and placed under a shadow, and how I should not worry about getting any sleep because I had to meet you this morning. So now you know what I know. Which has in no way helped me pick out the fiction or the reality. Sorry, best I can do."

"Hell," Dorsey said, "you did just fine. Much more honesty that I expected, really."

"I suppose I should say thanks."

"Then I suppose I should say you're welcome." Reeves was all right, Dorsey thought. He had expected a prolonged cat-and-mouse game, one with far more teeth-pulling for information. Jim Reeves, reluctant messenger. Maybe for a reason. "During your time at Lambert, did you ever run into Filus? Work on anything with him?"

"Never, not once." Reeves held his silence for a moment. "Ah, in a way, I guess I did work with him. I was the attorney who handled the estate, it was done as a courtesy by the firm. So I did get to know the family, the wife and the two boys."

"Rough time, I suppose."

"There was some concern about the two boys," Reeves

told him. ''I was told they really took their father's death hard, really messed them up. So much so that the mother thought it might be good for them to help out in handling the estate. Some kind of therapy to work out their grief, I suppose.''

Dorsey thought back to the afternoon in the Hillman Library when he had reviewed the estate's final disposition. There had been a lot of money to account for and spread around, but it was carefully planned for by the CPA while he was still alive. ''How could those kids help?'' he asked. ''They were only freshman in college at the time. And besides, Dave Filus had his estate planned long before his death. Handling it would have been a cakewalk.''

''Oh, it was just a matter of double-checking a few numbers and the present value of some accounts.''

''So what did the sons do?'' Dorsey asked.

''I gave them the gofer work, and they were happy,'' Reeves told him. ''My boss insisted, so I played along. I sent those two muscle-bound no-necks all over the courthouse, made them do my leg work. It worked out, for the most part. Only one problem, and that was with the death certificates. You know, the small ones that have to be sent out to every financial institution the man ever dealt with so they'll believe he's dead and come across with records or money? One of the boys lost a few of them during the two block trip from the courthouse to my office. Cost us a few bucks to replace, but I didn't make a fuss. All in all, the kids seemed to do okay.''

''What'd you think of the widow?'' Dorsey asked.

''I'm married and I'm just the hired help. I don't think along those lines.''

20

Father Crimmins had cleared out by the time Dorsey had returned home. He checked the kitchen, the second story, and called down the stairway into the cellar. No response. Ah, hell, he thought, just when you had an opportunity to call Meara with only good news.

"So, where'd he go?" Meara asked over the phone. Dorsey, still in his exercise gear, was seated behind the desk in his office, feet up and across the desktop. "Not to the parish house," Dorsey told Meara. "That was the first place I tried."

"How about the girlfriend? Maybe he's seeking comfort at the Filus residence."

"That was the second number I called," Dorsey replied. "There was no answer. Maybe the two of them are off somewhere together. Not that it means anything at this point."

"Bullshit," Meara told him. "Find out where he's at. Not knowing where he is, it's just another pain in the ass that I don't want to experience. You were supposed to keep a leash on him."

Dorsey decided it was his turn to get rough. "Wait a goddamned minute. You put me on the payroll as an investigator, not to be a fuckin' nanny. Now let's put this shit aside for a second and let me tell you what came out of this morning's get-together in Schenley Park."

Meara kept silent, allowing Dorsey to give his report

without interruption, leaving Dorsey with the impression that Meara was taking notes as quickly as he spoke. This was confirmed when he repeated it all back to Dorsey afterward with little paraphrasing. "I've got this right?" Meara asked.

"Yeah, yeah," Dorsey said. "So, you'll contact Turner, give him the bad news?"

"I'll have to kick this around a little bit," Meara said. "But, yeah, I'll get together with him. Meanwhile, you sweep up any of the mess that might still be around. Check out the Sutton woman, make her talk to you. And just check to see where Father Crimmins has gotten to. When I drop this bomb on Turner, I want a direct hit. No response, no hidden hopes for him to cling to. I want him to pack up his tent and get lost. Maybe I'll even suggest that I plan on running against him in the next election."

Carnegie Place is a block-long stretch of road between Penn and Reynolds, lined on both sides with neat brick homes with large front porches, some with canvas awnings. Except for one house in the middle of the block, the one that Dorsey was watching from the front seat of the Buick. Parked halfway down the street and at the far curb, he could see a gray-and-white outline that framed the first story brick, suggesting that at one time there had been a porch that matched those of its neighbors. A second door had been installed at the front of the house, newer and well-pointed brick surrounding it. It led, Dorsey was sure, to the second-floor apartment occupied by Alice Sutton.

Surveillance was a drag, and it always has been, Dorsey thought to himself. A real take-no-breaks, pee-in-a-bottle-if-you-have-to, never-take-your-eyes-off-the-house drag. Because you wait for hours for something that might never even happen. Or when luck is with you, and something happens, like someone coming out of the house carrying a television, the critical period lasts only moments. So there are no paperbacks on the front seat to sneak glances at, no crossword puzzles to distract yourself with. Because distraction, when you need it the most, could kill a career.

Dorsey checked his watch, made a mental note that forty-five minutes had passed without incident, decided that enough was enough, and climbed out of the Buick. Dressed in a sport shirt and a pair of older, unpressed cotton slacks, he walked up the opposite side of the street until he was even with the apartment entrance. The windows were shut despite the heat, and there were no air-conditioning units. Dorsey didn't figure the place for central air and decided that Sutton was out. Time to try the neighbors, he thought, and crossed the porch of the home opposite to Alice Sutton's place and rang the doorbell.

"This the Sutton residence?" Dorsey asked a man who chose to stay behind his locked screen door. Apparently dressed for golf and in his early sixties, he wore yellow slacks, green sport shirt, and a white cap with visor. "Alice Sutton?" Dorsey clarified. "Maybe I'm wrong, but this was the address I was given."

From beneath his cap, the man gave Dorsey a slow examination before responding. "Not here," he said, his voiced low and cragged. "Wrong place. Might be across the street. Lemme ask." He turned and shouted back into the house. "Hey, Lil!"

"What?" the voice that shouted back was older and female. "What're you shoutin' about?"

"There's a guy here, I don't know who the hell he is," the man said. "He's looking for some woman named Sutton. That the skinny one, lives upstairs across the way?"

A woman dressed in an outfit that nearly matched the one her husband wore, came to the door. "Who wants to know about Alice?" she asked the man, ignoring Dorsey.

"This guy here," the man said, gesturing to Dorsey. "Hell, I told you I didn't know who he was. Alice Sutton, she the one lives on the second floor over there?"

"That's Alice's place," the woman said, now addressing Dorsey. "You lookin' for Alice? She won't be home now, she works at that food co-op they run for people during the summers. You could try there, it's just a block down Penn

Avenue. We have to go now to my daughter's place, it's her little girl's birthday. So you better try the food co-op. Sorry, we have to go. Try the food co-op.''

Dorsey thanked them and walked back to the street, heading for Penn Avenue. He couldn't help but wonder if their daughter had a putting green, at least for grandpa's sake.

The food co-op was housed in a small commercial building on Penn Avenue with a sign that directed customers to the loading dock at the rear. Dorsey rounded the block and entered an alley that was strewn with sheets of clear plastic, metal packaging bands, and the wooden slats of broken pallets. There were two panel vans at the loading dock and four teenaged boys were filling them with hand-carts of canned foods. He climbed the steps to the dock level and entered the building. Inside was a long bay where customers wandered about, looking over nearly fresh produce and packaged foodstuffs. When Dorsey first saw the woman he knew had to be Alice Sutton, she matched the age in the file and was the only female employee in sight; she was carrying a large cardboard box and bitching out the boy who trailed behind her.

"No, no, all of it has to be picked up. That alley looks like shit, absolute shit. If it gets left like that, the neighbors complain to the city. And then some inspector will be here going over everything, looking to shut down this place. So get some help, do it all yourself, I don't care. Just clean up the alley for godsakes!''

Yeah, Dorsey thought, she's Sutton all right. Mouth like an ex-nun, tough and freshly profane. He hung back among the other customers, watching as she added the carton to a corner stack and then set about rearranging another. She wore jeans and a light denim workshirt, sleeves rolled to the elbow. Her hair was a solid gray, and she had it parted over her right temple and pushed back behind the ears. Steadily at work, moving boxes, bossing teenagers, and haggling over prices with customers, she gave Dorsey an impression of determination, and of being single-minded once the task was set. And that, he thought, might just be the source of

Tommy Crimmins's troubles. Morally dedicated and end-lessly driven. She's bad news.

Dorsey slipped out of the food co-op and returned to his car, stopping along the way for a coke and a newspaper at a small grocery store. Settled into the front seat, he cracked open the can and sipped slowly to make it last, unsure of how long his wait might be. Knowing where she was and from what direction she would be approaching, he felt more secure in paging through the news. The first article to draw his attention was in the lower corner of the front page and concerned itself with speculation about why Father Crimmins had been interviewed by the District Attorney. It seemed that the priest was not available for comment. No shit, Dorsey thought. Let me know when you find him. I have some comments of my own.

Alice Sutton arrived home in thirty-five minutes, just as Dorsey was finishing a piece on how the Pirates were on the brink of leaving town, again. She stayed inside for only ten minutes before reemerging onto the sidewalk dressed in shorts and T-shirt, a large camera case hanging from her neck and resting at her midsection. Dorsey watched her head toward the intersection with Reynolds Street, gave her a half-block lead, then started after her on foot.

By the time Dorsey had stopped at the corner of Carnegie and Reynolds, Alice Sutton had set up shop at a picnic table on the lawn of a small park on the far side of the street. The camera case was on the table and she had extracted several film canisters, a 35-millimeter camera, and an attachable telephoto lens. Ten feet beyond her was a three-foot-tall cyclone fence that surrounded a number of lawn bowling lanes, long rectangles of grass trimmed as closely as the eighteenth green at a country club. Several groups of older men, dressed like the one living across the street from Alice Sutton, were gathered at the head of each lane and Dorsey could hear the clacking of wooden bowling balls as they struck one another. His father's place was only six blocks away, and he could remember watching an earlier generation of old men playing this game that he would later hear someone call WASP boccie. He wondered when his turn was coming. This game, he thought, or maybe the horseshoe pits would be his last stand. At least it was outdoors; beat being a shut-in with a stroke, like his old man. Ah, hell, he'd just spent all his time figuring out a way to fix the game.

Apparently satisfied with her choice of film and lens, Alice Sutton sat down on the tabletop and faced the bowlers, her feet resting on the attached bench. Dorsey watched her sight her shots and crossed over to the lawn, moving slowly. He had considered springing his presence on her, quickly stating his business and trying to get down to business, but now thought better of it. She was too damned intense; he had seen that at the food co-op and recalled it from her file. Her first response to a frontal attack would be to raise her hackles and strike back at whatever moved. Remember Father Kelly and the pepper spray? No, no. Better to ease your way in. She'll get angry soon enough, hopefully it can happen incrementally and you can gain some information before the final eruption.

"Pentax?" Dorsey asked coming even with the table, but keeping a polite distance away. "The camera," he said, gesturing toward it after she had turned and given him an annoyed look.

"It's a Leica, got it on a trip to Europe." She turned back to the bowlers and again sighted the camera.

"That's a great subject you picked," Dorsey said. "There have been men their age playing here for years. I remember from when I was a kid." He stepped a little closer, focusing his attention on the camera. "You do this professionally? Working on some kind of collection, maybe some sort of coffee-table book?"

"Hopefully," she said, keeping the camera trained on the men beyond the fence. "Maybe someday. But then again," she continued, bringing the camera away from her face and turning on Dorsey. "But then again, I'll never be on the same professional level as you. Taking action shots through car windshields and smudged windows. That must take talent.''

The hell with it anyway, Dorsey thought, so much for the slow and sneaky approach. ''Mind if I just sit here at the edge of the table? Safe enough distance?''

''They said there'd be some slimy bastard like you coming around,'' Alice Sutton said. ''I'm not supposed to speak to you. Not a word.''

Dorsey gave her a thin smile. ''When'd you learn to follow orders? Before or after you were tossed out of the convent? Literally.''

Her eyes were an icy gray, much like her hair, and for a moment Dorsey thought he saw them grow even colder. But the recovery was quick and he was relieved to find that he hadn't lost her. ''In reflection, I find that night to be one of my finer moments. That old priest didn't care much for it. But they washed out his eyes and put some ointment on his cheeks and he got over it. But you just remember, I still carry the pepper spray.''

''Just trying to find a way to talk you.'' Dorsey settled a haunch on the table's corner. ''No reason to get violent.''

''Keep your distance, keep it civil, and we'll be fine.''

''Sure, no sweat,'' Dorsey said, mentally agreeing only to keeping his distance. Damn right I'll keep my distance. ''They tell you anything else about me?''

''The slimy bastard part,'' she said, ''they told me that early on. Then later, just recently, I got a call from a DA's assistant and they gave your description and background. That's how I was able to spot you at the co-op this afternoon.'' She cut him a smug little grin and returned her attention to her camera.

''Actually, I'm glad they did,'' Dorsey said. ''Told you about me. Makes conversation a lot easier. I suppose you realize I've taken a peak into your personal history, too.''

Alice Sutton snapped a shot of the bowlers. ''The crack about getting thrown out of the convent gave that away.'' She reset the shutter speed and again took aim with the camera. ''But I remembered some of your exploits in the news a few years back. Done any other damage to the labor movement since then?''

"You've got me wrong, I've always been pro-union," Dorsey told her. "The matter you're referring to had an awful lot to do with insurance fraud. And a harmless retired guy I'd known for years died in the process. More of a byproduct to the process, maybe. But he's still just as dead."

Alice Sutton put the camera aside and turned to Dorsey. "I know about that, too. And I think it was a terrible thing that should never have happened. But you should understand that when a popular upheaval begins, which is what that was, there is a lot of unforeseen damage. To things and people. Homestead Strike, Haymarket Square Riot, every striking autoworker that GM ever starved out. Your friend was a casualty of world history."

What a load of shit, Dorsey thought, trying to avoid a few ugly memories that were getting the better of him. A nice but tough old guy with a dent in his head left by a length of hard metal swung by what this woman might call a member of the labor movement's maniacal fringe. But he died in the maniac's attempt to protect a criminal scheme, which didn't have a thing to do with anyone getting health benefits or a dime-an-hour raise.

"He was a friend," Dorsey told her, "not a quarter inch on the universe's time line. I find it hard to think of him as an historical increment." He watched her shrug and go back to working her camera. For a short time, he looked off past the bowling lawns into the trees of Frick Park, watching a few joggers headed into a wooded trail. He used the time to regroup, to size up the job at hand and get on with it. She was just what he thought he would find. Someone who was extremely intelligent and strongly opinionated. About everything, including the way history and the world will and should march on. And, of course, she couldn't keep it to herself. She had to talk, had to demonstrate all of her certainties. Just keep pecking at her, Dorsey told himself. She'll give you all you came for. Like she said, she's been expecting a slimy bastard like you to come along. She's also been looking forward to this opportunity to straighten you out.

"Kind of a complication, isn't it?" Dorsey asked her.

"How's that?" She trailed one of the bowlers with her camera, a frail man on a cane, as he took his position to pitch the wooden ball.

"C'mon, you spout all this revolutionary, there-are-no-civilians-in-a-war philosophy. But you're a solid Catholic. A pious Christian. So every Sunday you hear the Good News of the Lord, who warns you that what happens to the least of His is also happening to Him."

Alice Sutton went on aiming her camera. "That's weak, a piss-poor effort of an intellectual challenge. Besides, why would you think I'd feel compelled to explain myself to you?"

Because you're dying to, Dorsey thought. The hell with talking to an investigator, you'd buttonhole the first guy on the corner and lay out your life as a spiritual journey, not to mention a moral crusade. "Sorry," he told her, "just struck me as odd."

"Odd for you, perhaps," she said. "Because you buy into all the bullshit that gets mixed into standard religious education. Manmade bullshit that gets sold to you while you're young. Instead of a progressive faith, you get this entrenching of authority, temporal authority. We never run short of rules. The reasoning for the rules gets murky and lost, if there ever was a legitimate reasoning, but the rules stay put. Tradition can be a comfort at times, but it can't be a basis for life's limitations."

Dorsey grinned. "How the hell did you ever end up in a convent?" He pointed to the tabletop, she nodded, and Dorsey sat solidly on the bolted planks. "What'd you think, you were going to work the system from the inside?"

"It was a mistake; I let myself get taken for a ride." Alice Sutton put down the camera and looked off into the distance. "Remember the times, things had changed. Nuns were able to dress like human beings and some of them lived in groups in the local community. It looked like a place I'd really like to be. But it was all bullshit. Mother superior maintained her authority whenever possible, really had your life in her hands. She was the power, unless of course a priest happened to be in the room. Then she might as well have been a waitress. What a load of crap.''

''And that load of crap led to your spraying a load of pepper spray into poor old Father Kelly's face.''

''Poor old Father Kelly, my ass.'' Alice Sutton grabbed up her camera and worked her fingers at the settings. ''As far as I'm concerned, the man was spiritual deadweight. Never had an original thought in his life. A religious yesman for the diocese. Didn't know the value of being a priest. Couldn't appreciate what he had.''

''But you wouldn't have that problem?''

Alice Sutton again let the camera drop to her lap and directed her eyes at Dorsey. ''You can bet the farm on that. The gift of ordination wouldn't be wasted on me. I'd use it to lead, not to fall into lockstep. I'd put my time into progressive matters instead of signing off on the weekly collection totals.''

''So how does Tommy Crimmins stack up in your scheme of things?''

''It's about time you got around to him,'' she said. ''I was starting to wonder if you really knew your business.''

Dorsey took the rebuke in stride; it just reinforced his impressions of her. ''Regardless of my motives in asking the question, I think it deserves an answer,'' he told her. ''I've had some talks with the guy recently and I've heard some nontraditional concepts being kicked around. Temporary priesthoods, women included. Sounds like your kind of man.''

''So what's he done with these concepts of his, besides using them as an excuse to get laid?'' Alice Sutton shook her head in apparent disgust. ''What's he do with his office as pastor? Keeps the congregation and the bishop happy in equal measure, that's what. CYO basketball games, fish fries, and a bottom line that's well into the black. And he's only done that through the good graces of Louise Filus. No, he's not my idea of a priest. He's all talk and no action, which is worse than being one of the hardliners. The ones who just talk, they make it legitimate for a lot more priests to sit on their ass and just talk. They never take action and the pace of change is set at a crawl.''

''So you hate the guy,'' Dorsey said, ''because he's one of those dumb-ass liberals who make things difficult on all those enlightened radicals. Besides the fact that he can't make you into a priest. Is that why you followed him around, documenting his affair with Mrs. Filus? To destroy him? Why? They wouldn't have given you the pastor's job. Most likely, you would've ended up with somebody worse; maybe Father Kelly would've come out of retirement.''

Alice Sutton got to her feet and faced Dorsey. ''No,'' she said, ''it wasn't to destroy him. You asked me before if I had any thoughts of working on a coffee-table book. Yeah, well, I have a collection of times, dates, and photos, a chronology of Father Crimmins's disloyalty to his vows. And I wanted to confront him with it, throw his hypocrisy in his face. It would have been a lesson to him, one he might've taken to heart. Something might've actually come of it. Some good. Maybe he would've left the talkers behind.''

''And then again,'' Dorsey said, ''you could've blackmailed him into being a radical, maybe? Hey, if there are no civilians in this war, then you can use any weapon at your disposal.''

''Not a bad idea, blackmail.''

''Still, trying to help get the guy indicted for murder is a little extreme.'' Dorsey leaned forward, returning the woman's glare. ''Jesus, there's no point in it. It's just cruelty, it's just because you hate the guy.''

''He murdered that man,'' Alice Sutton said, the words slipping out over a clenched jaw. ''The two of them planned it. Then he did it while she sat in the church hall having dinner.''

''Father Crimmins was hearing confessions at the time. Check the schedule.''

''I don't give a damn about the schedule,'' Alice Sutton

said. "There's no way to confirm it. He can't give the names of anyone whose sins he heard that night; he's barred from doing that. And who the hell can remember when they went to confession on a specific night three years ago? He shot that man."

"How in the hell do you know that?" Dorsey asked. "Besides, wasn't Dave Filus just a casualty in someone else's war?"

"It was murder," Alice Sutton said. "This wasn't a stray bullet in a great struggle. They murdered him."

"Again," Dorsey said, "how in the hell do you know that?"

"Because, you bastard," she said to Dorsey. "Because I've seen the gun they used. I was able to snap a picture of it. The telephoto lens came in handy. The two of them in her car, the gun on the front seat between them. After the killing. How long after, that I can't remember offhand. And don't bother asking, I gave the photo to the DA's people and they've confirmed it as a thirty-eight, the sort of gun that killed Dave Filus."

Ah, hell, Dorsey thought. The murder weapon. No wonder Turner is so hot for this. And there's no wonder why he hasn't arrested Crimmins. He has no idea where the gun is at. Otherwise, Tommy Crimmins and Louise Filus would be writing to each other from separate wings of the Allegheny County Jail.

21

Early evening found Dorsey flopped on one of the white Adirondack chairs on the front porch of St. Anne's parish house. On the lawns, with temporary soccer goals sitting at opposite ends, Bill Sargent was putting his squad through some final drills, occasionally taking a player aside for individual instructions. From the cemetery and from the hedges that surrounded the lawns, the rickety song of crickets and cicadas grew more insistent while shadows grew across the grass. Dorsey liked the effect. The grass was a richer hue of green in this light, like the felt on a particularly expensive billiard table, and the insects' call almost crowded out his thoughts. Almost. They never do, he thought, nothing ever does. Except for deep, black sleep. And that only comes when you're at peace. So wait for that to come along. It always makes an appearance, but it never calls ahead to let you know when it can be expected.

It was his third trip to the parish house looking for Father Crimmins since his conversation with Alice Sutton. He had also swung by the Filus residence twice, finding it and the garage empty both times. Interspersed with all of this running around had been three attempts to call Bill Meara. The last one, made from a pay phone in a bar on Penn Avenue called the Evergreen, had caught him at his desk.

"A fuckin' gun?" Meara had said after hearing Dorsey's report. "She has a photo, or the DA has a photo, of these two lovebirds sitting around in public admiring a gun? You met her, tell me what you think. She giving you the straight shit or not?''

''Sounded like square business to me,'' Dorsey told him, sitting on a wooden stool at the end of the bar. ''But keep this in mind, this woman believes in her own version of the world. You can see it; she reaches a conclusion, then she looks around and studies the facts. And if they don't agree with her opinion, she says fuck it, let's get some new reality out of an old trunk some where. Anyways, her story makes as much sense as the one I got out of Reeves this morning. And Louise Filus, she already told me how Sutton had been on to her and Crimmins, followed them every chance she got.''

''I'm not saying we shouldn't look into this,'' Meara had replied, ''because we may have to explain it away sometime. But right now, the Rosenthal theory is golden. Yeah, sure, find out where the Father has gotten to, that's first priority. And find out why he took off. Then do whatever you can to bolster up this Rosenthal thing.''

Dorsey had assured him he'd handle both matters, although he wasn't certain how in either case, then he hung up and bought a six-pack of Rolling Rock on his way out.

Watching soccer practice, he was now three cans into the six-pack, empties and torn plastic ringlets littering the porch about his feet. Other than checking real estate transfers on the riverbank properties, he knew of no other way to find supporting evidence for the Rosenthal hit. As nebulous as a smoke cloud, the possibility would remain a myth, believed because it had a persuasive spokesman or laughed at as a spook story because it seemed outrageous at first blush. The first priority seemed to be the only one. Find Father Crimmins and figure out why he and Louise had taken off.

There was the squeal of unoiled metal hinges and Dorsey turned to see a gray-haired priest standing at the open screen door. A thin man from a religious order that Dorsey couldn't place, he wore a black cassock with pleated skirting, and a rosary hung down from his neck and Roman collar. The replacement for Father Crimmins sent out by the bishop.

"This doesn't look good," the priest told him. "I asked you before not to drink out here on the porch. At least be sure to clean up after yourself."

"I'll do that."

The priest stayed at the door. "There's very little chance that Father Crimmins will be back this evening. So, really, there's no need for you to hang about. I'll certainly call you if he comes back."

"Ah, you're right," Dorsey said, wondering if going home would do him any good. "Just let me finish this beer, the one in my hand, and I'll clear out. But I'll hear from you pronto if anything develops, right?"

"Absolutely," the priest replied, then said good night and went inside.

Dorsey slumped a little deeper into the chair and drank most of his beer. He wondered how much the replacement priest knew about the situation he had been dropped into, and decided it was precious little. Ignorant and planning on staying that way, blissfully. Lucky guy, smart guy. All he needs to deal with is a depressed beer guzzler, taking up space on his front porch, before the neighbors start to call. Lucky guy, smart priest. Take a lesson.

But curiosity was his stock in trade and Dorsey couldn't stop thinking of the long day's events, the telling of two stories that didn't mesh. The story he had gotten out of Reeves didn't hang together if Crimmins and Louise had the murder weapon. Because, he thought, if you have the gun, you're the one who used it. A simple rule of investigation. Unless, of course, you have a great story that puts you in literally another state at the time of the murder, which Crimmins does not. At least the gun hasn't been found. If he did it, Dorsey thought, maybe he had the brains to dump the thing. Dump it for real, not just hide it under the kitchen floorboards. Take a quick run up to Lake Erie and throw it in. Or drop it into a newly dug foundation for a downtown office building. Make sure it's gone, long gone and for good.

Dorsey watched Bill Sargent dismiss the soccer team and begin stowing away the equipment into the back of a minivan and wondered if Father Crimmins was up to all of this. Not just the killing. Hell, that may well have been the easiest part. It's all the other things, the funeral that he presided over, continuing to see Louise Filus, and the careful lies for three years. And wrapping the lies with half truths and philosophical speeches. Admitting to the affair but not the killing. Explaining away the affair with the possibility of a new priesthood staffed with temporary ministers who knew that a more personalized life was theirs after their time in office. Just like former presidents, he had said. Could Father Crimmins be that good? If he was, you had to wonder where he got all the practice.

Bill Sargent came up the steps and took a spot at the porch railing in front of Dorsey, resting his haunches against the iron bar. Dorsey offered him a beer, warning him that they hadn't seen a cooler or ice cube in sometime. Bill took off his wire-framed glasses, polished them with the hem of his T-shirt, and accepted the beer. "Hear anything from Father Crimmins?" he asked.

"Not a thing," Dorsey said. "How about you? If you have, I think I better know about it."

"I wish I had." Bill sipped at his beer. "I don't know what I'm supposed to do with this soccer team. I head back to school in a week and somebody has to take over. Besides, I'm worried about him. What with that business on TV about him at the courthouse. I'm not a church member, but we've gotten to be friends."

Dorsey sized him up for a moment and decided that he probably knew already. "How about Mrs. Filus? She's dropped out of sight, too. Any worries about her?"

"I hear what people are saying," Bill told him, "but not being Catholic, it isn't such a big deal for me. I never understood a celibate priesthood anyways. If there's something between the two of them, it's just nature taking its course."

"There's a dead husband in the picture. Murdered."

"That happened three years ago." Bill went silent, apparently thinking. "Is that why you've been coming around? You suspect Father Crimmins?"

"Not me," Dorsey told him. "But some other people have ideas on the subject. And Mrs. Filus might figure into things, too. I guess you can't have one of them without the other."

Bill shook his head and shifted his position on the railing. "That's bad, really bad. She's one of those people, I guess, that always has troubles."

"How's that?" Dorsey asked him. "She and the mister fight a lot, something like that? Bad childhood maybe?"

"I couldn't say anything about those areas of her life, don't know about them."

"So?" Dorsey said, gesturing for him to continue.

"I guess," Bill said, pulling on his beer before continuing. "I guess I was thinking more along the lines of her sons."

"The twins?" Dorsey asked. "Mark and Greg?"

"The Beefers."

"The what?"

"The Beefers," Bill continued. "Side of beef one and side of beef two. The Beefers, that's what they called them in high school, but never to their faces. You know, they were on the football team. Linebackers, big necks and small brains. They were pretty good. And they stayed in shape during the off-season by kicking the shit out of guys."

"Is that right?" Dorsey asked.

"Oh, sure," Bill said. "They were a holy terror. Really knocked guys around. I remember a couple of big fights over in Mellon Park, in the basketball courts along Fifth Avenue. Some kid from over in Oakland had to get his face rebuilt when they were through with him. I don't think they ever had police trouble, but Mrs. Filus had to come up to school a couple of times because of fights. They really gave it to people. Especially the Jewish kids. The Beefers always had a few they targeted for abuse."

"You graduated the same year?" Dorsey asked him. "See much of them since? During the summers, picnics, things like that?"

"Not much," Bill said. "I hear things from other guys,

like that the Beefers are still the Beefers. Only maybe a little worse. And with money to spend.''

Dorsey thought back to the disposition of the estate. There was money for the sons, but it was in trust for a few more years. "Good summer jobs, maybe? Or maybe Mrs. Filus is trying to use money to make up for the loss of their dad.

Bill shrugged. "I'm not sure what they do for summer work. But from what I hear, they both have these four-wheel-drive vehicles. And if tattoos cost money, they've dropped a bundle on them. I heard they got insurance money from their dad.''

No, Dorsey thought, Mrs. Filus received the insurance money and a chunk of that went to clean up the parish's financial mess. Still, she could have showered riches on the boys and maintained her lifestyle.

"I gotta go," Bill said, and shook the beer can, indicating that it was empty. "I'll throw this out when I get home.''

Dorsey watched him turn away and flashed back over his talk with Reeves. The boys had helped out with the handling of the estate. Just as gofers, but they couldn't even get that right, the pains in the ass. Lost one of the small death certificates that you send to the creditors, like the gas company, and to the banks to close accounts. And to the insurance companies to collect the death benefits. Ah, for Chrissake.

"I'm with you," Dorsey said, gathering up the debris of his beer drinking. "I gotta get going, too.''

22

Dorsey returned to the row house, completed the summer-time ritual of propping open the office windows, and dug into the file cabinet at the far wall. Extracting the case file he had been keeping on the Crimmins matter, Dorsey went to his desk and lit the goose-necked reading lamp. He inched his way through the file, looking for anything that pertained to the final disposition of the estate. Just as he had recalled, the Filus boys weren't due to gain control of their trust funds until age twenty-five. Dorsey made notes of their full names, including middle initials, their social security numbers, and the year of their birth. Setting down his pen and taking a long slow breath, he lifted the telephone receiver and punched in a local number. After six rings, a nervous sounding man answered.

"Teddy?" Dorsey asked. "How's it going? Any chance that the office is still open? Even if it isn't, I'd pay for you to reopen for the evening."

"This important? Really?" Teddy replied, his voice beginning to relax. "It has to be important, and when things are important they're usually expensive."

"Just name your price," Dorsey said, reminding himself that Meara was footing the bill.

"I will. You want me to call you with the results?"

"No, no," Dorsey told him, "I'm coming over. Here's the background you'll need." Into the telephone, Dorsey read his notes on the Filus twins.

* * *

Night had fallen completely when he parked the Buick in the unpaved driveway of a suburban home just west of the city limits. The house itself, Dorsey thought, was a miniature of the parish house at St. Anne's. Wooden frame painted white with green trim, it was a small house with dormer windows for added space on what must have been a cramped second floor. At the far end of the driveway was a matching garage. Between the house and garage's side door was a metal-framed breezeway that was covered to the ground by a striped canvas awning. The garage windows were painted black and cut into the side wall was an aperture that held an air-conditioner, humming and dripping run-off water. Dorsey counted three telephone lines coming into the structure. He knocked at a second door, opposite from the breezeway, and a shout told him to count to three slowly before entering. Ah, hell, Dorsey thought, Teddy was supposed to be getting better, what with the medication and all.

Teddy Majus, his gray-hair trimmed into a crewcut and dressed in a tanktop and a pair of ageless high school gym shorts, was seated at a computer printer with his back to Dorsey. "Is the door closed?" he asked. "Tell me when it's shut. All the way shut."

"I got it," Dorsey said, giving the knob an extra twist and click. "It's okay."

Teddy stood and turned to Dorsey, gesturing him into a cramped work area that was fully illuminated by high-intensity track lighting. The walls were lined with folding tables that held the components of a least three personal computers and cable lines ran to three modems mounted on the back wall. At the near end of one of the tables was a cardboard box filled with business cards that bore the heading I.D. INCORPORATED (INSURANCE DATABASES).

"How's business?" Dorsey asked, pulling up a folding metal chair and settling in.

"Comin' along," Teddy said, looking at him over the edges of his half-moon reading glasses. "It's coming along.

Word's out that I do a thorough job at the right price. Low overhead and no payroll to support.''

What a goddamned shame, Dorsey thought. Thaddeus Majus, the best claims examiner Backwell Insurance ever had. Hell, he was the best around. Until he came apart, or fell apart or had a breakdown. Dorsey smiled for a moment, thinking that all the polite terms for mental illness suggest that our brains are put together by tongue-and-groove work. But the joke was on Teddy and he wasn't laughing. Dorsey hadn't been there, but he had heard all about the crying and trembling and the paramedics who escorted Teddy from his office desk. He functioned, used all his knowledge of the profession, but only within his personally structured environment. Teddy Majus was a severe agoraphobic who hadn't seen unfiltered daylight in three years.

"So how'd you do for me?" Dorsey asked.

"All you could ask for," Teddy told him, and took an oversized folder from a metal basket next to the laser printer. "These brothers leave a hell of a trail, if you know how to look for their tracks." He pulled over matching chairs for him and Dorsey and opened the folder. "Where do you want to begin?"

Dorsey shrugged. "The money, where else? That always seems to be the head waters for most troubles."

"Life insurance death benefit," Teddy said, handing over a printout. "Three hundred thousand dollars, paid out four months after the death of their father. Mutual of New Hampshire was the carrier. Looks like it was a credit card rider. Accidental Death and Dismemberment.''

Dorsey looked over the printout and thought over how easy it must have been. Your credit card statement comes in with the offer of five-figure coverage on AD&D for pennies a month, the first three months of coverage free. Or the phone rings and a telephone solicitor from your credit card company makes the same offer. All you have to do is say yes or check the right box and name your beneficiaries. Then the premiums are just added to the monthly statement. Which presents a problem. David Filus was a CPA, just the type to closely scrutinize his monthly statement, his bill at a restaurant, and keep the receipt when he bought a gallon of milk.

"I know what you're thinking," Teddy told him. "It was a Visa card from one of the thousands of banks in Delaware, the land of credit. And just after it was issued, probably resulting from a blind offer in the mail, a change-in-address was sent in. The statements have been going to a post-office box in Brooke, West Virginia. Other than a few purchases here and there, the only charge has been the premium."

So, Dorsey thought, unless he asked for a full credit report on himself, very unlikely, David Filus would have never known about the card or the policy. For the boys, it was just a matter of forging his name on the credit card and policy applications. The credit card people would never check it out and the folks at Mutual of New Hampshire wouldn't have given it a thought. Accidental Death and Dismemberment was a moneymaker, the next best thing to selling flight insurance at the airport. And murder, with no indication that the beneficiaries were involved, is considered an accident. In the wrong place at the wrong time. The claim investigation would have been a joke. Hell, a little operation like Mutual of New Hampshire might not even have a claims department. All that would have been required of the Filus twins was to provide that misplaced short death certificate with their claim forms. If an investigation had been done, the insurance company would have had a local independent investigator obtain the police report. A report that suggested a random shooting and theft and confirmed that the two beneficiaries were away at school, probably in their dorm room, cramming for tomorrow's psych exam.

"What else is there?" Dorsey asked, setting the printout next to him on the tabletop.

"Bank accounts," Teddy told him, again consulting the folder on his lap. "Checking accounts here, checking and savings at a bank in Wheeling. And get this, the Wheeling accounts have fake social security numbers on them. The names and approximate birth dates match up so it must be them. Must of thought they were being clever, real smart-asses. Between the two of them, there's still about eighty-five grand left in the accounts.''

Dorsey squirmed in his seat. He had known what to expect, but the truth never reveals itself gracefully in these matters. He wondered how Meara would take the news. Hey, Bill, if the Rosenthal theory doesn't impress Doug Turner, there's a little backup scenario I've put together. You'll love it. It's much closer to home than you might have liked, and Tommy Crimmins'll still have a bit of a smear, but the Father's indictment is very unlikely. Ah, shit.

"Teddy, how about the cars?' Dorsey asked. "Bill Sargent, the guy who put me on to most of this, he said they both had four-wheel-drive vehicles. Supposed to be nicely tricked-out, too.''

"Two Explorers,'' Teddy said, back into his file. "Purchased about a year and a half ago. What they call the Eddie Bauer editions. Maybe they look like rolling catalogs for expensive outdoor wear. Sort of a West Virginia–prep school hybrid is what I'm thinking. Registered in West Virginia, by the way.''

More meaningless trickery, Dorsey thought. Understanding how to go about collecting on the insurance, that showed some brains, a little knowledge of how those things worked. Maybe they picked that up from their father the CPA. But this other stuff, out of state registrations on the vehicles, fake social security numbers on bank accounts that had their real names and birth dates, that should embarrass even the most rank of amateurs. Did they dream that up themselves or were they getting sloppy advice from a real half-assed mentor?

"Now,'' Teddy said, handing a few more sheets to Dorsey, "there's nothing in the civil court records, in Pennsylvania or West Virginia, naming these two. But on the criminal side, they've been arrested together and singularly, in the area around Wheeling and that school they go to. Mostly drunk and disorderly charges. Bar fights, that sort of thing. Mark has a DUI conviction and did a few hours of community service. And Gregory Filus had a Protection From Abuse order slapped on him by a girl named Beth Feldman. He can't come within fifty feet of the girl without her having his ass hauled off to jail. Maybe a girlfriend he roughed up."

Might have harassed her, Dorsey thought, maybe even roughed her up, but she was no girlfriend. Not a girl named Feldman. Bill Sargent had said that the twins liked to kick ass, and that they had a particular hard-on for their Jewish schoolmates. So unless Greg and Beth were as star-crossed as Romeo and Juliet, this was no love affair that had gotten too physical. Poor girl just chose the wrong school and wrong semester. Higher education strikes again.

"You've put in a hell of a night, Teddy. What'd you have to do, push four buttons or five?"

"The art," Teddy told him, "the art is in knowing which four or five buttons to push."

Dorsey looked around the room. "I can see that. The right buttons, ten thousand dollars in computer equipment, and two or three telephone trunk lines. And, of course, years of experience."

"Oh, just a few years, with this machinery." Teddy closed the folder, straightening the contents, and turned it over to Dorsey. "The invoice is inside. Payment in thirty days, please."

"Depends on my present employer's bookkeeping practices." Dorsey got to his feet. "Do the best I can."

"That's good enough," Teddy said. "I guess it'll have to be. Just remember, this was a rush job. No discounts, no negotiation on the bill."

"Sure, sure," Dorsey muttered, flipping through the folder. "Anything in here about gun registrations? Rifles, pistols, anything?"

"Nothing in Pennsylvania," Teddy said. He was on his feet now, moving about the room, shutting down monitors and flicking off one of the printers. "In West Virginia, who the hell knows? There's boys back in the hills secretly armed to the teeth, I'll bet. Some still have great-granddaddy's flintlock. You heading down that way, have a talk with the Filus boys?''

"That's the next logical move," Dorsey said, "get a look at them in the flesh."

"Better watch your ass."

"Damned straight," Dorsey replied, thinking he had a stop to make in the morning, just after the banks opened. "How do you want to work this? Me leaving here, I mean."

"Gimme a minute," Teddy said, turning away from Dorsey.

Dorsey opened the door and stopped. "Teddy, man, you ever miss going outdoors? Ever want to try it."

"I miss it like hell," Teddy said, still facing the far wall. "But I don't want to try it. It scares me shitless. Just the thought."

23

At the stroke of nine the next morning, Dorsey stepped through the doors of the Iron and Glass Bank on Carson Street and made the necessary arrangements to get his safety deposit box. Alone in a private viewing room, he removed the purple felt Crown Royale sack and loosened the gold-colored drawstring. He reached inside and extracted a revolver, a Meridian break-top six-shooter, and loaded it with the .38 shells that weighed down the bottom of the sack. Once the gun was in his waistband and covered by the tail of his sport shirt, Dorsey went back to the purple sack and took out a spring-loaded switchblade with a four-inch cutting surface concealed in the handle. He checked the mechanism, working the toggle that released the blade, sending it forward and locking it in position. Satisfied that it would respond if called upon, Dorsey worked the blade back into its hidey-hole, dropped the knife into the hip pocket of his khaki shorts, and returned the metal box to its perch in the vault.

Dorsey headed south on Interstate 79 from Pittsburgh, moving toward that concrete gash of a right angle where it met I-70 west at Little Washington. From there he would proceed into the West Virginia panhandle, a finger of land that rode along the Ohio River, slipped between Pennsylvania and Ohio. Brooke College, by his reckoning, sat about twenty miles short of Wheeling. And at Brooke College, hard at work in football training camp, were the Filus twins.

Dorsey wondered what type of madness he would find there. What level of violence had the two linebackers reached over the last few years? You'll find out, he told himself. That's what the hardware is for. For the unknown, which can be pretty damned scary.

The hardware, that was the term his last partner at the DA's office had used the day they had lifted the gun and knife from the evidence locker. It was his partner's last week before retirement and the theft had been a last prank of sorts, the bestowing on Dorsey of throwaway pieces in case he ever found himself in a shooting that needed an explanation. Like the shooting of an unarmed man. The weapons had been used by a deranged college student at Pitt who had killed a classmate for his Norton's literary anthology. Well boys, Dorsey thought, addressing the gun and knife, we're headed back to school.

Dorsey took the interstate to Wheeling and backtracked eastward to Brooke College, traveling across two-lane county roads dug along hillsides and dropping to the flat bottoms of hollows. He crossed three very thin silver-and-rust bridges that spanned the same meandering creek, stopping twice to make room for delivery trucks coming from the opposite direction. Along the roadside, which was often obscured by the encroachment of trees and wild vegetation, were occasional patches of homes, mostly trailers, huddled around dirt driveways that showed signs of being dug and redug each spring. Just as the road signs told him that the school was only a mile away, Dorsey encountered a stretch of straight and severely inclined road, straining the Buick's engine as had the trips up South 18th Street. It reminded Dorsey of a bar argument he had seen years before between a fellow from Morgantown and a Pittsburgh native. The fellow from Morgantown had just been called a hoopie, the favorite derogative used for West Virginia residents. In reply, he told the Pittsburgh native to take a look around, to take a close look at his hometown. "It's the same hills," he had said, pointing the neck of a beer bottle at the other man. "You've got the same fuckin' geography, y'all just put houses on top of 'em. I'm a hoopie, and you're nothing but a fuckin' urbanized hoopie.''

The college, quiet without the student body, was constructed on the ridges around the town of Brooke, which Dorsey found to be little more than a village sitting in a hollow. Translating it for himself into approximately six city blocks, Dorsey did two laps through the town, noting a small grocery store and a collegiate-looking bar mixed into the brick or wood-framed homes. He made short stops at both.

"Never again, those two don't ever get back in this store." The elderly woman behind the grocery store counter shook her head, apparently disgusted with the Filus boys, if not with the entire student body that would soon invade her shop. "Shoplifters," she told Dorsey, "and smart-asses to boot. Catch 'em red-handed and there's no shame at what they're doing. No saying I'm sorry and paying for the merchandise or putting it back. Just a grin on their faces and out the door they go. With my goods. I would've had the constable on them, but that smile they both had was spooky. Weird is the only way to describe it. The kind that stays with you. Scary. I just avoid 'em. But they don't get back in here.''

Out on the sidewalk, Dorsey went back to the Buick, unloading the revolver from his waistband, where it had become sweaty and uncomfortable, and locking it into the glove compartment. He hustled across the street and went into the bar, a single large room cluttered with rough wood tables and iron-backed chairs. At the far corner, standing beneath a directional sign that indicated the restrooms, were two lonesome looking pinball machines, dusty from a summer's lack of players. On the walls were pennants from Brooke College, their nearby small college rivals, and unplugged neon beer advertisements. And behind the bar was one of the largest and fattest men Dorsey had ever seen. He was sucking in air as he stocked a cooler with quarts of beer. Dorsey rested a haunch on a barstool and asked about the Filus boys.

"Take-out customers," the fat man said, setting aside his

work and mopping his face with a paper towel. "Best ones I have. That's how I prefer it, with those two, anyway. Silly, goofy bastards. Don't know how to act, especially around girls. Gross, that's what the girls call 'em. I hear they do their outside beer drinkin' up the road at the Gardens, which nobody seems to mind. There's not many girls up there. Mostly local boys go there."

"Ever hear about the two of them being involved in any fights?" Dorsey asked.

"Not recently," the fat man said, setting his wide ass against the backbar, causing the wall studding to groan under the strain. "Last winter I think there was something. Something to do with a fraternity over at West Liberty State. Those two aren't all bad, I suppose. Good ballplayers, from what I hear. Somebody said they made all-conference last year."

The fat man gave Dorsey directions to the football field and told him it was within walking distance. "Not for me," he said, "but you look like you're up to it."

With the exception of a few maintenance men putting a coat of dark green paint on the bleachers and repairing the track surface that enclosed the playing field, Dorsey found the place to be empty. He did an about-face and went back to the Buick, cranked down the windows, and drove up and out of the village, hoping to create a slipstream of cool air. On the ridge top was a long classroom building of dark stone academia and beyond that were several dormitories and the campus library. Only one of the dormitories, large and modern-looking, appeared occupied, and Dorsey pulled the Buick to the front curb. Sunbathing on the front lawn, clothed only in shorts, were two out-sized youths, arms and chests expanded from hours spent in the weightroom. Dorsey approached them and asked if the Filus boys were housed inside.

"Supposed to be in Room two-eleven," one of the sunbathers said, his face held to the sky, eyes closed. "But you won't find them there. Go up if you want, but they have a place, a farmhouse, where they stay most of the time. There might be some of their stuff up there in the room, but I kinda doubt it.''

Dorsey decided to check the room and made for the front door. "Almost forgot," the sunbather called after him. "Both of them are on a three-day suspension from the team.''

"What's that all about?'' Dorsey asked, turning back to him.

"Beat the shit out of some freshman punter. A guy named Grossman.''

Two-eleven was at the end of a tile-floored hall and was cleaned out, for the most part. The only furnishing was an ancient-looking refrigerator with a beer tap driven into the door. Inside was a keg attached to hosing that led into the door wall. Okay, Dorsey thought, the boys move out and the team uses the room for the community keg. Some good is coming out of these two.

Dorsey checked the closets and found them empty. The cinderblock walks were unadorned but he could tell that they had been freshly whitewashed with cheap paint. Unintelligible graffiti was struggling back to the surface, but Dorsey didn't get the message until he inspected the back of the room's door. Carved into the wood in six-inch block letters was the phrase LIBERATE THE Z.O.G.

Z.O.G. It was a term that Dorsey had heard only recently on a televised documentary. Learned it just in time, he thought, how goddamned lucky can one guy be. Z.O.G., Zionist Occupied Government. A government that needed saving from those rich banker-intellectual-internationalist Jews that congregate along the East Coast. A term used by right-wing militants. So Greg and Mark were planning to liberate the Z.O.G., and the plan was to start off by beating the shit out of the Jew closest at hand. Like the guys in high school. Or Grossman the punter. Or that poor co-ed Feldman. But Dave Filus was Catholic. So maybe they're not to blame. How fortunate, maybe they're not killers. Just anti-Semitic, asocial psychotics. Which should certainly put everyone's mind to rest.

Back outside, Dorsey hit up the sunbather for directions to the farmhouse. "You know the street were the bar is? Okay, just keep going straight out of town on Route 331, headed east. You cross two bridges and then you'll see the Gardens, right by the creek side. Go another hundred, hundred and fifty yards, you'll see the farm house. Left side of the road, away from the creek."

"Thanks," Dorsey said, heading for the Buick.

"Makes no difference to me what your business is with them two," the sunbather said, propped up on both elbows. "But you better watch your ass. What's your name? You know, in case you don't make it back."

"Murray Benkovitz," Dorsey told him.

Following Route 331 as instructed, Dorsey passed over the two metal-and-concrete bridges back into a heavily wooded countryside. The foliage was thick with several shades of green, and the air had the near-jungle smell of moist plant life. The smell he had heard about in the army, from brother soldiers fresh back from Vietnam. The big party he had missed, despite four years in the service during those worst of times. Thank God, Dorsey told himself, thank God that invitation never arrived. Even if it's become fashionable to have been there and survived. But then it's always fashionable, and romantic, to be among the damaged.

The trees gave way to a poorly mowed lawn that sloped downward to the creek bed. There were a few old picnic tables and just beyond the lawn was a red painted shack with a plywood sign, hand painted the same red color, that read BEER GARDENS. Dorsey pulled into the parking lot on the far side of the shack, leaving the Buick between the only other parked cars, a Dodge pickup and a white Ford Explorer, Eddie Bauer edition.

Dorsey stepped into the shack, expecting to get his first look at at least one of the Filus twins. The inside consisted of a small bar counter, two tables at a window looking out over the creek, and a back screen door leading out to the lawn. Behind the bar was an elderly woman talking to her lone customer, an equally old man dressed in matching workman's greens. Dorsey went to the bar, tried to order a Rolling Rock but had to settle for a pint bottle of Iron City Mountaineer. He commented on how slow things seemed to be.

"Just us," the woman said, setting herself onto a stool of her own behind the bar. " 'Course it's early yet. After three, that's when the road asphalt crews come in. Till then it's just us in here and that bunch outside." She nodded her chin toward the screen door.

Dorsey went to the screen door, peered outside, and saw what had to be Mark and Greg sitting in the sun, resting themselves atop one of the picnic tables. They were the Beefers, all right. Indistinguishable at this distance, they both had freshly shaved heads, save for a small tail at the neckline. Hard muscled with heavy shoulders and legs, they were dressed in cut-off fatigue pants; one of them wore a tanktop and there were quarts of beer at their sides. Accompanying them were two dark-haired girls that looked about high school age. Both girls were giggling and seemed to be admiring the tattoos that wrapped about one of the boy's legs.

Must've just missed them, Dorsey thought. They must have gone out as you came in. The woman behind the bar interrupted his thoughts.

"Those are good boys out there," she said, directing her words at Dorsey. "May look a bit funny, even scary, but they're okay. Always behave themselves in here. Get along with everybody. That's why I trust them with the beer around them girls, who really shouldn't be here anyways. They won't share with the girls, you'll see."

Don't need to give up any beer, Dorsey thought, the tattoos seem to be working just fine. Ought to do the trick on their own. "Look like football players," Dorsey said. "They're from the school, I guess."

"Yeah, they play for the school," the woman said. "Must be a day off from practice, though. They usually don't get here till later. Anyways, they just got here."

Good, that's good, Dorsey told himself, slugging down

most of the pint. This way he'd have some time to look around.

Dorsey drove out of the parking lot and headed east, keeping the speedometer around twenty miles per hour. The farmhouse was almost totally obscured by the heavy thicket, and he nearly passed the site before he noticed the beginning of a dirt driveway. He stopped for a moment and took in the partial outline of a small house through the leaves, then went on another thirty yards until he found a bare spot at the berm on the opposite side of the road. After pulling the Buick as far as possible away from the road, the front end covered by low-hanging tree limbs, Dorsey trotted back to the driveway and headed inward. The driveway was only fifteen or so feet long and hidden within the shade was the second Explorer, navy blue in color. It was parked at the side of a one-story brick house that was quickly losing its coat of dull yellow paint. The widows on either side of the front door were trimmed in a dirty white and had screens propping them open. Dorsey tried the door first, but found it locked. Bright boys, very bright. He eased up one of the windows, slipped the collapsible screen from the sill, and heaved one leg inside.

All the way in, Dorsey unfolded to full height and found himself back in basic training. The room's floor was bare wood and the furnishings consisted of a cot with gray wool blanket, foot locker in its proper position at the end of the cot, and a metal upright locker by the wall, all of which had clearly been purchased at a war surplus store. Dorsey tried the footlocker, found it padlocked, and moved on to the upright locker. Inside the unsecured door hung two sets of fatigues, one pair of tiger pants left over from Southeast Asia, and three drab olive T-shirts. On the single shelf were toiletry items and a green paperback book, plain military lettering across its front cover. Dated as being issued in the mid-1980s, it was an army-prepared manual on interrogation techniques to be used against insurgent forces. Dorsey remembered hearing of this in the news as well, manuals issued to our democratic partners in Central America. Why the hell didn't these two just enlist and leave the rest of us alone?

Curious over the padlocked footlocker, Dorsey fished around in his pocket for the switchblade. He worked the blade tip into the padlock's keyhole and tried, unsuccessfully, to spring it. Frustrated, he gave up the effort, put the knife away in his pocket, and moved through the house. Beyond the bedroom door was a short hall that led to a kitchen, which held two chairs and a flimsy-looking card table. A second bedroom and the front door were beyond that. No bathroom, Dorsey thought. These guys are into serious training.

The second bedroom mirrored the first, with the exception of double-doored cabinets hanging on the far wall. Dorsey fingered his way through the upright locker and found the same clothes and toiletries but no interrogation manual. The footlocker was padlocked so Dorsey moved on to the wall cabinets.

The cabinets had a veneer of plastic oak and opened outward from the center. Dorsey checked for locks and booby-traps, his paranoia increasing, then took hold of the handles. What he found inside was a madman's shrine. "Fuckin' Adolf, goddamned Schickelgruber," Dorsey muttered. "Should've guessed that you'd be in on this."

The cabinet was shallow, about four inches deep, and the shelving had been stripped out. On the back wall were four photos, apparently pages torn from a variety of history textbooks. At the base was a fullfaced shot of Adolf Hitler, clearly a posed shot for a state occasion. Above him were three smaller photos, all of which had names captioned beneath. Dorsey recognized Himmler immediately, his neck held straight, that thin mustache in perfect trim, the monocle screwed into his eye. The next photo was of an older man, Julius Striecher, publisher and ideologue of the party, Dorsey recalled. The final shot was of Adolf Eichmann and Dorsey pictured the man in his Berlin office, manipulating train schedules, commandeering rolling stock, and reviewing the latest report on a newly developed lethal gas.

At first, the arrangement of the photos seemed odd to Dorsey, as if they constituted an inverted organizational chart of the party. But then again, he told himself, think of the designers, that's why these three have ascendancy over the Fuhrer. Striecher, the man who spent so much time dreaming up this shit and putting it into attractive words. Himmler and Eichmann, the men of action, like Mark and Greg. The ones who had the supposed strength to carry out their duty, the necessary dirty work that would result in a better, cleaner world.

Inside the left door, secured with thumbtacks at the corners, was a map of eastern Europe. It didn't take much guessing as to its purpose once Dorsey had read the names of the circled towns. Sobibor, Birkenau, Thereisenstadt. Maybe after college, Dorsey thought, maybe after graduation, these two plan on making their version of the Grand Tour of Europe.

The inside of the right door, for Dorsey, was much worse. Near the center was a brown leather wallet, pinned to the wood with a penknife. The wallet's edges were eaten away and the corners were green with mold. With these signs of age, Dorsey could think of only one person whose billfold had gone missing. About three years ago.

Dorsey yanked out the penknife and caught the wallet as it fell. Using the tiny blade, he worked his way through the contents. There were sixty-three dollars in cash and a three-year-old bus pass for the month of November. These boys are slipping, Dorsey thought. Those heroes of theirs in the cupboard had always made use of the victim's valuables, right down to the gold teeth and eyeglasses. In the identification compartment was a driver's license, American Express and Visa cards, and a donor card from the Central Blood Bank. All belonging to David Filus. Dorsey noted, absentmindedly, that Filus had a B+ blood type.

Pretty ballsy, Dorsey thought, holding on to a souvenir from a killing. A souvenir that was the only connecting evidence, short of a murder weapon, to the shooting. Held on to it for three years, with never a fear of discovery, because the police had always blamed some black junkie, a member of the other subhuman class. Damn it, they've got balls. And one other thing is for sure. We all owe an apology to Chick Rosenthal.

Dorsey thought about taking the wallet, then thought about a breaking-and-entry charge he might face with the local sheriff and pinned the wallet back in place. He slipped the cabinet doors shut and decided to make a quick search of the kitchen.

"I'm Greg."

Dorsey pivoted and found the shirtless twin framed in the doorway. The boy's right hand was extended, and in it was the revolver Dorsey had left in the Buick's glove compartment.

"The big mouth old lady at the Gardens, right?" Dorsey asked.

"Yeah," Greg said, calmly. "She said you seemed pretty interested in us. Told us you didn't say much, but you seemed curious. And you drank up and left in a hurry."

Dorsey fought an internal battle to remain composed. "I'm not the only one interested in you, and in your father's death. There's a new DA who thinks it was a family matter, done by a relative. The black-junkie theory is out the window. I was sent here to see what you might have on hand. So my presence here is well-known. I can't just disappear. That won't work for you. Maybe you can take off, make a run for it. But if I don't show my face somewhere soon, you'll be in trouble just that much faster. Give it some thought."

Greg held his thoughts for a moment, then shouted his brother's name. "He's in here! Get in here, we gotta think about stuff!"

Dorsey heard the front door being unlocked and then Mark Filus came into the room. Twirling his key ring in his hand, he seemed to take Dorsey's measure before tapping on his brother's shoulder and whispering in his ear. Greg nodded at Mark's words, then turned to his brother's ear and gave a near silent response. Jesus Christ, Dorsey thought, these guys should be in a laboratory, their brains wired and strapped down into matching chairs. Hell, they act like they're joined at the hip.

"You've seen our stuff?" Mark asked, as if taking his turn at speech.

Dorsey shrugged. "Yeah, I've pretty much seen most everything, I guess. But I was just telling your brother, Greg, killing me won't get you anywhere. The law is on to you, why else would I be here?"

"You're no cop," Greg said, "nothing in your car says you're a cop. Especially the car."

Shit, Dorsey found himself thinking despite his fear, I don't make fun of your car. "Naw, I'm not a cop, that's the good thing for you. Cops don't go places alone. But what I said was true, the cops are on to you and they're not far behind. You've got my car, there's no phone in this place, and the woman at the Gardens doesn't care for me. I can't alert anyone, so you can take off, get a good head start. You've got the equipment, probably trained yourselves for it. The two of you could get back into these hills and never be found. Leave me here and take your stuff, burn the wallet. It's the only connection. Do it. Just take off."

Dorsey watched another whispered conference, each brother taking his turn, after which Mark produced a green paperback from his back pocket. Dorsey figured it for another copy of the army's interrogation techniques. This wasn't good. These sick bastards saw the opportunity to try a few things out.

Mark went to the room's footlocker, freed the padlock with his key, and came away with an army-issue bayonet and police nightstick. He stepped around his brother and went into the kitchen. Greg gestured for Dorsey to come forward and backed out of the room. Dorsey moved ahead, feeling the switchblade's weight at the bottom of his hip pocket, hoping they were too intent on their plans to search him and wondering if he might get a chance to use it. And wondering if he could make use of it if the chance came. He had always done his best to keep his few violent moments at his own chosen level and on his terms, allowing time for mental preparation. This time it might be a cold start. When he got into the hall, Greg waved him into the kitchen with the gun barrel.

"Just grab a seat," Greg told him, indicating the card table with chairs.

Dorsey turned for the table but never got there. First there was the sunburst of pain from his lower back, the result of a sold rabbit punch to the kidney with the nightstick. Next came a blow to the back of the knees that sent him forward, his forehead catching wood slivers as it hit the bare floor. And the beating went on, without break, for the next ten minutes. Kicks to the back, punches to the face.

24

On the floor with his back to the wall, Dorsey took a physical inventory, evaluating his situation. His nose remained intact, but the swelling beneath both his eyes was growing. The three previously fractured fingers of his right hand had been stomped and now appeared dislocated. A tightness was gripping his bad knee and he had thoughts of blood streaming into the joint space. But most of all, he sensed the weight of the switchblade in his hip pocket.

Watching the twins standing across the room, studying their manual, Dorsey was surprised by his ability to think straight and amazed at his mind's capacity to compartmentalize all that was going on. The pain was real and God how it sang out to him. He fully realized the extent of the danger he was in and panic was creeping in from the edges. But a third portion of his consciousness, the spectator mind, allowed him to observe and evaluate the other two. It allowed him to take in all that was around him. And it allowed him to plan and look for opportunities.

"That was to prove the seriousness of our intent," Mark said, pointing out a passage in the manual to his brother. He looked over at Dorsey. "It's a necessary stage in the process. Not just to soften you up for more. You probably noticed that neither one of us has asked any questions. We weren't supposed to before now. The whole idea was to show you how ruthless we are, how we're willing to beat the hell out of you for no reason. To scare the life out of you, make you beg to cooperate.''

Well, Dorsey thought, it worked. Score one for the army. ''Listen, you want to know something, just ask,'' Dorsey said, tasting the cuts inside his mouth. ''No shit, you ask and I'll answer, because this is completely unnecessary. What I know about you is not a military secret. I had to put a few things together, figure out a few things, but what I did doesn't come close to the splitting of the atom. So just cut me some slack here, and we can talk.''

Greg smiled and kept the gun leveled at Dorsey. ''Okay, first question. Who the fuck are you really?''

Dorsey rocked over onto one hip and undid one of his rear-flap pockets, taking out his wallet. He slid it across the floor to Greg's feet before he was told to do so. Anything, he thought, anything to avoid a frisk. The switchblade was hope, possible salvation.

Greg did a one-handed search of the contents and then gave it over to Mark with what Dorsey now took to be the required whispering between the two. ''Private Investigator, pretty neat shit, huh? Who you working for, and don't give me any of that client confidentiality bullshit.''

''Like that means something, here and now,'' Dorsey said, then proceeded with an abbreviated version as to how he ended up on their floor with the stuffing knocked out of him.

''They really got things all fucked up,'' Mark said, and looked to his brother, both of them grinning. ''The perfect crime. Three years go by and the geniuses who run this country still haven't figured it out. When the time comes, it's gonna be easier than anyone figures. The Take-Over is gonna happen fast.''

The Take-Over Dorsey thought, stretching his good leg, assuring himself of his remaining powers. The Take-Over must be the latest version of Come The Revolution. Somebody's been teaching them. Z.O.G., The Take-Over. The Point Breeze thugs have found themselves a guru down here in the woods. Nice to see the molding of raw material into the final product. Ah, Christ. The worst of humanity always knows where to find each other.

"So," Dorsey said, hoping to keep them talking and prolong the break in his interrogation, along with his life. "So, what do you say you tell me how we got to this sorry-assed state of affairs. How about your father? You guys did him in, right? For the insurance money?"

Greg kept the revolver pointed at Dorsey, apparently considering the issue before him. "What do you think?" he asked his brother, surprising Dorsey by speaking out loud to his brother. "We got to kill him anyways. No sense in being closed-mouthed about things."

Mark consulted his manual, seemingly to double-check an important point. "The book," Mark said, joining his brother in audible speech, "the book says we're supposed to keep him in the dark about most everything, like why we're even talking to him and who we are. It's supposed to heighten the sense of terror. It confuses the subject of the exercise. That way, they don't know which bits of information are important, they don't know what information has to be protected. But, I guess we've already gotten past that point. Shit, we did the best we could, considering the situation and what we had to work with."

"Sure," Greg said, "that's the best way to look at it. You know how it is, even the best instructions don't cover every situation. You have to be ready to improvise."

Dorsey found himself wondering if this was what it was like to be one of the newly convicted. The trial was over, the jury had returned a conviction, and now lawyers and judges were bargaining over your fate. Trying to determine how best to administer your sentencing. It was like being the elderly and now irrelevant relative who sits in the corner of the room while the rest of the family decides who gets him or whether there's a nursing home in his future, the discussion conducted as if he weren't even present. You better keep them talking. And you better find a way to bury the switchblade into Greg before he can get off a shot, thought Dorsey. Then work your way past Mark before it's over. Yeah, it's coming down to that.

"Well," Dorsey said, "your old man is dead and his missing wallet is pegged to the wall at the Nazi shrine in the next room. You two, unknown to just about everybody up until now, have made out pretty well from his death. Several hundred thousand each, new vehicles, and all the fatigue outfits you can handle. Then there's the trust accounts. C'mon boys, I've put a lot of time into this thing. You killed your father for the money, just say it."

The twins looked at each other and sly grins worked across each of their faces, followed by uncontrolled laughter. "You're getting close," Mark said, the words struggling to get out. He went back to his laughing and tossed the interrogation manual at the ceiling, letting it fall into one of the room's empty corners. "The money was good, though. We kept some for ourselves, a little reward for our effort, and the accomplishment. The rest will help finance the Take-Over. When it gets here. Think about that. Insurance company money, banker's money, Jew money, it's gonna be used to free the country."

"The country's true owners," Greg added. "White men, Christians."

An odd look passed between the twins, something conspiratorial yet also shame-faced, but Dorsey took only minor note of it as his mind filled in the story's gaps. Two amateur Jew and nigger haters, demented little bastards, graduate from high school and go out on their own. And the raw material they represent is noticed by a more practiced and darker mind. One that can add some ideology to the hate, give some kind of whacked-out rational basis to it. Then add just the right touch of messianic duty, murderous evangelism, and you've got two loyal soldiers anxious to prove themselves in battle. Militia, Free Americans, Aryans, these woods are probably full of them. Call them what you want. How about simpletons? Or maybe pissed-off white boys who twist reason and religion into a vehicle that reinforces their belief that they've been cheated out of something big.

Something that God meant for them. And guess what, Dorsey old boy, you just put yourself between them and what they want.

"This killing of your father," Dorsey asked, "was that supposed to be some type of initiation rite? Is that how city boys get themselves accepted by the good ole boys down here?"

Again, the expression of shame passed between the boys and this time it registered with Dorsey. What the hell is that? he thought, some twisted deep-down remorse? Like hell, not from these two. But it was an indication of a weakness, something that Dorsey was searching for. "The hell's the matter with you two? You look like you just had your wrists slapped, like you just got caught with your hands in your pants. C'mon, tell the dead man what's on your mind."

It looked like he had gone too far. The shamed faces turned red with anger, and Greg thumbed back the gun's hammer with a slow mechanical click. "Dead man, that's right, sooner the better." Fortunately Mark's composure seemed to return to him and he went to his brother and massaged the base of his neck. "Not yet," he whispered. "Things need to be done, but always in the proper way. Remember your discipline."

Dorsey watched the immediate storm pass, thinking again of the knife that uselessly weighed down his hip pocket, when he took in the sound of an automobile engine idling outside. The humming and whirl ended, followed by the opening and closing of car doors and the crunching of feet on gravel. Mark gave his brother a final pat on the shoulder and went to the hall and the front door.

"Of course," he said flatly, the door open a crack. "Of course, they would be the next ones to show up. Makes sense."

Dorsey was at a loss. Cops, maybe? Or a few of the twins' fellow travelers with the shovels that would prepare his eternal resting place? Despite the gun that Greg still pointed at him, Dorsey worked his shoulders into the wall and used his good leg like a tire jack, cranking himself into an unsteady standing position. He tried some weight on his injured knee, found it could take a little, and decided that he had gone as far as he could. Hell, let's see who's come acalling.

Mark flung open the door and stepped aside. "Your friend is already here. We haven't done much with him yet."

Louise Filus stepped into the small corridor and came into the kitchen. Instinctively lowering his head as he passed through the doorway, Father Crimmins followed close behind.

25

Father Crimmins moved ahead of Louise, disregarded the twins, and helped Dorsey to one of the chairs at the kitchen table. He had a grip on Dorsey's left arm and shoulder and together they moved slowly, Dorsey trying his left knee, at first with resistance and then finishing the step with more confidence. Once in the chair, Dorsey kept his hands below the tabletop.

"Where have you been the last few days?" Dorsey asked. "People were starting to wonder. And worry."

"Let's look after you first," Louise Filus said. She took a handkerchief from the blue cotton shorts she was wearing, soaked it at the kitchen sink, and washed Dorsey's face. As she did so, he could see the looks of disgust in the faces of the twins. "Put that gun away," Louise told Greg.

"I'll hold on to it," Greg said, but he let the gun fall to his side, his grip loosened. Dorsey took careful notice.

Louise addressed herself to Dorsey and his care. "We thought you might come down here. Tom spoke to Bill Sargent and he mentioned your conversation the other night. We've been at Wilson Lodge, it's on the road into Wheeling. It's a good place to get away from things. We figured if Tom couldn't go back to the parish house, if he had to stay away, well, we could use the time. To talk and all."

Dorsey let her finish with his face and then took the moist handkerchief and pushed it through his hair. "There's a lot of talking still to be done. Let's just try to do it without my taking any more of a beating. What do you think?''

"We were practicing,'' Mark said, holding the bayonet by the grip, leaving the nightstick on the tabletop. ''Questioning techniques. We needed whatever intelligence we could get from this person. It was the perfect opportunity.''

Dorsey let the handkerchief slip onto the table and returned his hands to his lap, apparently unnoticed. He looked to Father Crimmins who was leaning against the wall. ''What the hell is going on here, Father? Any comments, conclusions? We've got two private sector Green Berets living in the woods and faking their way through a college education. In the next room is a shrine to some long-dead false gods and enough evidence to send these two to death row by express train. Early yesterday, I met with a guy in the park and had you in the clear. And then I spoke to Alice Sutton, who has a personal hard-on for you, and she mentioned a photo she had of you and Louise admiring a .38 revolver. So I make two stops and then come here. Where I get the shit kicked out of me. C'mon, you've got to have something to say.''

''You've seen the evidence,'' Father Crimmins said. ''These two boys killed their father.''

''That's it? Things are that simple for you?'' Dorsey fell back into his chair and made a show of shoving his hands deep into his pockets, disgusted. Pain roared through the damaged fingers of his right hand and Dorsey bit into the inside of his cheek. But he had his working thumb and forefinger on the knife hilt. So, he thought, what the hell happens next?

Father Crimmins came off the wall, stepped between Greg and Mark, tapping each of them on the shoulder, asking for more room. Mark held on to the bayonet, and Father Crimmins sat down.

''No, things aren't that simple. Well, they weren't that simple,'' the priest said. ''But I had to make them simple, just to survive this. This is how I did it, and it worked, at least until Turner started his investigation. And then you had to follow up, too. It's what kept me sane, and in the church, but it looks like that's all changed.

"Murder is a sin, and sin is a simple matter of temptation and the giving into that temptation," Father Crimmins said. "That simplicity is what makes the possibility of forgiveness and redemption such a logical next step. If anyone understands redemption's power, it's someone like me—who got himself into an army jail cell and found God there. You're right, it's a horrible and ugly crime. But at the same time, and this may seem very strange, don't make more out of it than it already is. Spiritually, universally speaking. In terms of Eternity, this is nothing that can not be gotten past." Father Crimmins gave Dorsey a grin that fell flat. "Our biblical heros," the priest said, "they spent an awful lot of time and effort cheating and injuring their family members. And always receiving a measure of forgiveness."

"Some punishment, as well," Dorsey said. He used his apparent interest to draw closer to the table's edge without notice.

"True," Father Crimmins said. "But even Cain, with the shame and punishment he had to endure, was given the mark of God to protect him."

Dorsey couldn't argue with the priest's spiritual position. It was what any believer would want for himself, and Dorsey was a believer. In God, in Jesus Christ, the Son of God. Despite cynicism, and wise-ass comments and Sunday mornings spent in a warm bed instead of a wooden church pew. He had been through sixteen years of Catholic education and training, and he knew full well that was a coat of paint that could never be scraped away. Once in, never out. But, Dorsey told himself, you also happen to be a true believer with a smashed hand, wobbly knee, and stuck in a room with two armed maniacs. So try to deal with the immediate situation. Get past this, and there'll be plenty of time for meditation. He brought the knife hilt nearer to the lip of his pocket.

"What about you?" Dorsey asked. "What about you and Louise?"

"I don't understand," Father Crimmins said, shooting a quick glance at Louise.

"Your involvement in all this," Dorsey said. "You are involved, right? Your presence in this room sort of indicates a connection." Dorsey went on to fully describe his conversation with Alice Sutton.

"We found out soon after," Louise said, folding her arms about her, warding off a shiver in the stuffy, overheated room. "I found the gun, by accident, in their dormitory after a football game. They beat Carnegie-Mellon that day. Shut them out."

Dorsey hunched his shoulders forward and let his head hang. Well, he thought, perhaps this society does put too much emphasis on sports. He also managed to get the knife onto his lap without detection.

"I took it to Tom and we discussed the matter," Louise said. "I suppose that's when Alice the Snoop got that picture she told you about. Anyway, we discussed it for days, almost turned the whole thing over to the police, really we did. But then we didn't see the sense in destroying their lives, too. David was gone, he wasn't coming back no matter what was done, and if no one else was blamed for the killing, we decided that we could handle it as a family. You probably think that's crazy, but these are my boys. So I don't care what you think."

"And the gun?" Dorsey asked her. "Whatever became of that?"

Father Crimmins answered. "Over the side of the Kinzua Dam. I had a retreat weekend in a cabin for some of the men in the parish. Up near Warren. I made a little side trip." The priest grinned sheepishly. "Like I said, I'm good at tactics."

Dorsey pictured the dam, an engineering landmark in the middle of the Allegheny National Forest. Near the headwaters of the Allegheny River. Hell, they won't find that gun until after the next ice age. "These boys killed their father," Dorsey said. "For money. To finance the Takeover."

Greg laughed first and then Mark joined him. Dorsey shot a look at Louise, who blushed and turned away. Father Crimmins had his eyes on the tabletop, his fingernail working at a chip in the cardboard surface. "The money was a nice bonus," Mark said, toying with the bayonet, applying the tip to a pane in the kitchen window. A thin white scratch line remained behind.

"Bonus?" Dorsey asked, his thumb playing at the blade release in the knife hilt. "The money wasn't enough for you two?"

"He had to go," Greg said. "He had to feel the consequences of his actions, to feel the pain he caused for us. As a race defiler."

"Tom," Dorsey said, addressing the priest. "What in the hell are these two talking about?"

Father Crimmins's gaze came even with Dorsey. "Louise is a Catholic convert. She was born to a Jewish family. To these guys, she's the enemy. She's a Jew."

26

"**So,**" **Dorsey** told the two boys, "you fellas are half Jewish and you also happen to hate Jews like your glorious leader has taught you. Ever give any thought to sparing your father and just killing yourselves? Or maybe just having a few parts of your body cut away in hopes of removing the Hebrew portions?"

"Fuck you, man," Greg said, momentarily leveling the pistol's muzzle at Dorsey. "She can't help what she is," he indicated his mother by waving the gun, "and me and Mark can't do anything about it, either. But my father knew what he was doing and he went ahead and did it. Mixing the blood. Now Mark and I have to live with it through no fault of our own. We can never be true brothers to the people that we belong with spiritually."

"So you have to try harder," Dorsey said. "To prove yourselves worthy of something you can't have because of blood. The loyal outsiders, tools of the masters. That's why your old man had to get it in the head."

"Exactly," Mark said, still holding the bayonet. "You got it figured out, even if you're too much of a goddamned fool to see the need for it. Blind son-of-a-bitch."

Beneath the table, Dorsey practiced his grip on the knife, testing his strength and holding his right wrist with his left hand, searching for the best support and leverage. His knee and hand ached but they were losing the competition with the anxiety that was playing at his spine and shoulders. He feared a muscle twitch or spasm might give away what little chance he had. "This situation," he asked the priest, "you felt you could handle this as a family matter?"

Father Crimmins looked about the room, seeming to take in all of the occupants, giving each a moment's consideration. "Strange as this may sound," the priest said, "yes, yes I did. I already gave you my spiritual reasons, but I did it just as much for Louise as anything else."

"So what you're saying," Dorsey told him, "is that if I came into the parish house and told you I just shot somebody, you'd counsel me to turn myself in and take it like a man. With the support of God and the Church, every step of the way. But if it so happens that you're banging my mother on the side"—Dorsey paused and gave each of the twins a sly grin—"well, if that's the case, it might be your advice that I keep things to myself, right?"

Both Greg and Mark began to close in on Dorsey, responding to his taunt, and Father Crimmins quickly got to his feet, giving each of them a gentle push backward. Dorsey had little in the way of a plan, but he knew he had to draw both of the maniacs close if he hoped to make use of his knife. Greg had to go first, the gun had to be taken out. Then, maybe, there could be enough of a scramble to try something on Mark. Dorsey knew the situation too well. They were both armed and had twenty years of youth and strength on him. And he told himself, they have every intention of killing you. Crimmins can't stop them. He wants to, he might even get physical, old bad-ass soldier that he is, but he can't do a thing without endangering his deal with Louise. So it's up to you. Sit on your ass and die or take the shot. So take the shot. Play out the scene if you have to, but take the shot.

"Well," Dorsey said, looking up at the three of them, "the past is the past. So let's move on to new business. I'm sitting here in front of a guy with a gun, one with a government-issue knife, and a priest. Looks like we've got the makings for Last Rites, a killing, and then the funeral. All in one convenient location."

"Don't be so dramatic," Father Crimmins said, leaning forward, his arms supporting him at the table's edge. "This is where things stop. You've caught up with them, and that's it." He looked away from Dorsey and settled on Louise, standing behind Dorsey at the wall. He shrugged his shoulders.

"The fuck it is!" Mark shouted, driving the tip of the bayonet into the cardboard tabletop. The flimsy material gave little resistance, dramatizing the action to the point that Greg again leveled the gun at Dorsey. "This is just the fuckin' beginning, goddamned silly-ass priest. You think this is your church? See any altar wine around here?" He pointed downward at Dorsey, jabbing his finger in the air. "This fucker is gonna die, understand? Me and my brother, we're too important. Jesus, can't you see that? We've made connections down here with the right people. We've got a part in things."

Father Crimmins pulled himself to his full height. Dorsey's eyes stayed fixed on the bayonet. He sent up a silent prayer that it would remain in place for the next few minutes.

"Mark," the priest said, looking at the boy. "I can't listen to this—this madness of your's anymore. You've got to see the reality of this situation. This isn't war games, you're nobody's soldier. I was one, remember? Nobody knows better than I what it's like, what it takes, where it takes you. This game of yours killed your father, for God's sake. A game that makes you think you're a soldier, a soldier for an evil idea. No more, Mark. No more."

"We've got a mission," Greg said, his voice low, almost forlorn.

"What?" Father Crimmins said, turning first to Greg and then back to Mark. "What's he saying?"

"Yeah, let's hear this one," Dorsey said. He held the knife between his knees, ready to release the blade.

"When the time comes," Mark explained, "when the Take-over happens, we'll play a part in it. And I'm talking about a couple of things. We're gonna be part of the Take-over, we've got an assignment, a government building to seize. And then afterwards, there'll be work to clean up the filth and make the country work like it should. A lot of people are gonna have to go. And this Dorsey guy is gonna be first. Only the first. Of many.''

''End of discussion, I guess,'' Dorsey said, addressing Father Crimmins. The bayonet was still in the tabletop; the gun was still pointed at him. ''But believe me, it's great to have a priest so close, me being at my final hour and all.''

''Louise?'' Father Crimmins said. ''These are your sons, you have to say something.''

Louise Filus came to her son Mark's side, running a hand lightly under his chin. ''How did you ever get like this? Both of you, how did this happen?''

''How'd it happen?'' Mark said, a grin taking over his face. ''It happened for the best. Understand, Jew? It happened for the best.''

''For the best,'' Greg repeated and laughed. ''For the best.''

The blood dropped from Louise Filus's face and her knees caved, dropping her against the sink and then down to the floor. What's so surprising? Dorsey thought, they already killed your husband, even if you were stepping out on him.

Then the moment came and Dorsey pushed aside all the bullshit and fear, his thoughts reuniting from their compartments. Survival. Stay alive. Take them out. Kill the gunman first.

Father Crimmins pushed past Mark to get to Louise, unwittingly running interference between Mark and the bayonet. Greg reached out his empty left hand, grabbing at the priest's back, apparently to yank him back into place. It was a long stretch and his right arm, with gun in hand, went backward for balance, away from Dorsey. Fuck it all, Dorsey thought, one mind with one purpose, and with his left hand he shoved the card table up and away, flying in the direction of Father Crimmins. The muscles of his right leg were bunched and the knee joint cocked, carrying his full weight. On command, the blade was released from its hilt. His left hand joined with his right and Dorsey pushed off, jettisoning himself from the chair, his body uncoiling and directing itself at a soft spot beneath Greg's chin. The hope was for the blade to enter on a slight upward tilt, as Dorsey had been taught by his army hand-to-hand instructor, and proceed through the windpipe into the brain stem, severing it and ending all motor function. It was a good thrust, with Dorsey missing only enough to allow Greg a few dying twitches. But it was a much too powerful one, and the blade passed through Greg's neck, snapped away from the handle, and pegged the boy to the wall behind him. Dorsey fell forward into the body then slipped to the floor, his eyes darting about, searching for the gun that the dead twin had dropped. He spotted it a few feet away, leaning against the baseboard, and awkwardly tried to get to his feet until his left knee buckled. Flat on his chest, he leveraged himself with his elbows, looking like a frog, and plopped himself on the weapon, taking it in his left hand.

By the time Dorsey had managed to roll onto his back, Father Crimmins was flat on his own in the far corner. Louise crouched beside him, checking his injuries. Dorsey figured he had tangled with Mark and lost, and he said a prayer that he would survive to ask the priest if he'd gotten in any good shots himself. But it was quickly back to the business at hand when he saw that Mark had pulled the bayonet from the tabletop and was approaching. Dorsey pointed the gun at him from the floor, left elbow locked, his whole being still intent on remaining alive.

"This is it kid," Dorsey told him between gulps of air. "One time deal, offer expires immediately. Set the bayonet on the floor."

Mark grinned and took another step forward. Dorsey shot him in the stomach. And he continued until the revolver was empty and Mark was on the floor. Jesus Christ, he thought, you made it. Against this whole crazy bunch. You made it. What kinda fuckin' family did you get yourself mixed up with?

27

Dorsey watched summer give way to autumn from one of the two white patio chairs in his backyard. Facing the alleyway toward the river and the bluffs that towered over the distant bank, he watched his patches of grass slowly move from anemic yellow to dusty brown and a tree in his neighbor's yard turn to orange and red before succumbing to winds and rain, emptying its branches onto the ground. Dorsey himself went from shorts and T-shirts to sweaters, scarfs, and corduroy slacks.

For most of this time, the fingers of his right hand were firmly taped to flat steel splints. Surgery had not been necessary, and in fact had been declared useless by several physicians who thought that Dorsey should be satisfied with whatever function he could retain through splinting and eventual physical therapy. He had taken the news with little reaction. Hell, Dorsey had thought at the time, so it'll slow down my typing.

His left knee had required draining and arthroscopic surgery. Bone chips and whatever cartilage were left behind from his earlier, conventional surgery were removed. A few days use of crutches, made awkward by his injured hand, had followed, but he soon advanced to a quick step of a limp and then back to full stride. Planted in his backyard chair, Dorsey did straight leg lifts, muscle-tension exercises, and gradually increased the degree of bending his leg could perform. All the while planning a return to his daily morning speed-walk.

For the first few weeks, Gretchen had moved into the row house to supervise Dorsey's care. Her first action, and one that met with surprisingly little argument, was the banning of all beer from the premises. She explained to Dorsey that the basis for her decision was two-fold. She wanted to minimize any weight gain based on his present inactivity, sure, but she was also concerned about his mental outlook. One of the worries she mentioned to Dorsey was that he hadn't switched on the radio or tape player since returning from West Virginia. Jazz was missing from the row house for the first time in her memory.

"Honestly," Gretchen had told him, a few days short of Labor Day. They were seated in the backyard. "You've got me worried. It's not my specialty, but you have enough of the signs of depression. Alcohol would only worsen things, maybe deepen the problem."

Dorsey had merely shrugged. "Sure," he had told her, "no sweat."

"Any time you want to talk," Gretchen said, "about anything that's on your mind, you just let me know. Any of the things that are bothering you."

"Well," Dorsey had told her. "I'm a little pissed off about the safe deposit box at the bank. With the knife broken and the gun confiscated, I'm paying rent to protect a sack with a couple of bullets in the bottom."

Gretchen's concern grew to the point that she convinced a colleague from the hospital's psychiatric unit to drop by and put Dorsey through an informal evaluation. A thin, reserved man, he observed Dorsey over the course of a dinner at the kitchen table, making apparent small talk that Dorsey knew to be a soft sell of an examination. But he had played along without any emotional disguises, his own curiosity about his present state forcing him to do so. After the meal, back out on the patio furniture, the psychiatrist told them both that treatment wasn't necessary. Sure, there was some expected reactive depression to the killing of the two brothers, but this was already showing signs of abating. However, he suggested, there might be a different, less medically definable problem. He suggested to Dorsey that he detected what he chose to characterize as a ''state of disillusionment.''

''You're responsive, which the truly depressed are not,'' the psychiatrist had told him. ''Very responsive, in fact, but not very spontaneous. And your responses to questions and comments are those of a wisecracker. Sarcasm is all one gets.''

''Worse than normally?'' Dorsey had asked, turning to Gretchen.

''Much worse,'' she had said. ''You're not nearly as funny. Not to me, anyways. You say rotten things, but you never follow up with a crooked smile or an explanation to let me know that there's more going on inside your head. The act doesn't come to an end. Ever.''

Soon afterward, Gretchen moved back to her Aspinwall home, visiting Dorsey as her work schedule allowed, keeping a healthy distance for their mutual protection. Henry and Al shuttled meals, but no beer, between the bar and the row house. Both visited during the day, giving Gretchen late-in-the-day phone calls with any comments, good or bad, on Dorsey, who was becoming a community project. Martin Dorsey called, anxious to schedule a meeting with Ed Shearing, but Dorsey had put him off, firmly in the end.

''There's no rush,'' Dorsey had told him. ''There's all the time in the world. All you've done these last few years is slow down. You're not at death's door; hell, you haven't even gotten to the front porch yet. We've got plenty of time. Tell Shearing to go resurface another road with peanut-butter strength asphalt and I'll call when I'm ready.''

And there had been the most extreme interruption of Dorsey's watch on the seasons, a coroner's hearing in Wheeling. A two-day affair that ended in a finding of self-defense and no charges filed. But it had required the testimony of Dorsey, Father Crimmins, and Louise Filus, who was clearly and admittedly under the influence of sedatives. It had also been necessary for Dorsey to retain local counsel to cut a deal with the Wheeling-based prosecutor. He had been operating in the state without a West Virginia private investigator's license; and more importantly, he had put six shots into Mark Filus when just one or so might have done the trick. After some give and take, it was agreed that Dorsey's gun would be confiscated, a hefty fine leveled, and that he would never again operate in West Virginia. Held in Wheeling, the inquest pulled only half of the media interest that a Pittsburgh-based hearing might have generated, especially from television. But both Meara and Turner had sent observers. This came to Dorsey's attention through two phone calls.

"Check's in the mail," Meara had told him over the line. "Don't bother sending a bill, Monsignor Gallard and I have come up with a fee amount that you can't argue with. The outcome wasn't what he had in mind, but your testimony about the twins, the way you made them out to be such monsters, kept Turner from filing any charges against Crimmins and Louise. Obstruction of justice, destruction of evidence, those kind of charges aren't very sexy, regardless of who they are filed against. There's just no political mileage in it."

"You're welcome," Dorsey had said before hanging up.

"Fuck you," was what Douglas Turner had said when Dorsey had come to the phone. "I keep a shit list, and you've just taken up a prominent position on it. I'll be checking my desk each morning, looking for a report that you somehow overstepped your legal rights. And your kind always does. I'll be waiting."

"You're welcome," Dorsey said again, and again he hung up the phone.

Father Crimmins came to the row house in late September when Dorsey was getting about on his own and painfully squeezing a rubber ball with his right hand. Dressed in slacks and a light sweater, Father Crimmins accepted a cup of coffee left over from breakfast and settled into the metal patio chair across from Dorsey.

"I'm moving away, leaving town," he told Dorsey. "Matter of fact, the car is packed and pointed in the right direction. I'm heading home for a while, up in New York, the Finger Lakes region. A few of my uncles still have a vineyard up there, and they can always use another hand. And it's remote enough for me to feel like I'm getting away from it all. At least for a while."

"But you couldn't leave town without saying good-bye," Dorsey said.

"Not really," Father Crimmins told him. "Part of me wants to avoid you at all costs. After all, you conjure up some shame-filled moments in my life. But we've been through most of those moments together, so I can't just walk away. Also, I had a conversation with Gretchen, Dr. Keller, and she told me you've been troubled."

"So how's Louise doing?" Dorsey asked, avoiding the subject.

Father Crimmins shrugged and went on. "She's away for a while, too. A little private place, rest home of a sort, down in North Carolina. I'm not really sure how long she might be away. And, to be honest, I'm not sure where things are going to stand between us when she gets back. Two dead sons, and every time she looks at me, they're what she's thinking about."

"How about you?" Dorsey asked. "What happens after your stay in wine country?"

"I'll move on to something." Father Crimmins sipped at his coffee. "I've made my formal request to leave the active priesthood, and I don't think it will meet with any resistance. The Church would rather I just walked away. This way, there's no debate about a possible censure or where I can be reposted. Being defrocked or excommunicated was never a possibility; with the total number of priests being so low, a poor one can always be rehabilitated. Anyway, it looks like I'm about to become one of the enlightened laity I proposed the last time I was over here."

"Best of luck."

"Thanks, I'll manage." Father Crimmins took another pull on his coffee mug. "Now, let's talk about you and you're apparent loss of faith."

Dorsey gave the rubber ball a hard squeeze, sending a flare of pain across his wrist and halfway to the elbow. "One guy says I'm disillusioned, now you come and tell me I've lost faith. I still believe in God, so maybe we should stick to disillusionment."

"It's your faith that's taken the hit," Father Crimmins said. "I've been around you long enough to see how you've become a cynic over the years. But even the cynical have faith. Things are bad, corrupt, inhuman. They never go as planned or for the best. Things aren't done in service to the greater or greatest good. But as a cynic you accept this, because that's the nature of the world. There is cruelty and very serious, unanswered questions. Yet we get along with a margin of happiness, contentment. Never complete, never fulfilling the human potential, but livable. From what I hear and see, you've lost that. You've gone from cynical to fatalistic."

"Two dead college seniors," Dorsey said. "I had to put them down because someone, a few people probably, had turned them into rabid dogs. Takes a lot out of a person, that sort of thing."

"I know," Father Crimmins told him. "It's been a long time, but I still remember the things I had to do with my M-16."

"That was war time," Dorsey said. "After the indoctrination of basic training, jungle-warfare school, and the short-timers who helped you learn the ropes. And always with a bunch of buddies who are in the same spot you are. This is different. I had no time to prep, no buddies to lay it off on."

"We were talking about you," Father Crimmins said. "I'm not the one hanging out in the backyard, staring at the ground."

"So what advice are you here to dispense?"

"That only time, in small increments, will heal what ails you."

"And that's the best you can do?"

"That's the best there is, my hopefully cynical friend," Father Crimmins said. "Nobody heals in one moment, nobody learns everything at once. We learn our lessons, repeatedly, over time. You just have to understand that."

"Well," Dorsey said, "I've certainly learned to take my time with things."

"Bullshit." Father Crimmins finished his coffee and set the mug on the ground at his side. "Time shouldn't just pass, you should participate in it. Let me try a little religion on you and boil down a lot of St. Paul into a few words. Patience leads to perseverance, which leads to faith. It all comes to you in time. But you have to keep an eye open for it. You have to keep an open mind."

Dorsey relaxed his grip on the rubber ball and slipped it into his hip pocket. He wondered if the passing of time was worth the wait, but he soon realized that the only other option was to cancel time. And the only way to do that was suicide, the opting out from time. The hell with that, Dorsey thought. "I don't see as I have any other choice," he told the priest.

"We never do."

A week or so later, Al made his last delivery to the rowhouse. He had been slowly weaning Dorsey from the bar's kitchen, and his visits fell to a more normal level. One that didn't cause him or Henry to juggle schedules behind the bar. But that last drop-off was not a meal.

From his chair in the backyard, Dorsey saw Al's familiar white refrigerator van pull into the alley and stop at his back gate. Al hopped out, dressed in his professional white shirt that had grown full sleeves for the cooler weather, came around the van's front, and opened the passenger door. Wrapped in a beige raincoat, Mrs. Leneski took Al's hand to steady herself and stepped out onto the sidewalk. Al waved a quick hello and then undid the gate, allowing Mrs.

Leneski to enter the yard in front of him. As she came closer, Dorsey saw the dark metallic ring that was bound around her ankle. For a moment he had some thoughts of wavelengths and megahertz and wondered if she could open automatic garage doors by crossing her legs.

"Special permission, written permission." Mrs. Leneski pulled an envelope from her purse while she took a seat. She shook the envelope at him. "From this goofy son-of-a-bitch in the probation office. Just to come over here to look in on you. This paper has three signatures on it. Like a goddamned passport. Like I was planning a trip to the old country."

"For the young twerps they probably have working there," Dorsey told her, "this is the old country."

"The hell's the matter with you?" Mrs. Leneski asked, her eyes boring in on him. "I hear you don't work; you sit out in the cold all day. I hope you at least have the sense to go inside when it rains."

"I've moved to that level just recently," Dorsey told. "If you're cold, I can offer you coffee. It's just in the kitchen. Sit, I'll get it for you."

"Don't," Mrs. Leneski said. "I probably wouldn't like your coffee."

Of course not, Dorsey thought, it's nothing like yours. It doesn't come in a container with Quaker State printed across the front. "You went to a lot of trouble to come here. To tell me something?"

"Go back to work. You look healthy enough."

"Sounds simple enough," Dorsey told her.

"Goddamned right it is," Mrs. Leneski said. "Just that simple. You gotta start acting like you're alive. And don't tell me about those two dead boys."

Dorsey squirmed in his chair. "Sure, what have they got to do with things? They've got no right to haunt me."

"You mourn them, but you can't do that forever." Mrs. Leneski shook the envelope at him again. "I can give you my black dress if you want. Even I don't wear it anymore."

Dorsey waved her off with a snort of a laugh. "Keep the

dress. I'd have to make too many alterations. I don't think I can let out the waist far enough.''

Mrs. Leneski stuffed the envelope from the probation office back into her purse and looked off toward the alley where Al had stayed with the van. "I'm only allowed out for a short while," she said, turning back to Dorsey. "So I better have my say. A while back I told you, you didn't know a damned thing about suffering. Well, now you're learning, like I did. I had to get over my granddaughter's death. Then I had to get over shooting that bastard doctor. Maybe for me it was easier. I'm a lot older, I seen more. So I know how to suffer. But I also know that it has to come to an end. That's something you haven't learned yet. It will end, and you at least have to act like it will. You have to get used to the idea. You gotta get off your ass and rejoin the world. Just go through the motions if you have to.''

Dorsey steepled his fingers below his chin, examining the lines and crevices in the old woman's face, running over what she had to say. He also thought of the things that Father Crimmins had said, things that had been forcing their way into his thinking since the priest's visit. Patience to perseverance to faith. And before him sat the embodiment of that process, the living end-product. Eighty some years, a husband who dropped dead walking home from work, a daughter who fried her brain on drugs, a granddaughter who had to be scooped from a secret grave just a few blocks from her home. She learned patience, she was forced to persevere, she found faith in God and his world. She's right, he told himself, you're a goddamned fool.

"Sure you can't stay for coffee? I'd like some myself," Dorsey said, rising from his chair. "Let's go inside. Kinda cold out here.''

THE TRAIL OF BLOOD

There was no one in the Lexus. Both doors were wide open. There was no sign of a struggle. Until Tawne walked into the headlights which blasted off twin shots into the trees and saw drops of blood on the ground.

She gasped, realizing her worst fears.

Tawne opened her mouth, sucking in a piercing lungful of the cold river air. She started to yell, "Delia?"

Instead, she let the air out in a slow gust and closed her mouth. She followed the trail of blood, stepping as quietly as she could without letting tiptoeing slow her down too much. The drops of blood became heavier, became patches of shiny oil beneath the headlight's beam. They were black on the dark ground not brightened by the glare that passed over it. She smelled a copper/salt stench which sharply contrasted with the sweet rot of wet vegetation and the fungal smell of the river.

Water splashed against concrete. This was where the county had stacked a section of drainage pipe in preparation for installation to help with flooding and erosion. It was eerie, loud and hollow but infinitely liquid. She imagined this was what it sounded like when blood went through one artery but not another because it had been severed.

It was into one of these pipes on the slimy bank that the ugly man was stuffing Delia's body.

This Symbiotic
Fascination

CHARLEE JACOB

LEISURE BOOKS   NEW YORK CITY

This book is dedicated to my husband, Jim,
without whose unconditional love and support
I would never have done a damned thing.

A LEISURE BOOK®

February 2002

Published by

Dorchester Publishing Co., Inc.
276 Fifth Avenue
New York, NY 10001

ISBN 0-8439-4966-X

The name "Leisure Books" and the stylized "L" with design are trademarks of Dorchester Publishing Co., Inc.

Printed in the United States of America.

Visit us on the web at www.dorchesterpub.com.

ACKNOWLEDGMENTS

I would like to thank the following long-dead poets whose work was quoted from: Lord Byron, Robert Browning, Edward Fitzgerald, and Robert Burns. Also Dire Straits because I borrowed a few lines from "Money for Nothin'." I would also like to thank Alayne Gelfand for publishing "This Marvelous Raven Image" in *Prisoners of the Night*, which I was still thinking of when I wrote the book, albeit in a different shade of darkness. I would also like to thank Glenda Woodrum and the Coyote, Andre Scheluchin, Ken Abner, Jeremy Johnson, Pat Nielson, Bryan Lindenberger, Wayne Edwards, and other editors who were always open to ideas of beauty that tend to repel a public obsessed with flawless image. My most special thanks to David G. Barnett for his suggestions and patience and belief.